CARVED IN ICE

BROTHERHOOD PROTECTORS WORLD

KRIS NORRIS

Carved in Ice

Copyright © 2018, Kris Norris

Edited by Chris Allen-Riley and Jessica Bimberg

Cover Art by Kris Norris

This book is a work of fiction. Names, characters, places and incidents are products of the author's imagination or used fictitiously. Any resemblance to actual events, locales or persons living or dead is entirely coincidental.

© 2018 Twisted Page Press, LLC ALL RIGHTS RESERVED

No part of this book may be used, stored, reproduced or transmitted without written permission from the publisher except for brief quotations for review purposes as permitted by law.

This book is licensed for your personal enjoyment only. This book may not be re-sold or given away to other people. If you would like to share this book with another person, please purchase an additional copy for each recipient. If you're reading this book and did not purchase it, or it was not purchased for your use only, please purchase your own copy.

Note: This book was previously released through Amazon Kindle World.

BROTHERHOOD PROTECTORS
ORIGINAL SERIES BY ELLE JAMES

Brotherhood Protectors Series
Montana SEAL (#1)
Bride Protector SEAL (#2)
Montana D-Force (#3)
Cowboy D-Force (#4)
Montana Ranger (#5)
Montana Dog Soldier (#6)
Montana SEAL Daddy (#7)
Montana Ranger's Wedding Vow (#8)
Montana SEAL Undercover Daddy (#9)
Cape Cod SEAL Rescue (#10)
Montana SEAL Friendly Fire (#11)
Montana SEAL's Bride (#12)
Montana Rescue
Hot SEAL, Salty Dog

To Kyle, Jared, and Sydney for being the best on-going story I've never written. You can't make up this kind of chaos. And I wouldn't change it for the world.

To those of you, like me, who hope to find their "Russel" one day. Never stop dreaming.

And to Elle James for creating a kickass world and letting me play in it, again. Can't wait to come back—yup, I said it. Because you all know Rigs needs a story.

PROLOGUE

Park County, Montana.

Snow. Christ, how long had it been since he'd driven in snow?

Russel "Ice" Foster stared at the expanse of white powder covering the lonely road, wondering if he'd ever seen anything so pristine. So pure. Growing up on the streets of LA, he hadn't encountered snow until his pararescue training. Oh yeah, he'd learned about the fucking cold pretty damn quickly. Nothing like a week in the Arctic to make those neurons fire—create permanent pathways that went on high alert whenever the temperature dropped below freezing. He couldn't walk into an ice rink without having a few flashbacks of that training session.

Not that he'd been in an ice rink recently. Been anywhere other than where his next mission had taken him. And, for the past decade, it had been the desert. *The*

Sandbox, as it had been affectionately termed, then on to Afghanistan. Heat. Sand. Dust that caked every damn inch of his skin for years on end. He'd had the occasional mountain rescue. Donned the odd parka and gloves. But nothing compared to the endless fields of snow he'd been driving through for the past few hours.

He scrubbed a hand down his face, shifted his truck into four-wheel drive, then started down the road. He hadn't seen another vehicle since he'd pulled off the main interstate and onto some shit backroad in the middle of nowhere, Montana. Not exactly nowhere, but it felt like it. Endless miles with nothing but the occasional ranch opening up the forest on either side. He'd checked the map a dozen times, had even inputted the address into his GPS. He was definitely on the right road, even if he felt lost.

Russel cursed the thought. He'd never imagined he'd ever feel that way—not after making a living out of finding people. A life dedicated to the military. A lifetime's worth of blood, sweat and determination to make it through Combat Rescue training. He'd been in the one percent of candidates who had actually reached the finish line. Who had earned the coveted PJ title and received their maroon beret.

Since then, he'd been on more covert rescue missions than he could count—dragging men back from places no one had ever heard of. Missions that wouldn't make the evening news. He was one of the guys who went in when special ops went down. Their only chance at getting back alive. Sometimes, with a team. Often, alone. Armed and ready to kill in order to bring his teammates back alive. His *brothers* back alive—men who'd dedicated their lives to fighting for freedom. Men who didn't surrender. Who didn't die pretty. Russel did anything and everything to uphold his sworn oath—that others may live.

And, here he was, in the middle of Montana, feeling lost.

He'd never considered a life beyond the service. Never imagined he'd have to learn how to integrate back into civilian life. He'd planned on dragging his ass through enemy territory until he either got old enough to retire or got himself killed. Either was fine by him. He'd never been afraid of dying. Had made peace with it, right from the start. And, now, he was faced with the possibility of a life so foreign to him, he didn't know where to start. How to fit in. All it had taken was one fucked-up mission, and here he was. On the brink of change. Caught in limbo until the review board gave their final decision. And it didn't take a psychic to know which side of the fence they were leaning toward.

He glanced at the GPS, again. Just another ten miles, and he'd reach Eagle Rock. A blip on the map. A town he'd miss if he closed his eyes for longer than a couple of seconds. And, yet, it might be his only chance at salvation. A Hail Mary in a lifetime of rolling sevens.

He laughed—out loud in the empty cabin. He'd been lucky his commander hadn't tossed his ass in jail straight off then tossed the key—due process be damned. Getting forced to take a temporary leave—yeah, it had been the best option in a list full of ugly alternatives. Not that the accusations had been justified. They weren't. And, given the same situation, he'd do it all over, again. Exactly the same. He didn't pull punches, and he didn't let his teammates down. Period. If saving that Marine's life meant

Russel might have to make a new one for himself—he'd accept it. God knew he had more than enough blood on his conscience, already. He didn't need any more.

The voice on his GPS broke the silence, calling out the next turn. He was nearly there. His last chance. One he needed to make count.

The ranch Russel pulled up to was impressive. The sprawling acres with majestic views of the Crazy Mountains behind it definitely surpassed his expectations. A modest house fronted the property, and he smiled when the door opened before he'd done more than jump out of his truck.

The woman standing in the doorway was breathtaking. Blonde hair and delicate features, she looked every inch the Hollywood starlet he'd been told she was, even with a toddler hitched on one hip, and her hair pulled into a ponytail.

She smiled as he climbed the few short steps to the porch. "Hey. You must be that para-something that Hank's been chattering about for days, now. Ice, right? I'm Sadie."

"Pararescue, or PJ, if you'd like. And, yes, ma'am." He extended his hand. "The name's Russel Foster."

Sadie laughed, waving him inside. "No need to be so formal, here. You can call me Sadie—all the guys do. And I doubt anyone actually calls you Russel. Swede's been using Ice this entire time."

"To be honest, I'll answer to just about anything."

She laughed, again. "Hank and Swede are in the office. Follow me." She took off, absently doting on her daughter before glancing back at him. "Please excuse the mess. Emma and I are heading off to LA in a few hours, along with Swede and Allie. I can't believe how much stuff I have to take along for one tiny person."

"I wouldn't call this a mess. You have a lovely home."

"Liar, but thanks." Sadie glanced back at him. "You know, when Hank told me you were large, I didn't imagine you might be bigger than him. Guess that's kind of necessary in your line of work."

"I do whatever it takes to bring my brothers back."

"Including carrying them?"

"If necessary."

She shook her head. "And I thought SEALs were crazy." She pointed to a door at the end of a hallway. "The guys are through there. Just go on in. They're expecting you."

She turned and headed back toward the entrance, stopping partway. "I hope you decide to join us, Ice. We can use all the honorable men we can find."

Russel nodded his thanks, doing his best not to flinch at the word "honorable". If the review board had its way, that was the last term anyone would use to describe him.

He waited until she'd disappeared into another room before covering the last of the distance. He knocked on the door, despite her instructions, opening it when a man yelled from within. He stepped into the large space, taking stock of the room.

It was uncluttered with some shelves on one side and a large desk in front of an immense window, giving a panoramic view of the mountains behind them. A few chairs were positioned around the room, with a couple sitting in front of the desk. Two men stood off to the right, mouths lifted into grins.

The taller of the two stepped forward, extending his

hand. "You must be Ice. I'm Hank Patterson. We talked on the phone. This is Axel Svenson, but we all just call him Swede."

"Russel Foster. Pleased to meet you. I've heard good things about you and your crew, both with respect to your service and your new venture. Brotherhood Protectors has been getting quite the chatter lately. Rumor has it you guys are making a real difference out here."

"We try." Hank motioned to one of the empty chairs. "Please, have a seat. I'm sure it was an interesting drive with all the snow we just got."

Russel chuckled, taking the chair closest to him. "It's been a while since I drove in these conditions. Though, it's not that different from sand."

"Nicer, though. Prettier, too." He folded his hands together on top of the desk, glancing at Swede. "Speaking of rumors, we've heard you might be going civilian, soon. That's why I called—asked you to come out. Thought we might do a preemptive strike, if you will. See if you had any thoughts on what your future plans were if things go that way? If you might consider joining our team?"

Russel clenched his jaw, studying both men. But, if they were concerned about how his career might end, they hid it well. "I'll get the final decision in a few weeks. And, no, I hadn't really thought that far ahead. Though, I'm pretty sure I already know what the outcome's gonna be."

Hank nodded, glancing at Swede, again. "The waiting is always the hardest part. We both went through it with the medical review board. All that fuss getting in, making it through to the Teams, and it seems as if they can toss you aside without a second thought."

"It's not the medical review board I'm facing."

Swede sighed. "We've...heard."

Russel fisted his hands then pushed to his feet, taking a few heavy steps away before turning. While he didn't regret his actions, he'd be lying if he said it didn't sting. That his fifteen years of service would be defined by a black mark he'd never erase.

He held his head high, eyeing both men. "If you've heard the rumors, then you know this is serious."

Swede twisted in his chair to face him. "We know the basics, if that's what you're asking."

"Then, you might want to think twice before asking me to sign up. I'm not like the other men, here. I'm not getting ousted because of a bum leg or because I decided it was time to quit. If the review board decides to discharge me—and we all know that's the way it's gonna play out. The only way it *can* play out without certain high-ranking officers losing face and possibly important connections. It'll be an other-than-honorable discharge. It won't matter how many men I saved. How many times I dragged my ass through hostile territory to get the job done. All people will see is that I wasn't *fit* to stay. That the Air Force deemed me a liability."

Hank rose, staying behind the desk. "Easy, Russel. We didn't bring you here to judge you."

"Then, you're crazier than I am for coming." He raked his hand across his scalp. Fuck, he'd have to start growing his hair before it became a constant reminder of all he'd lost.

Hank looked at Swede then slowly made his way around the desk, stopping next to his friend. "We're not crazy. And, as far as your situation goes, I'd appreciate it if you'd answer three simple yes or no questions. Then, if you want to get the hell out of here and never come back, I'll respect that."

Russel crossed his arms over his chest. "Shoot."

"First, did you save that Marine's life?"

He frowned. "Yes."

"All right. Second…were your actions that might get you this unwanted distinction a direct result of saving that Marine?"

"Of course. Whatever it takes. Period."

"Understood. And, finally…" He moved closer until he was up in Russel's face. "Would you do it, again, knowing the outcome you might face?"

Russel held his gaze, feeling the truth down to his soul. "In a heartbeat. Exactly the same. I took an oath. I don't go back on my promises."

Hank smiled, clapped him on the shoulder then walked back to his desk. He looked at Swede. "That's good enough for me. What about you, Swede?"

Swede grinned. "The man had me at the first 'yes'."

"Then, it's unanimous." Hank returned to his chair. "We all know it's a bullshit charge. But…like you said. Someone has to take the fall, and you rolled the snake eyes, this time." He leaned back and kicked his feet up on the desk. "Just do me a favor?"

Russel nodded, not sure how to respond. Getting an other-than-honorable discharge carried serious ramifications. Ones Hank and Swede didn't seem to care about. "What's that?"

"Stick around for a while. See what you think of Montana. Shadow some of the guys. I'm actually meeting up with a buddy of yours tomorrow night, and with

Swede heading out shortly, I could use an extra set of eyes. Not to mention this buddy is your number one fan. He's managed to bring your name up in conversation a lot. Swears you're the only reason he made it back alive."

"Does this fan have a name?"

"The guys all call him Midnight."

"Sam Montgomery?" Russel chuckled. "I'd heard he'd been medically discharged. Didn't realize he was working for you. I haven't seen him since... Well, since that night. The guy's hardcore. Carried his buddy five miles with four broken ribs and a buggered knee and shoulder before finally passing out, still holding him. Probably wouldn't have punctured his lung if he'd stayed put, but he knew Gray wouldn't have even had a chance if he had, so.... Killed a part of me not to save Gray. It still haunts me."

"All the more reason to hang around. I'm sure Midnight would love to catch up."

Russel walked over to the window, staring out at the mountains. While he'd figured Hank had called the meeting to offer him a job, he'd expected the man to rescind it once he'd discovered the reason Russel was getting ousted. Not being judged... He glanced at Hank over his shoulder. "You sure you're not making a huge mistake?"

Hank's smile faded as he straightened. "That Marine you saved? The one you broke ranks for—risked your life and honor over? I knew his brother. Ran a few covert ops with his unit. The guy never thought twice about putting his ass on the line to help his teammates. He got hit on our last mission together. He didn't have someone like you to go back for him. We tried, but..."

He cleared his throat. "So, no, I don't think I'm making

a mistake. And I personally don't give a shit what the review board says. If they're stupid enough to lose someone of your caliber over some screwed-up politics, that tells me all I need to know. But… This is just a friendly meeting. Let you test us out. See if you could put up working with a bunch of ragtag ex-veterans. We both know you'll be able to get a paramedic job without trying."

"Right up until they ask to see my discharge papers."

"I doubt many places are going to ask to see anything once they hear the word pararescue. So, what do think?"

He focused on the mountains, again, then smiled. "I think Midnight owes me a beer."

CHAPTER 1

One month later. Seattle, Washington.

"What can I get you?"

Russel focused on the woman standing behind the bar, a towel slung over one shoulder, her platinum-blonde hair swept up into a messy bun. Jet-black eye-liner ringed her eyes, highlighting the light blue of her irises.

He smiled. "Pale ale. Whatever's best out here."

She cocked one eyebrow then grabbed a bottle from beneath the counter. "Manny's is a local favorite." She cracked the cap off. "Glass?"

"No, ma'am."

"Ma'am? Wow, you really aren't from around here, are you?"

The truth hit home, only it wasn't just Seattle or Washington State that seemed alien. It was the whole package—civilian life. Christ, just thinking those two words made his skin crawl. After all his years in the service, he'd never imagined he'd be sitting in a bar, his career in the crapper, and his damn head so fucked up, he wasn't sure whether to laugh about it or start a fight. Or maybe he'd come here hoping to hook up. A few rounds of hot sex generally took the edge off.

Right. As if sex was going to make him forget getting kicked out. Forget the stain on his record—the one that virtually erased all those years of risking his ass to save someone else's. That mocked the oath he'd lived by since joining. While a part of him had known the inevitable outcome a month ago, it hadn't lessened the stab of pain when he'd gotten the official ruling.

Russel forced a smile. "That obvious?"

The woman laughed. "No one says ma'am around here. At least, not without a thick southern accent. I get called babe. Darling, sometimes. Besides, you've got the look."

"The look?"

"There's a reason people pour out their hearts to bartenders, sweetie. We're pretty good at reading body language. The way you're scanning the bar, looking like you're about to jump out of your skin... Either you're a spy, or this isn't your usual scene." She stepped back, crossing her arms over her chest. "Let me guess. Based on your freakishly large frame, short hair, and what looks like possible dog tags around your neck, you're either a wrestling pro in town on a tour, or..." She grinned. "You're military."

He snorted, the word stinging the raw wound still bleeding beneath his skin. "Not anymore."

"Ouch. Doesn't sound like it ended well."

"Most things involving war don't."

"So, is this a stop on your way home?"

He shook his head. How did he say that he'd come here to deliver a dying message to a dead soldier's wife? That every tear she'd cried had been like a knife across his flesh. That having her thank him for his kindness had cut deeper than his other-than-honorable discharge. She wouldn't have thanked him if she'd known he'd abandoned her husband's dead body in order to track down the men who'd captured his partner. That Russel had disobeyed direct orders in an effort to save a soul—atone for arriving too late. For not saving the other half of hers.

He worked up a quirk of his lips. "I had a promise to keep."

She frowned then sighed, leaning her elbows on the bar. "Sounds like you need more than just one beer. Like I said, I'm a pretty good listener. How about you and I…"

Her gaze drifted to somewhere over his right shoulder. "Shit."

Russel glanced behind him, but to him, it was just a sea of people—endless leather jackets, jeans and cowboy hats. Nothing looked out of place. Guys hitting on girls. A couple of boys shoving each other off to one side. Exactly what he'd expect in this kind of establishment.

He arched a brow. "Something wrong?"

The woman huffed, fluttering a few wispy hairs around her face. "I'll say. Looks like Red, over there, has some unwanted company. The kind that's gonna either break out into a brawl or get the cops showing up at my door. Maybe both."

He swiveled on the stool, searching the area more closely until he narrowed in on a pretty little redhead on the far side of the room. She had her hair in a similar bun, only half of hers had slipped out of the knot, cascading around her shoulders in a messy curtain of auburn curls. She was sitting alone at a table, nursing a drink, while three guys hovered around her. One of them slid his hand along her shoulder before she knocked it off, clearly mouthing for him to "fuck off".

Russel grinned. He had to hand it to her, she had guts. She didn't look big enough to take on one of the men, let alone all three. Though, he knew better than to judge people by their appearance. He'd witnessed more than a few female soldiers half his size kick guys on their asses without breaking a sweat. So, maybe the girl could handle herself.

The bartender muttered something under her breath then sighed. "Girls like that don't belong in this kind of place. Not alone, anyway. Most of the men that frequent this bar aren't the kind you want to take home—not unless you're a damn black belt. Or heavily armed."

"Do you know her?"

"She's like you. A first-timer. And the way she's been belting back those coolers, I'd say she's either going through a breakup or lost her job. She doesn't seem like the typical party crowd we get. Casual clothes. Very little makeup. Girl's out of her league, here."

She tossed the towel on the counter. "I'll grab one of my guys. Have them step in before it gets ugly. Or bloody."

Russel snagged the woman's wrist, giving her a genuine smile, this time. "No need. I've got this."

She tilted her head. "Looks, manners, and a gallant knight? You must have been some kind of soldier."

"Nothing special. Just did my job." He stood, reaching for his wallet. "How much do I owe you?"

She smiled and waved it off. "That one's on the house. Consider it a thank you for your service. Or, if that bothers you, it can be payment for helping me out."

Russel nodded. He didn't like getting special treatment, but he knew by the firm press of her shoulders that she wasn't going to take no for an answer. He turned, staring at the redhead, again. The guy who'd touched her had shuffled closer. He seemed determined to drape his arm around her shoulder, despite the way she continually batted away his advances. A light flush now colored her cheeks, and her back looked stiffer. A few more minutes, and Russel bet his ass things were going to get physical.

The guy bent lower and reached for her thigh, rewarded with a face full of whatever cooler she'd been drinking. He startled back, scrubbing his hand down his face before glaring at her. "Shit. Why the hell did you do that?"

She tightened her grip around the bottle, looking as if she was considering smashing it over the guy's head, when Russel moved into her sight line. She froze, her gaze shifting toward him. Her eyes widened as her head tilted back to meet his gaze, and her mouth gaped open slightly.

He smiled, hoping the simple gesture put her at ease, before addressing the men. "I don't want to speak for the lady, but I'm pretty sure that's the universal sign for all of you to get lost."

The guy glanced up. Whether it was Russel's size or how he carried himself, he wasn't sure, but the man straightened, nudging his buddies then lifting his chin higher. "You're right. You don't speak for her. So, why don't you go back to wherever you came from? We're in the middle of a conversation."

"You mean the one where she told you to 'fuck off' a few minutes ago?" He took a step closer, placing his beer bottle on the table. "As I see it, this can go down two ways. You boys can disappear on your own, or we can take this outside."

"You think you can take all three of us on? Alone?"

"It won't be a fair fight, but I can wait while you try to convince a few more of your friends to join in, if you'd like?"

A smile twitched the woman's mouth before a bemused chuckle made it past her pursed lips.

The guy behind her sneered, glancing between her and Russel a few times. "You must think you're something."

He reached for the woman a moment before Russel moved. Within seconds, he had the asshole off to the side and on his knees with his wrist bent backwards. The man grasped at Russel's arm in an attempt to release his hold, cursing when Russel increased the angle.

Russel leaned in, still eyeing the other men as he dragged the jerk toward him. "I don't think you understood me. Try to touch her, again, and I'll break more than your wrist. Now, I suggest you all leave."

The creep nodded, cradling his hand against his chest when Russel released it as he shoved him onto his ass. His buddies helped him up, all three giving Russel a wide berth as they headed for the door.

Russel waited until they'd stumbled outside before

gazing down at the woman. "My apologies, ma'am. Men like that give the rest of us a bad name."

She stared up at him, blinking several times, before shaking her head. "You... I didn't even see you move. Then, you had his hand, and—"

"I hope I didn't frighten you."

"Hell, no. That..." She whistled. "Is it bad that I kinda wish they'd been stupid enough to go outside with you? Because I would have enjoyed watching them get their asses handed to them."

He chuckled. "For a moment, I thought you were gonna cold-cock that one creep with your cooler."

"I was." She motioned to the chair across from her. "Would you like to sit? Can I buy you another beer as a thank you?"

He scraped the chair out then slid onto the seat. "You don't have to thank me."

She scrunched up her nose. "Are you seriously for real? Is there a hidden camera or something?"

"You act as if no one else would have done that."

"That's because no one else would have, other than maybe one of the bouncers. Even then, he would have probably asked me to leave, too. Haven't you heard? Chivalry is dead, and nice guys are extinct."

He laughed. God, it felt good to do that. "So, you're saying I'm a throwback?"

"In a good way. Though, I'm surprised they tested you, because..." She waved at him.

"Because I'm freakishly large, as the bartender put it?"

Her lips quirked. "I wouldn't have used the word 'freakishly'."

Russel smiled as he leaned back in the chair. He couldn't remember the last time he'd enjoyed easy banter with a lady. "You're…unique."

She pouted. "Unique? Isn't that guy-speak for crazy?"

"It has multiple meanings."

She arched a brow as she copied his position. "Sure. Just like, 'she's got a great personality', right?"

He laughed harder when she made the air quotes with her fingers. "I was right. You are a ball-buster. So, tell me. If I hadn't happened along, what were you planning on doing, other than breaking the bottle over his head?"

Her lips lifted, and it was as if someone had beamed a spotlight on her. Her smile lit up her entire face, accentuating the even symmetry of her features and the devilish gleam in her eyes. Her insanely *green* eyes. Fuck, how had he missed that before? Missed how beautiful she was? How smooth her skin looked or how full her lips were?

Her smile flourished, and his damn chest gave a hard thump, as if his heart had just flipped over. "I'm not helpless. I can punch a guy without crying over breaking a nail. And I have a full can of mace in my purse. I only needed enough of a distraction to get some distance."

He leaned in, bracing his forearms on the table. "Let me get this straight. You were gonna hit that asshole over the head with your cooler bottle. Then, while he was working himself up into a lather, you were gonna slip out, punch anyone who got in your way then hold them all back with a can of mace?"

"Well, when you say it like that…" She scowled. "What else was I supposed to do?"

"How about not put yourself in this position to begin with?"

He sucked in a deep breath then eased back, taking another pull of his beer. He wasn't sure why he was so worked up, other than picturing all the ugly ways her night could have ended.

She stared at him for a while. "So, I'm not allowed to come out and have a few drinks by myself because I have a vagina?"

He choked on his beer, nearly spitting it across the table. Damn, he liked this woman. Feisty. Beautiful. A dangerous combination, but Russel wasn't known for shying away from danger. "You're right. It's not fair. But places like this don't care about equality. And guys like that take what they want without any regard to who they hurt in the process."

She leaned forward, this time, that green gaze locked on his. "Trust me. I'm *intimately* aware of what guys like that are capable of. I know the moment I step into a room who's safe and who isn't."

Russel studied her, her words making the hairs on his neck prickle. The bartender wasn't the only one who was good at reading people, and he knew there was far more to this woman than he'd initially thought.

"I see. So, who else in here is safe?"

"Besides you?" She chuckled as she leaned back, again. "No one."

"And you're sure about me? I could have chased those guys off so I could get you alone."

She snorted. "Please. Everything about you screams honorable. I wouldn't be surprised if it was tattooed across your chest."

Except for the part where the Air Force had deemed him anything but.

"Besides, it would be a pretty stupid move—making a scene like that—if you planned on being anything less than a gentleman." She nodded toward the bar. "I'm betting the bartender would remember you to a tee. She hasn't taken her eyes off you since you sat down."

He glanced over his shoulder, grinning at the blonde watching them from behind the counter. "You have a point. But, if you know how dangerous it is in here, why come in?"

She shrugged. "I wanted to go somewhere…different. Off-character, I suppose."

"You mean, somewhere you wouldn't be found."

Her expression sobered. "I just didn't want to bump into anyone I knew. Not tonight."

"Something happen tonight?"

"Do you always ask strangers this many questions? Christ, I don't even know your name."

He extended his hand. "Russel."

She stared at his palm then slowly placed her hand in his. "Quinn."

"Quinn?" He gave her hand a gentle squeeze. "That's pretty."

She didn't answer, placing her fingers back around her cooler once he'd released her. "So, what's a nice guy like you doing in a place like this?"

"Isn't that my line?" He fiddled with the label as he watched her watch him. "Similar motivation, I suppose. I kinda wanted to disappear, too."

She nodded, downing the last of her drink then signaling to the bartender for another.

Russel frowned. "Rumor has it you've been pounding

those back. Don't you think it might be time to call it a night?"

Her face lit up, again, and he felt another hard thump in his chest. "A night? It's ten o'clock. Even Cinderella got to stay out until midnight."

"But Cinderella didn't have a bunch of assholes trying to get in her pants."

Her smile widened. "Neither do I, anymore. Thanks to you." She handed the bartender some cash when she arrived with another hard lemonade. "Thank you. And could you bring my friend another Manny's." Quinn arched a brow. "Unless you're done? Or moving on."

Russel cracked a smile, nodding at the bartender. She glanced between them then shrugged, heading back to the bar. Russel waited until she'd returned with another beer and taken his empty away before focusing on Quinn. She really was beautiful. The way her hair set off the pale, creamy tones in her skin and brought out the flecks of amber in her eyes. And, with half of the silky locks falling out of her clip, he had no trouble imagining what she'd look like after a night of tumbling between the sheets. Or against the wall. Bent over the couch.

He cleared his throat as he gave himself a mental shake, watching her work her way through her drink. A drop beaded on her lip, and he nearly creamed his damn pants at the way she licked it off.

Quinn glanced at him, her gaze raking up and down his body. "So, Russel…what brings you to Seattle?"

He took a swig of his beer, grinning at her. "What makes you think I'm not from around here?"

"Call it an educated guess. I saw you walk in. You looked…out of place."

"Funny. The bartender said the same thing about you."

"Did she?" Quinn sighed. "She's right. I don't go out that often. I'm not much of a drinker."

"Says the woman who's working her way through another cooler."

"Like I said. Tonight's different. And don't think I didn't noticed you didn't answer my question."

He pushed down the resulting sting. "Let's just say I'm in the midst of a career change."

"Ahh. One you're not happy about. I can appreciate that."

"Is that why you're here? Drinking your way to oblivion?"

"It's…complicated."

"Most things are." He arched a brow when she drained the last of her drink. "That didn't take long. Tell me, how are you planning on getting home?"

A furrow creased her brow as she stared at him, looking as if she was deciding how much to tell him. "Taxi."

"By yourself?"

"I'm a big girl. I got myself here. I can get myself home."

"You weren't drunk when you got here." He scrubbed a hand down his face. He didn't want to come across as a sexist asshole, but damn… He wasn't from Seattle, didn't know it that well, but even he was aware that the girl was asking for trouble traveling in this part of the city, alone.

She giggled. "Who says I am, now?"

"That giggle to start with. Do you have someone you can call? To meet you or pick you up?"

Those fucking sexy lips of hers quirked, the barest hint of gloss glinting off the overhead lights. "You mean like a *boyfriend*? No, I don't have one of those. Besides, I already told you. I'm not helpless."

She pushed to her feet, swaying unsteadily. Russel jumped up and hooked his arm around hers, planting his other hand on her waist. She leaned against him, and a sweet fragrance filled his senses. He tried not to inhale, but it wove around him, sinking beneath his skin until he was sure it had infused his blood.

She laughed, attempting to push off, only to teeter into him, again. "I guess I shouldn't have gotten up so fast."

"The speed had nothing to do with it, sweetheart. It was the half a dozen coolers you drank."

"I only had five…I think." She giggled, again. "Or was it seven?"

"Whatever it was, it was more than enough. And it seems to have hit you all at once. Can I take you home, now? Or are you determined to keep drinking until you can't even stand?"

"But… I haven't figured it out, yet?"

"Figured what out?"

She shook her head. "I need more time. I don't know what to do? What's right?"

"More alcohol isn't going to help you think clearly. Just… Let me take you home. I'll see you get tucked safely in bed. And you can think about whatever is bothering you, tomorrow. Okay?"

She glanced up at him. "You're gonna take me home and tuck me in bed?"

"You said you knew who was safe and who wasn't."

"I do, and you are." She sighed. "I guess I *am* a bit…unsteady."

"Is that a yes?"

She tilted back her head until she could lock her gaze on his. Her tongue darted out to wet her lips before they curled upwards. "Yes. It's a definite yes."

CHAPTER 2

Harlequin Scott, or Quinn, as she was known, now, settled into the passenger side of Russel's truck as he moved in beside her, closing out the wind and rain then starting the engine. The truck hummed to life, accompanied by a blast of cold air through the vents, and the hushed sounds of country music playing over the speakers.

Russel muttered something under his breath as he flicked some switches, deflecting the air away from them. He sighed. "Sorry. It's gonna take a few minutes to warm everything up."

"That's okay. Beats the taxi I was going to take." She arched her brow. "Are you sure you still want to drive me home? It's across town."

The look he gave her answered her question. "Having second thoughts about riding with me, sweetheart? Afraid you might have read me wrong?"

She studied him, trying to ignore the way the buzzing in her head made his silhouette occasionally double.

Granted, she'd had a lot to drink—an obnoxious amount, actually. But she hadn't been lying. Growing up amidst dangerous men, she'd learned quickly how to gauge risk factors—the man's build, his movements, his hands. If his voice rose or lowered. If he made eye contact. True, Russel outweighed her, and she wasn't naïve enough to think some fancy moves and a can of mace would be enough to fight him off.

But the longer she stared at him, the more at ease she felt. No tingling awareness at the base of her spine. No raised hairs along her nape. And, while her heart raced whenever he smiled, she suspected it had more to do with attraction than worry.

Of course, accepting a lift home was completely out of character—much like going to the bar in the first place. She never took these kinds of risks. She couldn't. Not when she couldn't be certain even a nice guy wasn't connected to her father's business. But there was something about Russel—something on an atomic level that reassured her.

She smiled, resisting another giggle. "No second thoughts. You're...safe. And I'm safe with you."

He gazed at her for what felt like an hour before smiling. "I am, and you are. But you're taking one hell of a risk. One, I hope you don't do often."

The giggle slipped free, earning her a stern shake of his head. "No. Not often. Actually, never. But even... slightly intoxicated, I still trust my spider sense. And it's not going off, at all."

"Pretty sure you passed 'slightly' three coolers ago. Okay, where to?"

She rattled off her address, watching him pull into the

street then maneuver through the light late-night traffic. Staring at how his hands dwarfed the steering wheel, his long, strong fingers barely gripping the leather wrapping. She'd felt those same fingers pressed against her lower back when he'd guided her out of the bar and over to his truck. He'd had to catch her a few times when her balance had shifted, but if it had been at all taxing, he hadn't shown it.

Another giggle threatened, but she managed to crush it. God, she hadn't realized how drunk she was until she'd stood. It was as if all the coolers had waited until that moment to enter her bloodstream, warming her from the inside out and making her feel as if she was moving in slow motion. If Russel hadn't insisted on walking her to his truck, she doubted she would have made it out of the bar without tripping onto her ass.

More likely, the bartender would have called her a cab and had one of her bouncers carry her out. And the last thing Quinn needed was a scene. She'd drawn enough attention to herself by having Russel ride to the rescue like some modern-day knight. She didn't need someone snapping a photo of her face-first on the old wooden floor that might end up on social media. She needed a place she could go without worrying anyone would recognize her—would know who her father was. Somewhere no one would ever think to search for her. She'd gone to extreme lengths to remake herself. But it wasn't something she'd bet her life on.

Thoughts swirled around in her head, muddied by the afterglow of alcohol. She pushed them away, content to worry about her problems tomorrow, then focused on Russel.

The man really was massive. Not outrageously tall, probably six-one or two, but… Damn. He was thick. His barrel chest pressed against his shirt, clearly outlining his chiseled pecs and upper abdominal muscles. His arms were larger than most men's thighs, matching the wide breadth of his shoulders. When he'd leaned forward to open the door for her, the back of his jacket had actually stretched from the strain of his lats, and she hadn't missed the way his torso tapered into lean hips and one hell of a sexy rear end.

Quinn drew her gaze up to his face. His square jaw was covered in a thick shadow of stubble—more than just a day or two's worth of growth. Not quite a beard, but definitely on the way. The dark color matched the chocolate brown hue of his hair, even if it was fairly short. But it was his eyes that she'd noticed, first. Green with flecks of copper around the iris, it had been like looking at spring amidst a brilliant sunrise. And she knew she could gaze at them for hours and still find them mesmerizing.

Russel must have felt her staring and glanced over at her as he changed lanes to take the next exit. "You okay? Do you feel sick?"

"I'm fine. Why? Do I look sick?"

"Your face is flushed, and you were staring at me with this odd expression. Thought it was worth asking. In case you needed me to pull over."

She laughed, the sound morphing into a snort. God, she really shouldn't drink. It went straight to her head, every time. "My face is flushed from the coolers, and I was staring at you because I was trying to figure you out."

No sense telling him she couldn't seem to take her eyes off him, or that her face was flushed because she'd just started to imagine what it would be like to kiss him. To slide her mouth over his full lips—feel his tongue caress hers. She'd never had a lover who was so innately male, and she couldn't help but wonder what it would be like to trace her fingers across his shoulders. Test the strength hidden beneath bronzed flesh. He'd obviously been somewhere warm recently, every inch of visible skin tanned from hours spent in the sun.

For a moment, she thought about asking him what he did for a living—mercenary immediately sprang to mind with his attractive, yet thug-like, appearance and overabundance of muscles, despite the trustworthy vibes he gave off. Though, she supposed a guy could be both—a mixture of violence and honor. It's how she'd always rationalized her feelings for her father. He'd never been anything but gentle and loving toward her. The kind of man who had always kept his word.

But she'd discovered there was a darker side to him— one he'd done his best to keep hidden. One she wasn't sure how to resolve. It was why she'd gone drinking to begin with. Hard problems were rarely solved by easy answers, and she'd needed the liquid courage to contemplate options that not only scared her, but had her questioning her own moral compass. After all, who betrayed their own flesh and blood?

She groaned inwardly, quickly dismissing any line of conversation that might give her more insight into her unlikely savior. The last thing she needed was to get to know Russel better.

This wasn't the beginning of a relationship. He was driving her home. Sure, she was seriously considering asking him to stay the night—give herself a few hours of sexual bliss. Make some lasting memories she could carry with her, especially with her future so uncertain. She hadn't been looking for a lover, but she recognized an act of providence when it slapped her in the face. And she'd bet her ass the man was good in bed. If nothing else, she could really get off simply touching every inch of him. Tracing his bulging muscles. Feeling him pressed against her.

But even if he was interested—if she was able to lure him into her bed—it was only for a night.

One-offs were her specialty. No commitments. No strings. Nothing meaningful. If she cared about someone, that person became a weakness others could use against her. A means to get her to comply. And she'd been excruciatingly careful about avoiding anything and anyone her father's colleagues could ever use to their advantage. Not when she suspected their business was far more gruesome than she'd ever imagined.

Russel turned onto her street, still glancing over at her. "Figure me out?"

She smiled at him. "You know, whether this is the norm for you—driving drunk girls home. Why you chose to step in, to begin with."

He shrugged, frowning as he stopped in front of what was obviously a warehouse. "I've taken a few ladies home when they've gotten themselves into dangerous situations. Made sure they got safely inside before seeing myself out. Not that I'd say it's a norm for me. And I stepped in because guys like those men in the bar are the reason women can't enjoy a simple night alone, like you wanted. They're the worst kind of predator."

He shook his head. "Did you give me the wrong address?"

She looked out at the old brick building, the red tones hidden by the foggy rain. "Nope. This is right. I live in the loft apartment. A friend of mine is a mechanic. He uses the rest of the space to store parts and old vehicles he's fixing up. It's actually a great setup. Quiet. Out of the way—"

"Creepy. Not to mention the perfect place for someone to get assaulted. Christ, do the cops even do drive-bys out here?"

"Do you view everything in terms of how dangerous it is?"

"Of course. Don't you?"

Where her family was concerned? Definitely. But she'd never questioned her decision to live here.

"Not everything. Besides, I see this place as safe. No nosy neighbors. No bars or clubs nearby to attract unwanted strangers. The only people who come around here either work here or are—"

"Serial killers?" He scoffed at her huff. "Come on, sweetheart, there are a million ways someone could stalk you here, and you'd be an insanely easy target." He gave her another stern look. "At least tell me you generally park inside."

"Of course. And it's key-coded. As is the old elevator. And my apartment has a security system wired to a monitoring company. Despite how tonight played out, I don't go looking for trouble, and I know how to protect myself."

Russel's frowned intensified, and he scanned the area, again.

She released her seatbelt then shuffled closer, placing her hand on his forearm. Strong muscles bunched beneath her fingers, and she couldn't stop from wetting her lips as her throat grew suddenly dry. Christ, not an inch of the guy was soft.

Russel glanced at where she touched him then slowly drew his gaze up to meet hers. The green in his eyes had darkened, and she didn't miss the way his breathing kicked up a notch.

She stayed close as she pointed toward a garage door off to their left. "That's my spot. There's a keypad on the post. If you drive up, I can input the code and you can park your truck inside." She inched closer, pressing her chest against his arm. "Unless you'd like me to get out, here?"

He clenched his jaw, flaring his nostrils before exhaling. "And chance you won't make it all the way to your door? I don't do anything half-assed. I said I'd see you safely home. That means locked inside."

With that, he inched his truck forward, inhaling sharply when she leaned over him to open his window and reach the keypad. He grabbed her around the waist when she lost her balance, one arm grazing her breast as he attempted to steady her. He mumbled an apology, parking his truck beside her motorcycle.

He frowned, again, as he stared down at her, helping her back to her side. "A bike? That's all you use year 'round?"

"I have a convertible, but the muffler went on it. My friend's fixing it for me next week. And, for the record, with the proper attire, you can ride a good ten months of the year out here."

"Yeah, if you have a death wish."

"Has anyone ever told you that you worry a lot?"

"Part of the job description, sweetheart. I can't help others if I get hurt because I didn't consider every angle. Every possible outcome." He sighed. "At least, it was."

She stiffened. There was a wounded edge to him she hadn't noticed before—one that made her chest tighten. Made it hard to breathe as the interior of the vehicle warmed to the point she felt light-headed. Who was this guy, and why the hell did the thought of him hurting tear at her? Make her want to slide back over and take him in her arms. Smooth out the furrow in his brow. Kiss away the pout curving his lips.

She steeled herself against the punch of emotion that welled in her chest. She didn't want to know any more. Didn't need to develop stronger feelings for him. Not when every moment spent in his presence felt this…right. As if he was some missing piece of a puzzle that finally completed the image.

She cleared her throat, grabbed the handle, then made a hasty exit. It would have been perfect if she hadn't tripped getting out. Caught her damn boot on the small step and tumbled onto the floor. Pain blossomed through her head and across her shoulder as the garage did a full three-sixty in her vision before steadying.

"Shit!" Russel was at her side, keeping her from sitting up as he did a visual sweep of her body. "Christ, you've got a fucking lump forming above your right eye."

He placed his hands on her face, pushing and rotating her head as he stared at her. Then, he opened her eyes wider, looking inside. "Are you dizzy? Feeling nauseous? Any double vision?"

She laughed then groaned. "Laughing hurts."

"Then, I suggest you don't. Especially, since this isn't funny."

"What's funny is you asking me all those questions. I was dizzy, nauseous, and seeing double before I got in your truck."

"Which further complicates this." He leaned forward. "Wrap your arms around my neck."

"Okay, but… Whoa!"

She gasped as he levered her against his chest then stood, looking as if it was normal to have someone cradled in his arms. He grabbed her purse off the seat then headed for the elevator doors on the far left.

Quinn tightened her hold, wondering how he was going to manage with her arms all the way to her apartment. "You don't have to carry me. I was just clumsy. I can walk."

"And have you upgrade your concussion when you fall, again?" The look he gave her clearly indicated that he firmly believed she *would* fall, again. "Not likely."

"I'm fine. Just a bit of a headache, but that's probably from the coolers, too."

Russel scoffed at her. "You just fell head first onto concrete. I'm going to err on the safe side until I can do a more thorough exam."

She opened her mouth to ask what qualified him to do any kind of exam then snapped it shut. This was exactly the kind of personal information she didn't need. If she found out he was a doctor or nurse or maybe a fireman, it would give her a means to track him down, later. To break all the rules that had kept her safely in the shadows. It would mean she cared, even if just peripherally.

Instead, she clung to him, secretly waiting for him to put her down when she got too heavy. But Russel simply moved along as if he were carrying some groceries. Or maybe he was accustomed to carrying bodies. Maybe he was an assassin instead of a mercenary. Or some kind of forensics guy who dealt with dead people all the time.

She nearly giggled at the thought. Chances were, it was just endless hours in the gym. But she couldn't deny the appeal of being with a man who knew how to handle himself. A guy who might actually be untouchable where her family was concerned. Someone not intimidated by the dark stain smeared across her DNA. Someone she could have more than just a fleeting moment with.

God, she must have hit her head harder than she'd thought if she was seriously romanticizing about being with a guy she'd just met. One who she was secretly hoping was an assassin, just to have more than a one-night stand with him. That's if he was even interested. Judging on how clinically he was holding her, he really had only planned on driving her home and dropping her off.

Great, now she'd become some kind of charity case. A drunk one with a concussion. Nothing screamed sexy like a bruised lump on her head. And, if she'd thought her hair was a mess before, it was wild, now. Anything left of the bun she'd made had let loose with the fall, the tangled curls bouncing around her shoulders with every step.

Russel stopped at the elevator, glancing at the keypad. "Do you feel well enough to put in the code?" He eyed her. "Can you even see the keypad?"

She scowled. "I told you. I'm fine. You're the one who's

blowing this out of proportion. I just fell. Trust me, I've had worse lumps than this."

Not that she'd tell him any of the details. Learning how to read people hadn't been easy, and she'd encountered a few "failures" along the way. Gotten too close to a few of her father's colleagues who hadn't thought twice about knocking her around when she'd accidentally walked in on a meeting. Until her father had found out, and the men had vanished.

Russel made eye contact. "Why does that singular thought make my skin crawl?"

Quinn ignored the remark, reaching for the keypad. It took a couple of tries with her hand shaking and missing the odd number, but she managed to disengage the lock. Russel stepped inside, still holding her against his chest. No heavy breathing. No outward signs that he found it at all stressful to hold her this long.

She tilted her head to the side, squinting when the scenery blurred. "I must be getting heavy. I swear, I can walk."

He rolled his eyes. Actually, rolled his eyes at her. "Please. I've carried guys my size for miles on end. Your weight barely registers."

She knew her mouth had gaped open before she'd managed to shut it. He'd carried guys *his* size for *miles*? Seriously? Who the hell was he? Who carried men anywhere?

Pain throbbed through her head, pushing away the thoughts. It didn't matter who he was. Where he'd come from or where he was heading. All that mattered was now. This moment, even if she'd managed to screw it up more. The chances of talking him into anything, now, seemed remote at best.

Russel stopped next at her alarm system, allowing her to push her thumb on the print reader before taking her inside her apartment. He headed immediately for the kitchen off to the right, sliding her onto the counter. Before she'd blinked twice, he had a cold compress on her head and was testing her eyes, again.

She grunted. "I'm fine."

He probed the lump, mumbling an apology when she winced. "So far, so good. But...I'm concerned. Between the amount of alcohol you consumed, and now this... I'm not sure it's safe to leave you alone."

Her heart fluttered at his words, the sensation moving lower to settle in her gut. Had he really just implied he wanted to spend the night?

She leaned against him, tracing the line of his jaw. "Sounds like you might need to stay. For safety, of course."

His jaw flexed, jumping the muscle in his temple as he took a deep breath, lips pulling tight at whatever it was he'd scented in the room. "Quinn."

"I wasn't lying, before. I never bring guys home. Not home. And never from a bar. But you..." She inched forward until she could kiss the spot just below his left ear. "You're worth breaking a few rules."

A deep rumble vibrated through his chest as she nipped at his earlobe then licked the slight hurt. His fingers dug into her waist, his breath hot and heavy against her neck.

She pulled back, staring up at his closed eyes before he blinked them open. "Unless, you're not interested."

That muscle in his temple jumped, again, a moment before he snaked his arms around her, dragging her against him. Her groin collided with his crotch, the hard, thick evidence of his arousal jabbing the soft vee of her mound.

Another deep rumble—somewhere between a growl and a purr—as he hovered a breath away. "Does it feel like I'm not interested? But—"

"No buts. You're hard, and I obviously want you to fuck me, so…"

"Christ." He closed the distance, claiming her mouth in a brutal kiss. It was all lips and teeth and tongues, mashing together. His erection swelled, increasing the pressure against her sex, and she ground herself against him, sure she wouldn't need more than a minute or two to get herself off.

Russel hissed out a breath once he'd eased back, his chest heaving, his dark gaze riveted on her. He didn't move, seemingly frozen to the spot as he stared down at her. "This is a bad idea."

She chuckled, kissing her way along his jaw then down his neck, nipping at his muscles through his shirt. "Actually, it's a fantastic idea. You. Me. Naked. I bet you can go all night long and not get tired."

He moaned as she arched against him, rubbing her groin up and down his dick. "Hell yeah. All night and all tomorrow. But…"

"Again, with the but?" She eased back enough to meet his gaze. "This is pretty brainless."

"It's not like I don't want to. And the but is because not only did you just whack your head, you're drunk."

"Not that drunk."

He continued as if he hadn't even heard her. "And I

make it a policy not to sleep with women when they aren't in their right frame of mind. That would make me no better than those assholes at the bar."

"I didn't want any of those assholes at the bar to touch me. But you... I want you to touch every inch of me with your hands, your mouth." She pressed against him. "Your cock."

"Quinn." He moved his head when she tried to kiss him. "How about we make a deal?"

She shuffled back, blinking against the sudden shift of the scenery. "I'm offering you a night of hot sex, no strings attached, and you want to make me a deal? I thought that *was* the deal?"

His smile made the room spin faster, and she had to hold his shoulders to stop from falling off the counter. He shook his head then sighed. "The deal is... You show me you can walk from here into your bedroom without falling down or puking, and I'll pound you into that bed for as long as you'd like."

Quinn smiled. "Seriously? All I have to do is walk into my bedroom, and you'll make me scream?"

"Scream. Beg. Come. Over and over, sweetheart. You have my word."

"Fine. Then, I suggest you take a deep breath because I plan on grinding myself on your face for the foreseeable future."

Russel's breath hitched, but he didn't move, waving in the direction of the hallway. Quinn allowed him to help her off of the counter, then steadied herself. Walk to the bedroom—piece of cake.

She set off, getting a few steps away before her head seemed to catch up with her. The floor tipped, and she had to palm the back of a chair to stop from crashing into the table. Russel tsked behind her but didn't stop her, staying in her peripheral vision as she made her way to the hall—using more pieces of furniture than she would have admitted to. But now… Now, it was clear sailing. Nothing in her way and a wall to brace against. She had this.

Until more than the floor tilted, and she had the distinct sensation of falling. Only, she didn't. Russel was there, catching her against him—taking her up in his arms, again. He said something, but it got lost in the hazy darkness slowly drawing her under. Images danced around inside her head, too fleeting to make sense of, when everything settled. She blinked, wondering what the ringing in her head was before she rolled over, staring at the alarm buzzing on the small side table. She reached for it, groaning at the pulse of pain through her temples. Light streamed in through the windows on the opposite side of the room, the brightness suggesting she'd slept later than usual.

A throat cleared close by, and she shifted her gaze, locking it with a pair of stunning green eyes. The guy smiled as he leaned forward in the chair, his muscled forearms braced on thick jean-clad thighs. Heavy stubble covered his jaw, the shadowed skin adding to his rugged good looks.

He smiled, and her damn stomach dropped. "Morning, Quinn."

CHAPTER 3

Russel stared at Quinn, wondering if he'd ever seen a woman quite as beautiful. Hair a tangled mess around her face. Eyes slightly reddened. A deep blush coloring her cheeks. She looked so perfectly—imperfect.

Quinn palmed her head, glaring at him through long lowered lashes. "I'm pretty sure there's nothing about this conversation that requires you to yell."

He smiled. Fuck, she was adorable when she got angry. And there was no doubting she was mad. The way her eyes crinkled as she continued to glare at him... Priceless.

He grabbed a glass of water off the table and held it out to her. "Here. Drink. It'll help with the headache."

She groaned, still palming her head. "Again, with the yelling."

She took the glass, managing half of it before handing it back to him. She glanced at the clock, squinting in an effort to see the numbers.

"It's almost eleven."

Her head wobbled as she turned it toward him, as if

she was trying to hone in on his voice before her eyes widened. "Did you say, eleven? As in, just an hour before noon?"

"That's generally how the clock works. First, eleven, then twelve."

"Shit!" She collapsed against the headboard. "This can't be happening. Not today."

Russel frowned. While he wouldn't question her being upset if she had somewhere to go—not that she'd mentioned anything before she'd passed out in his arms last night. Of course, he hadn't really asked her too many personal questions. Any, really. Not when he got the distinct feeling she wasn't looking to share those kinds of details. In fact, he was certain she'd gone to great lengths to keep herself as anonymous as possible. But the way her voice had cracked slightly. The raised pitch and uneven tone. She wasn't disappointed. She was nervous.

The thought scratched at his protective instincts. There had been several instances during the evening when he'd wondered if she was actually running or hiding from someone. Tidbits of information coupled with her usual residence. Not to mention the part where she claimed she never brought anyone home. Hadn't asked him anything remotely personal in return, even when he'd given her the perfect opportunity to do so.

He'd grown up in a troubled home. Had been roused in the middle of the night and spirited away into the dark. He'd been too young at the time to appreciate what his mother had done for both of them. Why she'd left everything behind in a desperate attempt to escape. But he'd clued in as he'd gotten older. Had watched her try to adapt to a life spent looking over her shoulder—always wondering if his father would show up. Drag them back.

While Quinn put up a good front, he'd noticed the slight cracks in her façade. The fingerprint reader on her door—definitely not standard fare. And her apartment lacked any type of personal items—no photos, no memorabilia. Nothing that couldn't be left behind at a moment's notice—pretty much the same as his house had been. He just needed to figure out a way to bring it up—see if there was anything he could do to help.

He nearly laughed at the thought. He barely knew the girl. Had spent the night watching her sleep, waking her every few hours in order to check her condition. For all he knew, this was a weekly outing for her, despite her claims to the contrary. And yet…

His years of training—of knowing when guys were lying to him about how badly they'd been hurt in order to stay in the field—told him she'd been completely honest with him. At least about the few details they'd discussed. And he wasn't about to abandon his instincts, now.

Russel shifted over to the edge of the bed, smiling at her when she wedged one eyelid open. "Late for something?"

"Not yet. But based on how bad I feel…" She managed to sit up, her head still bobbing around a bit. "So, um…"

He groaned. "Fuck. You don't remember my name, do you?"

Her chin jutted out as she attempted to stare him down, only to close her eyes for a few moments. "Of course, I remember you name. It… It starts with an R…" She looked at him, again. "Russel."

"Score one for the home team. Now, what about last

night? Do you remember anything after leaving the bar?" He frowned at the way she squinted at him. "Do you even remember leaving the bar?"

"Why do you seem to think I've got amnesia or something?"

"Because you're staring at me as if you've never seen me before."

"It's not that I don't remember you. Things are just a bit…fuzzy." She glanced down at herself. "I'll assume that since neither of us are naked and you were sitting in the chair, we didn't…" She waved her hand between them.

"Didn't what? Fuck? No, we didn't, because I prefer my sex partners to be conscious. Crazy, I know."

She furrowed her brow. "So, you spent the entire night sitting in the chair? Watching me sleep? I thought you were just going to drop me off then go home?"

"That was the plan until you Peter Panned out of my truck and hit your head on the cement floor. Someone had to make sure your concussion didn't get worse. Or that you weren't suffering from a bout of alcohol poisoning. With how much you drank…"

She stared at him, mouth hinged open, eyes wide.

He arched a brow. "Quinn? You okay?"

She opened her mouth wider as if she was going to say something then shook her head and closed it, doing her best to swing her feet over the edge of the bed—wedge in beside him. "Christ. You really are some kind of knight, aren't you? One of the last few good guys out there."

"You say that like it's a bad thing."

"Not bad, just not what I'd imagined." She glanced over at him. "I suppose this means you're not an assassin or mercenary?" She inhaled. "Shit, you're not a cop, are you? Or a fed? Damn, you're probably a fed."

He grasped her shoulders when she went to move, keeping her still. "You might not want to stand up that quickly or you'll just end up back on this bed. And, for the record, I'm not a cop or a fed. Actually, I'm—"

"Don't." She held up one hand. "I don't want to know what you do. In fact, I already know too much."

Too much? They'd barely talked about anything.

He snorted. "Is that so? You already think you know me?"

She locked her gaze on his. "I know enough."

"Really? And what is it you think you know about me? Because I'm pretty sure I didn't tell you anything remotely useful."

"I know you're a man of your word. That you have an insanely strong moral compass. That you know at least some form of martial arts, and you seem to have medical knowledge." Her gaze dropped to his arm, a hushed curse lighting the air. "You've got a tattoo? One that looks like…"

She didn't finish, choosing that moment to push to her feet. She took a couple of staggering steps away then turned to face him. "Thank you for bringing me home. For watching over me. But… I have somewhere I have to go, so… If you'll excuse me, I'm going to attempt a shower." She stumbled over to the adjoining bathroom door, glancing at him over her shoulder. "It was nice meeting you."

Russel watched her grope her way into the bathroom before closing the door. He waited until the shower turned on then made his way to the kitchen. She didn't have much in the way of food, but he managed to toast them both a bagel and make some coffee before returning to the bathroom. He'd been standing outside the door for a couple of minutes when it opened and she nearly crashed into him as she barreled through.

He caught her, somehow avoiding spilling coffee on her skin as he waited for her to regain her balance before releasing her.

She blinked, frowning at him. "You're…still here."

"You need to eat something. Here." He handed her the bagel. "I've got some pain killers in my bag. I'll grab a couple for you. But they'll just make you nauseous if you don't eat."

She stared after him, one hand fisted around her towel as the other held the plate with the bagel. "Your bag? When did you have time to bring in a bag?"

"You've been passed out for nearly twelve hours. There was plenty of time to go to my truck and grab my kit."

"You have a kit?" Her eyes widened when he retrieved the smaller of his medic bags from the hallway. "Christ, this is crazy."

"Crazy is not being prepared." He unzipped it, then grabbed one of the bottles. He shook out a few pills, closed everything up, then walked over to her. "Take these."

She arched a brow at him.

He chuckled. "Seriously? You've been unconscious all this time—completely at my mercy—and now, you think I'm going to drug you or poison you or something?" He offered her the pills, again. "It's just some Tylenol and some Naproxen. Trust me. It'll help with the hangover and any residual pain from that lump on your head."

She studied him for a few more moments then took the pills, downing them with a swig of coffee. "Thanks. And how did you know what to put in my coffee?"

He shrugged. "You wouldn't have flavored coffee creamers if you didn't use them. And no one keeps a small sugar bowl unless they use it for things like tea and coffee. I played the odds that you'd like it similar to mine."

She snorted. "Great, now, you've got me thinking you're a spy. And no. I really don't want to know if you are."

"Wouldn't spy trump assassin or mercenary?"

She smiled, and his damn heart gave a painful thump. "I suppose it would." She headed for the closet, pulling some jeans and a sweater out as she looked over at him. "Not to sound ungrateful, but... Is there a reason you're hanging around? I realize I pretty much threw myself at you once we got here. And it's not like you're not tempting, but..."

"You have somewhere to go."

The lines around her mouth deepened as she pursed her lips. "Yeah."

He didn't miss the way her pulse fluttered faster at the base of her neck or that her breathing had increased. "You don't sound too happy about it."

She lifted one shoulder then broke eye contact. "It's...complicated."

"That seems to be the definition of your life."

She looked over at him, and he turned in order to give her some privacy to dress. Soft rustling sounds drifted across the room, followed by the dull thud of the towel hitting the floor.

Russel steeled himself against any unwanted thoughts.

Now wasn't the time to imagine her swaying his hips back and forth to get into her jeans, or how smooth and pale her skin had looked above the edge of the towel. He'd already switched into PJ mode. Not quite full on, like in the field. But enough he was shutting off the other parts of him—the part that still felt her lips molded to his or her sex pressed against his aching dick. But it wasn't because she was avoiding his questions. It was what he'd glimpsed in her eyes before she'd looked away. He didn't need his years of training or endless missions in enemy territory to recognize fear. And Quinn had it in spades.

Footsteps.

He twisted as she walked back over, going for her purse, which he'd placed beside her bed. She thumbed through a few things then turned to face him.

Small creases furrowed her brow, and she seemed hesitant. "Bet you're regretting coming to my rescue, now."

"Nope. In fact, best decision I've made in a while." He took a step closer. "This place you have to go, is it the reason you were drinking last night? The thing you needed to figure out?"

Her eyes rounded for a moment, and her face paled. "Shit. I really need to respect my limits. And trust me. The less you know, the better."

He moved in front of her when she went to walk past. "I realize we barely know each other, but… I'd have to be blind not to see that you're in some kind of trouble. Maybe I can help?"

She snorted, waiting until he'd moved before heading for the hallway. He grabbed his bag then followed her out, watching her gather a few things before sitting on a chair to tug on a pair of boots. Her phone jingled, and she muttered a curse when she read whatever message flashed on the screen.

Russel leaned against the wall. "I'll go out on a limb and say you're not happy about that message you just received, either."

She huffed, zipping up her other boot. "Not really."

He handed over her coat once she'd stood, slipping on his. "At least let me give you a ride. You said your car's in the shop, and it's too damn cold for your bike. Not to mention the fact you're probably still over the limit."

"I'll call a cab."

"On a Sunday morning? In this neighborhood? Are you nuts? It'll be at least thirty minutes before anyone shows up. And you already said you were late."

"I said, not yet."

"Pretty sure we've passed that point, judging on the scowl you gave your phone a minute ago."

Quinn groaned, dragging in a few deep breaths before chuckling. "If I'd known good guys were this hard to get rid of…"

"I'll take that as a yes." He waved toward the elevator. "After you, sweetheart."

She rolled her eyes but headed out, strangely quiet as they rode down to the garage then got into his truck. Even after he'd backed out, she hadn't spoken a word.

Russel gave her a gentle nudge. "Where to?"

She scanned the area, looking as if she might have another option just waiting for her, before sighing. "There's a funky little café down on Western Ave. It's only open to the public in the evenings, but… They allow private gatherings. Just get me within a block or two."

He frowned, wondering if there was a reason she wasn't telling him the name or why she didn't want him to drop her off at the door. "Okay."

He looked up the street on his phone, memorizing the route, then drove off. Quinn sat rigidly beside him, staring out the window as the buildings rushed by. This was definitely a different woman from the night before. This Quinn was focused. Distant. Her hands gripped her purse, and she looked ready to jump out of his truck at a moment's notice.

Russel gave her some space, winding his way to their destination. Unfortunately, they were closer than he would have liked. Not nearly enough time to question her the way he wanted. Especially when her phone kept jingling. She ignored it, but the way she repeatedly clenched her jaw suggested she knew who it was—what the texts would say. While he didn't expect her to open up to him, he hoped she'd let something slip, and he'd know whether or not her life was in danger.

Music played softly in the background before his patience waned. He took a deep breath then glanced at her, once again, nudging her arm. "How's the head?"

She shrugged. "Not as good as I'd like it to be, but the drugs are helping. If I manage not to puke for the next hour, I'll consider myself extremely fortunate."

"If you're not feeling well, maybe you should cancel? I'm sure whoever you're meeting would understand."

She laughed, the sound hollow. "Trust me. Canceling is *not* an option. He'd only send some of his colleagues to check up on me, and that would be far worse than eking my way through brunch."

"This guy sounds…dangerous."

Quinn froze, as if just now realizing what she'd said out loud. Her breathing sped up, that fluttering pulse throbbing at the base of her neck. She peered at him, eyes wide. He didn't move, didn't talk, just kept driving, glancing over at her whenever he could.

Silence stretched between them for a while before she sighed and collapsed against the seat. "It's not what you think. I'm not in any danger—not from him. But the men that work for him…"

He didn't miss the shiver that shook through her before she managed to draw herself up—regain the stiff posture she'd had when she'd first jumped in. Not in danger his ass. All he had to do was glance at her, and he could see the fear etched in the smudges beneath her eyes. The firm line of her jaw. Regardless of what she claimed, the girl was scared.

"If you're nervous, I could come in with you."

She coughed, as if she'd been in the midst of swallowing, then spun to face him so quickly, he half expected her to knock her head on the side of the chair. "You'd what?"

"I said, I could come in with you. Have your back. So, you didn't feel as vulnerable."

"But…" She shook her head, mouth hinged open, eyes overly wide. "Why would you offer to join me when you don't even know what you'd be walking into? That's…insane!"

"I can handle myself. Whatever the situation."

"Even if that's true… No. Just, no." She pointed to the next stop sign. "You can let me out there. We're pretty close."

Russel pulled over to the curb, twisting to face her as he reached for her hand. "I mean it. Outnumbered.

Outgunned. Doesn't matter. I don't scare easy, and I don't back down."

Quinn stared at him, chest heaving, her fingers clamped around his arm. She seemed torn between wanting to push him away or press into his touch. A few minutes passed before she finally released an audible breath. "I knew you were trouble the minute you walked over to my table. My damn heart skipped when you smiled. I never should have asked you to sit. Guys like you… I doubt there are any other guys like you."

She shuffled closer, moving in like she had the previous night. She lifted one hand then thumbed his jaw, sliding her fingers back along his neck until she could palm his head as she brushed her mouth across his.

Russel tugged her closer, snaking one arm around her waist as he kissed her back, licking his way inside. Warm velvety softness filled his senses, the sweet taste of her pounding the blood in his ears. The loud beat echoed inside his head, drowning out every other sound until Quinn moaned into his mouth.

He felt that moan all the way down to his toes. Deep. Gravelly. As if she'd had to rip it out of her chest. He responded in kind, letting her suck in a quick breath before angling his mouth over hers, again.

This kiss was harder. Much like the one they'd shared on her counter before she'd all but begged him to make love to her—fuck her, he reminded himself. And he'd come damn close. The medic side of him had been appalled. The girl was drunk. Concussed. And yet, he'd wanted her. Had barely been able to pull himself back enough to make his proposal. And, damn, he'd been rooting for her. But he'd known, as soon as she'd tripped against the chair, she'd be lucky to make it to the hallway.

She'd surprised him and gotten a few feet in before she'd tanked—keeled off to her right. He'd been ready. Had caught her long before she'd been at risk of hitting the floor, because he was *not* going to let her get hurt, again. He'd fucked up getting out of the truck. He'd witnessed how unsteady she'd been walking out of the bar, falling into his arms several times before reaching his vehicle. He should have guessed she wouldn't make it down from the high step without incident.

Thankfully, it hadn't been more than a cosmetic injury—a small raised bruise the only proof of his failure, now. And she'd done a good job of hiding it behind some kind of makeup. She'd used more to hide the smudges under her eyes—the redness across the lids. Not that he thought she needed it. Her kind of natural beauty didn't need enhancing. But he suspected walking into this "brunch" as she'd called it, wouldn't have gone over well with a visible mark on her head. Or obvious evidence that she'd been out on a bender. She'd told him point blank that she'd gone somewhere she didn't think anyone would find her. And he suspected she wanted to keep it that way. Meeting up with this guy looking hungover would have raised suspicions. Maybe have his "colleagues" searching around for where she'd been.

Shit. The more he ran it over in his head, the more he realized this was way worse than he'd thought. He just hoped she'd let him help.

Quinn stared up at him when he finally let her come up for air. Green eyes nearly black, her lips swollen and wet from his kiss. Her chest heaved against his with every frantic inhale as her fingers scratched at the back of his neck.

He nuzzled her nose, wishing he could turn them around—take them back to her apartment. Then, he'd keep his promise. Spend the rest of the day—the night, too, if she'd let him—learning every sexy inch of her body. All the ways he could make her fly apart.

She must have recognized the predatory look in his eyes because she inhaled and held it, releasing it in a shaky exhale as she swallowed with effort. She closed her eyes for a second before smiling up at him. "Damn. You really are something else."

"Then, let me help you. Or let me take you home. Or wherever is safe. I—"

She silenced him with one delicate finger. Her eyes grew watery as she sighed. "I can't." She shook her head when he tried to talk around her finger. "Russel. You need to listen to me. I'm not…"

She huffed out a breath. "I'm not like other women. I try to be. Do everything I can to pretend I'm someone else, but the truth is… My family's dangerous. If you hang around, you'll get hurt. And that's just not something I'm willing to risk. I… I like you. You're the kind of guy I've always wanted to date. To get serious with. Fall in love with, so…"

She cleared her throat, moving decisively back and out of his immediate reach. "So, I won't risk it. Please don't ask me to."

She grabbed the handle and stepped out before he could register anything past the hard pulse of desire fogging his brain. The one focused on the shade of her skin and how it felt pressed against his.

He shook off the shock, reaching for her, but she was already standing on the sidewalk, the door held in her outstretched hand. "Quinn. I can help you. I'm not a normal guy, either. I'm—"

"I know. But it doesn't matter. He's got too many connections. And, if his right-hand guy ever discovered I had someone special…" Tears pooled in her eyes. "You need to go. Drive off and don't look back. Please."

"That's not who I am… Quinn!"

But she'd closed the door and stepped back.

Russel opened the window. "At least tell me your last name."

She smiled. "Just in case you were wondering, drunk or not, I never would have regretting spending the night with you. Never." She took another step back, motioning him on. "Goodbye, Russel."

Russel growled, his hand already on the handle when her phone rang. Her face paled, and she reached in, answering it. He couldn't hear what she said, but it obviously wasn't a pleasant call. She nodded then ended it, once again, waving him on.

She sighed. "Please. I don't want them to see your truck. Lying to them is…risky. I'm fine. The only thing that will put me in danger is if you stick around."

Anger burned beneath his skin, and it took every ounce of training he'd had to give her a curt nod then pull away, instead of jumping out of the truck and staying by her side. But endangering her life without knowing what she might face wasn't doing her any favors. And it was evident from the way she clutched at her purse—back straight, chin held high—she was determined to go in.

He considered parking a short way off and waiting for

her, but if she really was part of something dangerous, the organization might have men watching—waiting to catch her in a lie. And that wasn't something he'd risk. The same applied to her apartment. Without a car, one of these "colleagues" might insist on driving her home. And, if they'd somehow spotted his truck, seeing it, again, at her place could put her in serious jeopardy. He'd taken an oath to help people, not screw them over by making rash decisions.

Russel slammed his hand on the steering wheel. This wasn't the military, and he didn't have any intel to fall back on. But, if she thought he'd walk away—forget her—she had a hard lesson coming her way. He still had resources—had already agreed to join Hank's team at Brotherhood Protectors. And Russel would bet his left nut that Hank could unearth more information.

All Russel needed was a bit of time and some patience. And, once he was armed with the details, he'd be back.

CHAPTER 4

Quinn waited until Russel's truck disappeared around the next block before quickly crossing the street then heading back the way they'd come. She'd made sure he'd driven a couple of blocks past the café in case Thomas was watching, which she was sure he was. He'd been blowing up her phone since before they'd left. And had basically just told her to get her ass there before her old man sent out a search detail. Exactly what she was trying to avoid. She'd made a point to never be alone with any of her father's associates.

Associates. What a joke. They were thugs. The kind of men to strike first then worry if it had been warranted, later. Especially Thomas. Just thinking the man's name made her stomach roil. Why her father had picked him to be his go-to guy, she didn't know. Thomas was mean—junkyard dog mean—always sticking his nose in her personal business. He'd been chasing her since she was sixteen, and despite telling him repeatedly that she wasn't interested, he still kept texting. Kept showing up at her usual hangouts, not that she had many.

She'd done everything she could to distance herself. Had blocked him. Avoided him. She'd finally gone to her father, but he seemed confused as to why Quinn wasn't interested in the guy. Her dad seemed to think Thomas was the perfect man for her. Thankfully, he had told Thomas to let Quinn decide when she wanted anything more to happen between them. It had been enough to get him to curb some of his usual behavior.

But Quinn didn't trust him. That's why she'd secretly moved into her loft apartment. As far as her father and anyone else was concerned, she lived in the bachelor suite above her small studio. She made sure to have her lights on timers, her mail delivered there. To stay a few nights whenever she got the impression someone would be checking up on her. Whatever it took to maintain the illusion.

A cold gust of wind whipped her hair across her face, the icy sting of rain making her shiver. She glanced over her shoulder—half expecting to see Russel's truck parked on the side of the road, his luscious mouth turned down into a hard scowl—and sighed in relief at the empty road.

Christ. He'd actually offered to join her. To walk through the doors with his hand on the small of her back, his side pressed to hers, completely unaware of what he'd face. What kind of situation she could have been leading him into. And he hadn't been scared. Not an ounce of fear had crinkled the lines around his eyes. Whitened his knuckles as he'd held onto her. Any worry had been directed solely at her—for her.

Her chest tightened, her heart pounding forcefully

against her ribs. Tears pooled in her eyes as his image wavered in her mind—eyes narrowed, mouth pinched tight. She hadn't been convinced he was going to listen to her until she'd pointed out he was putting her at greater risk by staying. Something had passed over his expression, and he'd relented—driven off.

She took a deep breath, dabbing at any residual moisture. She needed to get back in control, and thinking about Russel wasn't going to help with that. Not after the way he'd turned her inside out with that kiss. Exposed the pieces of her she'd hidden away. Buried so deep no one could find them, least of all her. She wasn't sure if love at first sight—or first kiss—existed, but he was definitely putting that theory to the test. And, while she vaguely remembered kissing him last night, today's kiss was off the charts. She'd wanted to climb on top of him, make love to him right there in the truck, idling beside the curb, in broad daylight. Then tell him to drive and never look back. It was crazy. *He* was obviously crazy.

Or crazy good.

She swallowed past the large lump in her throat. She'd recognized the tattoo on his arm. Military. Special Forces. While she couldn't remember exactly which division, she knew she'd seen a similar one when she'd been doing a photo shoot at Fort Lewis—a charity calendar with the proceeds going to wounded veterans. All of the men had ink, and she'd seen her fair share of emblems. They had been SEALs, Marines, Army Rangers—the elite. Men who didn't shy away from a fight. Who didn't know the meaning of the word surrender. Men just like Russel.

She would have figured it out sooner if she hadn't been smashed the night before. Looking back, Russel screamed military. His hair, his moves. His sense of honor. Why she hadn't considered it before, she wasn't sure. But everything had clicked into place when she'd spotted that one mark.

She'd done her best to hide the fact she'd clued in to his profession, not wanting him to offer any other details that would make finding him, again, easy. That was a road she couldn't go down. While he might have the ability to keep her safe, she'd never put that kind of burden on him. Fighting a war was one thing. Going up against organized crime—never knowing who was on the payroll. If you were putting friends and family at risk—that was entirely different. And the last thing she wanted was to have his blood on her hands. She already had enough guilt weighing her down.

Quinn hurried toward the door, cursing under her breath when it opened before she reached it as Thomas walked out into the rain. He smiled smugly at her, stepping in front of her when she went to dart inside.

His fingers wrapped around her wrist with brutal force. "You're late, Harlequin."

She shivered at the way he drew out her name then yanked her arm free. "I've told you not to touch me."

"Your father was getting worried. You know better than to worry him."

"I came. That's all that matters."

"Where's your car?"

She stilled. Damn, had he spotted Russel's truck? Better to give him a version of the truth. "In the shop. A friend gave me a lift."

"A friend? What kind of 'friend' are we talking about?"

"The kind that gives you a ride last minute when your

car breaks down. That kind of friend. I'll assume my dad's at his usual table."

Thomas moved with her, still keeping the entrance blocked. "You can change your name. Make as many identities as you want. Live in that pathetic excuse of an apartment. Refuse to be seen in public with him. Severe every tie to this family. But you're still Harlequin James—Henry James' daughter and heir to his estate. You can't escape that."

"You're not *part* of this family. I've kept my promise. I don't interfere with his…business. And he stays clear of mine. And, by he, I mean you and all of your minions. Now, if you'll excuse me, I've kept my father waiting long enough."

Quinn pushed past him, breathing deeply as she headed for the table and chairs near the back of the café. Her father turned once she'd rounded the corner, holding his arms out to the side.

He arched his brow, glancing at his watch. "I was starting to think you weren't going to show."

She flashed him a small smile. "Sorry. Got tied up."

"You could have called me."

She nodded, though they both knew she'd never willingly call. Wouldn't leave any kind of physical evidence on her phone that they were connected. It was bad enough her father sometimes texted her, or had Thomas do it, like today. She didn't need to initiate anything. "I'm only fifteen minutes late. Hardly a reason to have Thomas send me a dozen texts."

"You're my daughter. I'll always worry. And I only asked him to check to see if you were still coming. It's not like you to be even a minute late."

And this was exactly why. "Car trouble." She held up her hand. "It's fine. I had a friend drop me off."

He arched a brow then motioned to the chair. "Sit."

She slid onto the seat, thankful for the chance to hide the way her hands were still shaking. Knowing Thomas was standing by the corner, watching her, make her skin crawl.

Henry sat across from her, his hands folded on top of the table, looking regal. He was dressed in a button-down white shirt and sports jacket, accompanied by a casual pair of tweed pants. Quinn wondered if he even owned a pair of jeans.

He leaned forward, smiling. "So, a friend. Tell me about this friend."

She plastered on the fake smile she'd perfected by the time she was twelve. "It's not like that. He's actually dating a girlfriend of mine. He'd asked me to hide her birthday present and was kind enough to drive me here when my muffler went. That's all."

He stared at her then sighed. "I was hoping that maybe you were seeing someone. Since you refuse to date Thomas, I thought you might have found someone else."

Good, she was obviously still skilled in the lying department, at least where her father was concerned. "You know I work crazy hours. Landing that magazine contract has made them even crazier. I don't have time for a boyfriend."

"You need to make time." He held up his hand. "I'm not getting any younger, Harlequin. I'd like to see my grandchildren before I die." He scowled. "I can't help but wonder if your mother was still alive, if you'd be less stubborn about getting involved in a relationship."

She cringed a bit at her full name. Only her father and anyone associated with him actually used it. None of her friends even knew it was her real name, and that's how she liked it. "Trust me, I wouldn't change anything. Besides, I'm only twenty-eight. I've got lots of time. And you don't look like you're on death's doorstep."

"Still, these things take time. And I'd feel better with you living on your own, going to some very questionable places, trying to capture...how did you put it? The real human experience? If you had someone to protect you."

"This isn't the nineteen fifties. I can fight my own battles, Dad."

"If you'd only agree to let me provide you with a bodyguard—"

"No!" She pursed her lips when he arched his brow at her sudden outburst. "Thank you, but no. I don't need a bodyguard. I'm fine."

He sighed, again, but the way he moved his cutlery around marked his displeasure. He stared at her for a few moments, glancing around before leaning forward. "I'm not a threat to you. You know that, right? Despite what people might say. What I do. You're my daughter. I'd never let anyone harm you."

She reached out and took his hand, a twinge of guilt eating at her stomach. This was why she'd turned a blind eye ever since she'd discovered his business empire was just a front for illegal activities. Money laundering. Weapons dealing. She suspected he did it all. That he was as cutthroat as the rumors she'd heard. As dangerous. But the man sitting in front of her, holding her hand as if she was made of glass, his worry etched in the lines across his brow and around his mouth... This was her father. And, despite everything, she still loved him.

"I know. But I promise you, I'm fine." She paused when Thomas appeared beside the table.

Henry turned. "Problem?"

Thomas glanced at her then focused on her dad. "Nothing you need to worry about. I just wanted to tell you that I have some business in the back office. You can text me if you need anything."

"That's fine, Thomas."

The man leered at her, making a point of ogling her breasts before spinning on his heel and disappearing down the hallway.

Henry gave her hand a squeeze then released it. "I really don't understand why you won't go out with him. He would definitely keep you safe."

But who would keep me safe from Thomas?

She smiled. "Not my type."

"I'm starting to think no man's your type." He relaxed back in his chair. "You look tired. And is that a bump on your head?"

"I dropped a lens and banged my head on the table getting up."

"You need to take better care of yourself. If you're working these insane hours because you're having money troubles…"

"No. I've got everything covered." She stood. "Though, I could use the ladies' room. Please order me the usual."

She dropped a kiss on his cheek then headed for the hallway. The washroom was down near the end of the hall, next to a couple of offices. Cool air swirled around her feet as the door closed behind her, giving her a moment's peace.

It appeared her father was in full coddle mode, and if she didn't stop his line of questioning, she'd scream. She didn't want his help, his money, or his men. She just wanted to see him once a month—pretend for an hour that he wasn't the head of some kind of crime syndicate. That he was Henry James, loving father and successful businessman.

Quinn ran the water, splashing it across her face. She'd hide out for five or six minutes, give her dad time to forget what other questions he was going to drill her with, then she'd make her way back. Choke down eggs and toast, call a cab, then head home. Alone.

Now was not the time to start thinking about Russel. He was gone. Period. And, even though she could probably find out which branch he'd belonged to, and ultimately his last name, she wouldn't. Couldn't. She'd been born into this life—accepted it as just a crappy roll of the dice. But she'd be damned if she'd bring someone else into it. Not willingly. And Russel was too stubborn, too proud, too much a soldier, to consider the danger before barreling in, guns blazing, all to save what he saw as the proverbial damsel in distress.

She took a calming breath, stilling when a series of dull thuds sounded through the wall. She pressed her ear against the cold surface, jumping when the next thud reached her, followed by a low moan. Like an animal that had been trapped so long it barely had the strength to call out. An angry voice came next, then another thud.

Quinn eased away. It didn't take a genius to deduce what was going on in the next room. And the thought that someone was getting beaten sickened her. Surely, this didn't have anything to do with her father. After she'd learned the truth, she'd confronted him. He'd calmly admitted to his "ventures" but had sworn to her that he'd never hurt anyone. That he didn't condone violence. That he'd never let anything like that touch her.

But, as she stood there, listening to the mumbled sounds in the next room, uncertainty surfaced. Hadn't Thomas said he had "business" in the back room? Which meant either her father had lied to her or he'd been kept in the dark, too. Shielded from certain undertakings.

She drew herself up then grabbed the door handle. She wasn't a scared teenager, anymore. If she'd had the guts to demand answers, then, she wouldn't balk at demanding them, now. She took a deep breath when the door down the hall opened.

"I'll be back in a few minutes. I suggest you reconsider our offer."

Quinn froze. That was definitely Thomas' voice. She stood motionless as his footsteps echoed down the hallway, toward the dining area, then faded.

Emotions warred inside of her, but curiosity won out. Maybe it wasn't what she'd assumed? Maybe she'd been wrong? Either way, she wanted to know the truth before she confronted her father, again.

She cracked open the door, made sure the hallway was clear, then darted out. She turned toward the office, quickly moving to the door before trying the handle—unlocked. She took a deep breath then peeked inside. A man was tied to a chair, head bowed, body slack against the bindings. Blood trickled down his face then dripped off his chin, pooling on a sheet of plastic covering the antique throw rug. His labored breath wheezed through his lungs, the light hiss to it sending shivers down her spine. She took a step in then stopped as her gaze dipped lower. His left knee was shattered, shifted off to one side at an unusual angle. More blood stained his pants, what looked like a piece of bone stabbing through his denim.

Bile burned her throat, and she turned, closed the door then raced back to the washroom. She made it to the closest stall before emptying her stomach into the toilet. Endless heaves that left her slumped against the metal divider, heart pounding, hands shaking. Maybe it was a by-product of the alcohol. Or the meds Russel had given her. Or just the cold truth that had slammed into her like a damn freight train. Whatever the reason, she wasn't sure she'd be able to get back up. Walk out the door.

Dear god. How had she been so naïve? So wrong?

Footsteps in the hallway. Two this time. One slower than the other.

She turned to gaze at the closed door, wondering if it would pop open—if she'd be the next person tied to a chair—when the footsteps passed by then stopped.

"God damn it, Thomas."

Another crest of bile rose in her throat, but she pushed it down. That was her father's voice. She'd know it anywhere.

She forced her legs under her, tripping her way to the door. She heard them step inside the other room followed by the distinctive click of the lock.

Quinn slipped out, once again, making her way to the office door. She glanced toward the hallway then pressed her ear against the wooden panel. She needed to hear what her father said. Needed to believe that his outrage was because he'd only, just now, discovered what Thomas was capable of. That he'd toss Thomas out on his ass.

More groaning, followed by incoherent mumbling. Nothing concrete until Thomas yelled at the man to just tell them already. The guy muttered something—it sounded like "fuck you"—before the room quieted. She stared at the door, wondering what would happen if she knocked, when a couple of dull pops broke the silence.

Quinn inhaled, placing her hand over her mouth to keep from screaming. There was no mistaking that sound. It had been a gun. The kind with one of those large black barrels that hushed the loud blast. The kind she pictured assassins carrying. Or mercenaries. She wouldn't have been surprised if Russel had pulled one out of his kit. If he'd had one stashed in his truck. He looked the part. Dangerous. But here? Her father? She'd never seen her father touch a weapon.

Not that it mattered. The harsh truth was that man she'd seen was likely dead. Dead and tied to a chair, and her father was in the room, just…standing there, staring at him. Letting it happen, unless.

No, no, no, no, no. What if…if…he'd fired the shot? If he'd…god…killed the guy? She shook her head, wild hair bouncing all over. This couldn't be happening. There had to be another explanation. She had to be wrong.

But, even as she tried to talk herself into it, she heard her father sigh. Sigh. Like it had been an inconvenience to kill the man. A drain. The same way he'd sighed after he'd asked who her friend was. Like it was nothing. Normal.

"How many times have I told you not to conduct business when my daughter is around? Seriously, Thomas. She's in the bathroom, for fuck's sake. What if she'd heard you or seen you? Knocked on the door and seen him? All bloody and tied to the damn chair?"

"Maybe it's time your precious Harlequin owned up to her birthright. Took her place in the organization before she topples it. Turns you, and everyone else here, into the feds."

A hand connected with skin. "Don't you fucking talk about my daughter like that. You know I want her shielded from this. It's bad enough I've got accounts in her name. Properties. I won't have her subjected to your mode of business. You know I don't approve of your methods."

Accounts in her name? Properties?

"Yeah? Well, my *methods* get the job done. Keeps your ass out of a federal prison and on your throne. The guy was an informer. He was going to tell the feds *everything*. You really think a slap on the wrist or a warning was going to change that?"

"What I think is that you're a necessary evil, at times, and that you could have done it anywhere other than here. While I'm having brunch with Harlequin."

"Please. She looks hungover. I'm betting she's hurling her guts out as we speak. She won't know a thing. I'll have this cleaned up before she's even out. By the way, she showed up in a truck. One I haven't seen before. A very large guy driving."

Shit. He had *seen Russel's truck.*

"She claims it was a friend's boyfriend helping her out."

"Want me to check into it?"

"I'm very protective of my daughter, Thomas. Very protective."

"Understood."

"Good. Now, make sure this place is spotless, and don't pull a stunt like this, again, if Harlequin is remotely close. I promised I'd never let anyone or anything hurt her. And I'm a man of my word."

Quinn backed away, forcing herself not to run down the hall and out the door. Run until her lungs burst or she died of a heart attack. Until she ran out of land or hit the mountains. Instead, she headed for the bathroom. She made a point of flushing the toilet several times—in case Thomas was listening. Waiting—before finally returning to the table.

Her dad rose as she stopped beside her chair, brow furrowed, eyes narrowed. "Harlequin? Are you okay? I've never seen you look so pale."

She feigned a half smile, gathering her coat off the chair. "Actually, I'm not feeling well. The truth is, I went out with some friends last night. You remember Rhonda? She's getting married, so we gave her a surprise bachelorette party. I'm afraid I drank a bit too much. I thought I was okay, but it turns out, I'm really nauseous. Would you be upset if we rescheduled? I know you're busy, and you go to a lot of trouble to arrange all this, but…"

Her stomach gave a short heave, and she had to palm her mouth to keep from throwing up, again. Right there on the table.

Henry sighed. Just like in the room. Like before. God, it made her want to heave twice as much. "Of course. Why didn't you just tell me? You could have called. You're young. You're supposed to go out then wake up with a few regrets the next morning."

"I didn't want to disappoint you."

"Not possible. I *do* remember what it was like to be your age, you know."

She feigned that smile, again. "Thanks. I promise I won't go drinking the night before, next time." She pulled on her coat. "I'll call the house. Tell Gladys what Sundays I have free. Like I said, the new contract…"

"Can I have Thomas drive you home? He's just tidying up in the back office."

She knew the color bleached from her face. She felt it. Like her skin just turned to ice. Frozen. Dead, like the man in the office. "No. I already called a cab in the bathroom. I'm just going to go home and sleep this off."

"You really do look pale. Please, promise me you'll take better care of yourself. Not work so much." He smiled. The kind he'd given her as a child. The kind that had always made her look beyond the surface. Only now, all she saw was that room. That man. "I worry about you."

"I know."

He shifted on his feet, looking slightly…suspicious. "You sure you're not really going to meet this 'friend'?"

"What? No. He's off-limits. And I'm in no condition for company."

"Still…" He took a step toward her. "You know, you can tell me anything. I only want you to be happy. That's all I've ever wanted."

"Nothing to tell. Promise. I'm going straight home. Alone."

And by home she meant her studio. No question that he'd have someone check up on her, now. And she couldn't risk he'd discover her loft.

She moved past him, using her impending bout of puking as an excuse not to kiss his cheek, again.

"Take care, honey. I'll see you, soon."

She nodded, aware if she opened her mouth that scream she'd somehow suppressed would break loose. She'd probably shatter all the glasses. Hell, maybe create a concussive shock wave. Instead, she walked a quickly as she could without looking as if she was escaping. The cold air bit into her skin as she hurried across the road then around the corner. As far as she could get before bending over—puking, again.

Images of the man flooded her mind. The blood. The white cast of his bone through his jeans. The way he'd slumped against the ropes. And she knew, she'd just jumped down the rabbit hole. That there was no coming back. No more pretending. It was time she decided which side of the line she was on. And what the hell she was going to do to stay on that side.

CHAPTER 5

"Ya know, if you keep coming in here, my regulars are going to think we're a couple."

Russel smiled at the bartender—Cynthia or Cyn to most of the men—ordering his usual soda. He hadn't caught her name that first night but had corrected that oversight when he'd walked back in a few days later. "Didn't I see you leaving here with Sean the other night?"

She blushed, wiped off a dry part of the counter, then smiled. "It's…"

"Complicated? Yeah, that seems to be the default answer of every woman in Seattle."

Of course, by every woman, he meant Quinn. It had been nearly three weeks since he'd been forced to drive away—leave her to what she claimed was a family brunch. Though, after digging as deep as he could, he hadn't found any family associated to her.

He released a weary breath as he paid for his drink then made his way over to a small table off to one side. It wasn't a great location, but it afforded him the best view of the entrance without allowing him to be seen too easily. The last thing he wanted was to have Quinn spot him before she'd gotten more than a foot inside the bar then bolt. He didn't want to have to chase her into the parking lot—look like some kind of crazed predator. But he would if it came to that. He'd do just about anything to get some answers.

Because, even with Hank's connections—with Russel calling in just about every damn marker he'd made while in the military—all he'd unearthed was her name—Quinn Scott—and that she was a photographer. He grunted. Fifteen years in the service. Fifteen years of dragging his ass through enemy territory. Reading maps. Gathering intel. Fifteen years, and he hadn't been able to get so much as an address of where her studio was located. Everything came back to a digital PO Box and an email.

No cell. No permanent residence.

And, if that wasn't bad enough, the few pieces of ID they'd unearthed not only had bogus addresses, they had all started ten years ago. Before that—nothing. Not a birth certificate, not so much as a library card in her name. As if she'd just appeared one day.

Which meant he'd been right. She was hiding. He just didn't know from what. Or who.

He'd gone back to her apartment. Had spent more than a few nights waiting for her to make an appearance, but it was as if she'd vanished. He'd finally managed to peek into her garage, only to curse when he realized her bike was missing. He just hoped she hadn't skipped town. Changed her name and left him with absolutely nothing to go on. No hope of ever finding her, again.

And, damn it, he needed to see her, again. Needed to

hold her in his arms, taste her lips. Feel her pressed against him. Proof he hadn't left her behind to die at the hands of some madman. If he'd learned anything during his years as a PJ, it's that family didn't guarantee you were safe. He'd treated almost as many civilians in the field who'd been harmed by their kin, than he had actual soldiers. Not every culture saw blood the same way he did. And he couldn't stop from picturing all the ways her meeting could have ended. All the ways she could have been hurt. And all because he'd done what she'd asked and driven away.

He pounded his fist on the table. Fuck, he hated this. Hated feeling out of control. He'd only been a civilian for a few weeks, and already, he felt like a complete failure. If it wasn't for Hank's help, Russel wouldn't have even gotten Quinn's last name. He was starting to see why his buddy, Midnight, had joined up so readily. Hank and his men were top-rate. Russel had been scheduled to take on a few new security cases, but Hank had given him a hall pass—told him to see to Quinn's safety before he ventured back to Montana. Had gone so far as to threaten to kick Russel's ass if he showed up without proof he'd finished his job here.

Except, there wasn't a job. Just Russel's paranoia. The one that couldn't stop thinking about a girl he'd known for less than twenty-four hours. One who had told him to leave and not look back. One who had messed more with his head in those few hours than any other woman in his life.

Maybe the Air Force had been right? Maybe he wasn't fit to be a soldier, anymore. Hell, he couldn't track down one temperamental woman—what good would he be still traipsing across the desert if his brain was this fried, already?

Russel leaned back, sipping his drink as he scanned the room. Left with few alternatives, he'd returned to the bar damn near every night, hoping she'd come back in. That she'd planned on using this place as a safe haven of sorts. But he'd struck out every time. And, after two weeks straight, he was starting to lose faith.

The night wore on, each passing hour adding another layer of tension to his shoulders. He'd probably drunk a gallon of soda by the time the clock finally registered eleven-thirty. Chances were, she wasn't coming, now. Not this late.

He pushed back his chair then rose, leaving the last empty on the table. He made a quick trip to the men's room before stopping at the long hallway to take one more look around. The guys he'd threatened that first night had ambled in a couple of hours ago, but they'd stayed to the other side of the room. Only occasionally glancing his way.

Not that he cared. The assholes could stare all they wanted. Try to ambush him in the parking lot. The way he felt, he could take on the entire bar and not work out his frustration. He was running out of time, and there wasn't a damn thing he could do about it.

He fisted his hand against the wall, stemming the need to punch a hole in it when a swirl of cold air breezed through the bar. He looked up and froze. Just like that. Rooted to the spot, eyes wide, breath held. He'd never frozen before. Not standing at the open door of a plane, waiting to jump into utter darkness on the wrong side of a border. Not when a teammate was down and bullets were flying. But standing there, staring at *her*... It was all he could do to draw in air then push it back out.

A tremor worked through his hands, and he swore it was the first time they'd ever shaken. Countless firefights. Rescues where he'd had to work huddled over a bleeding soldier while trying not to get his ass filled with lead, and he'd always had a steady hand. There was a reason he'd been nicknamed Ice—nothing got to him. Ever. He was always stone-cold focused. Yet, seeing Quinn walk into the bar—alone—had him looking like a junkie needing a fix.

Quinn picked her way to the bar, glancing around until Cyn approached her. Quinn's lips moved, and Cyn nodded, handing over a bottle. Quinn reached into her purse just as Cyn looked over at him, eyebrow arched. Russel shook his head. He wanted to approach Quinn after she'd settled in. When she wasn't twenty feet closer to the door than he was.

He slipped back into the shadows, waiting until she'd headed for the same table he'd been sitting at before melting into the crowd. He'd watch her for a while, let her relax a bit before confronting her.

Quinn slid into the chair he'd been sitting at just minutes earlier, cooler clasped in one hand as she scanned the crowd. It looked innocent enough. Every woman there had taken stock at some point during the evening. But the way Quinn's gaze paused at each face, a small purse of her lips shaping her mouth before she moved on to the next person, was anything but routine. She was searching the crowd; he just didn't know if she was looking for him, or someone else.

Creases formed along her brow, those green eyes of

hers refocusing on her drink as her chest heaved, her shoulders slumping. She took a pull of her cooler, staring at the bottle as she thumbed the label. She'd left her hair down, the auburn mass cascading over her shoulders—a few bouncy curls grazing the top of the table. Her skin looked paler than he remembered, and he noticed the dark smudges beneath her eyes—not from a hangover. These were darker. As if they'd been etched into her skin. And he doubted she'd slept much since that night three weeks ago.

God, he hated being right. Hated that she was in danger. That she hadn't felt she could confide in him. Sure, he was essentially a stranger. But she had good instincts. He didn't doubt that, now. He'd been undecided if she really could sense trouble. If she'd actually read him that night or just lucked out. But standing there, watching her, he knew it hadn't been luck. The way she studied the other patrons, stopping at anyone Russel considered a possible threat to the other women in there, eyeing them as if mentally noting not to get close, assured him she'd developed highly attuned senses. Which only solidified his theory that she'd grown up amidst violence. Had learned to read people out of necessity. As a means of survival.

Well, those days were over. She was done living in the shadows—looking over her shoulder. Russel hadn't known how to help his mother all those years ago, but he'd learned. And all Quinn had to do was trust him.

His chest tightened at the thought. If he'd thought finding her had been difficult, convincing her to let him help her was going to be next to impossible. She seemed to have this notion she'd get him hurt. And maybe if he hadn't spent his entire adult life learning how to deal with threats—with people who'd trained just as hard and long as he had to be deadly—she'd have a point. But there wasn't an assignment he'd ever turned down, and right now, she was his mission.

He switched into PJ mode. Tactics, first. He was good at that. Planning then executing. He never went in blind, and this situation warranted the same thorough thought process. She was already on her second drink, which meant her inhibitions were starting to slide. He didn't want her to be mentally compromised. But waiting until she'd downed half of her cooler wasn't a bad idea. Let her relax a bit. Less likely to just up and run the second she saw him.

Next, he'd slide into the chair beside her. He'd make sure she wouldn't even know he was there until he cupped her arm. He'd have to be prepared for an elbow or maybe the mace or the cooler bottle aimed at his face, but that was minor. She could draw a knife, and it wouldn't faze him. He was already running through a dozen deadlier scenarios, most of which weren't really possible, but he planned for them, just the same.

He'd talk calmly. Use language that made her feel like she had some control. Which she did. It wasn't like he could hike her up on his shoulder and carry her out of here like some kind of caveman. God knew, he wanted to. Wanted to eliminate all the talking and compromising he knew was ahead and just take her away—ensure she was safe.

But kidnapping her didn't seem like the best way to convince her he was still one of the good guys. That he was better than whoever had put the fear in her eyes—had made her beg him not to stay. That she could trust him to keep her safe. That he wanted to keep her safe. So, he'd use every trick he knew to slowly topple her walls until she came to the same conclusion—that he was her best shot.

Russel wiped his palms on his pants, cursing at the clammy feel. He wasn't used to being nervous. Fear had been beaten out of him in week after week of training. He'd faced each mission prepared to die. No regrets. No second thoughts. Feeling a cold sweat break out across his skin, his stomach clench at the thought of her turning him down—it hit him hard. Just how hard he wasn't ready to acknowledge. He barely knew Quinn. Had nothing but a bunch of circumstantial evidence and one hell of a gut feeling that she was even in trouble. And yet, the thought of failing her, of not protecting her, stole his breath. Made it hard to do his job—to scour the crowd for any threats. To work through all the possible outcomes. To focus on anything other than finally holding her in his arms.

He realized a part of him had feared the worst—that she was dead. That he'd willingly driven away when he should have been busting through the door. He had a few weapons stashed in his truck—a Beretta M9. Walther PPK and an M5. And he always carried a couple of knives on him. But he hadn't been facing an insurgent camp in Afghanistan. He'd been in the middle of downtown Seattle. He couldn't just waltz into some café, armed to the teeth, because he had a "feeling" she'd been in danger. The rules out here were different. And Russel needed to learn how to navigate this new world. How to keep those he valued safe without starting his own private war.

He scrubbed a hand down his face. He'd do one more

loop of the bar then go in. Pray she'd listen to reason because he really was considering hoisting her onto his shoulder and carrying her out if she refused.

He started toward the bar then stopped. The hairs on his neck prickled, a heavy feeling building between his shoulder blades. Russel changed direction mid-stride, quickly disappearing into the shadows along the hallway, again. Something was off.

He searched the crowd, pausing on three men who had appeared on the opposite side of the room—close to the employee entrance. They were new. Russel had already memorized every face in the bar. Had watched each patron enter and leave, mentally adding or removing them from his list. But these guys—they hadn't walked through the front door.

He did a quick body sweep. Bulges beneath their armpits. Hard edges to their faces. A light sheen reflected off the overhead lights, making their skin glow. They were sweating.

Shit. Armed and nervous usually meant something was going down. Either they were here to rob the place or they were hunting. The thought had him moving. Had him circling around. He doubted they'd make a scene. No way they were packing enough fire power to take out everyone in the bar. They'd need bulkier clothes to hide those kinds of weapons. Which meant they'd play it safe. Wait. Watch. Execute their plan at closing time or when their target left or headed for the washroom.

Russel settled in off to their right. They'd commandeered a table in the far corner—one eclipsed in shadows with a fairly good view of the bar. He wanted to know if he should have Cyn call the cops or see if he could figure out who their mark was before making his own move. The last thing he needed was to get caught in the middle of something as he was trying to get Quinn out the door, assuming they weren't after her.

They ordered a beer then sat there, constantly shifting their gazes to…

Fuck. It was Quinn.

They could only see half of her, but there was no doubt she was the focus of their attention. Especially the taller guy with slicked back brown hair. He looked fairly polished—hair styled, nicely fitted clothes. Not quite out-of-place in the bar, but definitely not the typical fair. But Russel recognized the look in guy's eyes. The lack of compassion. The cold determination. Functioning sociopath was one of the clinical names. And Russel would bet his life this was one of the "colleagues" Quinn had mentioned.

Time to switch tactics. Plan A was gone. Obliterated. He wouldn't risk having them see him talking to Quinn. Hell, he wouldn't risk having them stare at her another minute. Which meant shifting to Plan B.

He made his way to the bar, careful to avoid being seen, not that they were really looking anywhere other than Quinn, now. Big mistake. Not surveying the establishment. Not considering they might face resistance. Russel knew how to capitalize on mistakes.

Cyn walked over to him, glancing behind him at Quinn before arching her brow. "What's wrong, tiger? Getting cold feet over that kitten?"

"See those three men at the table in the corner behind you? The ones who ordered a beer ten minutes ago?"

Cyn frowned, glanced to her left then nodded. "Yeah. What about them?"

Russel gave her thirty bucks. "I want you to wait two minutes then take them all a round of Manny's. Stand in front of them and lean over. Tell them that blonde near the jukebox bought it for them."

Cyn's eyes widened. "Bella? You know she's part of that biker crew that comes in here, right? The ones playing pool in the back room that will tear those men apart if they so much as smile at her?"

"Yup. Just do me a favor and try to linger. All I need is thirty seconds, but I'll take as long as you can give me."

She cocked her head to the side. "Do I want to know what's going on?"

"Probably not. In fact, the less you know, the better. Just…trust me. Please."

"Right. Trust the guy who's been coming in here every night just to meet up with the redhead, again, who he avoids the moment she walks in. Nothing suspicious there."

He smiled. "Exactly."

She snorted. "Fine. But I swear I will send you a bill if this turns into a full-out brawl."

"Deal."

She rolled her eyes but motioned for him to get lost. Russel nodded his thanks, carefully picking his way back to the hallway. He was already working through steps four and five when Cyn loaded three bottles onto a tray and headed toward the men. Russel watched each step, judging when she'd block enough of their view, then slipped out, mentally counting out the time in his head.

Ten seconds.

He was at Quinn's table, ass in the chair beside her, his hand on her shoulder.

Fifteen.

He'd avoided the elbow she'd directed at him followed by a swing of the cooler bottle in her other hand.

Twenty seconds.

He had her attention, her green eyes wide, her mouth open. She inhaled sharply then held it, as if she couldn't quite remember how to breathe. How to speak.

Twenty-five.

He leaned forward. "You have five seconds to decide if you're leaving here—alive—with me, or dead at the hands of those men that are watching you from the corner of the bar. Because, sweetheart, they aren't here to buy you a drink."

Quinn's gaze flew to where he motioned with his head. Cyn was standing in front, blocking most of their view as she leaned in low, no doubt flashing them a healthy dose of cleavage before pointing to Bella. The men all looked that way, giving Quinn a clear view of one of the men's profile.

Quinn gasped, most of the blood draining from her face. Her fingers tightened around the neck of the bottle, bleaching her knuckles white. "Thomas."

"He and those other two came in the back. And they're armed." Russel cupped her chin, tilting it toward him. "Time's up. What's it gonna be?"

CHAPTER 6

QUINN STARED into Russel's eyes and wondered if this was all a dream. If the sleepless nights had finally caught up to her, and she'd passed out in her studio, scanning through the last of the photos she'd taken—photos that guaranteed to either take down Thomas and his goons or get her killed.

Russel squeezed her shoulder, and everything snapped into focus. This wasn't a dream, and if she didn't get out of the bar right now—didn't convince Russel to get in his truck and leave, again. For good, this time—they'd both die.

Her stomach protested the thought. She couldn't imagine him dead, his blood on her hands. She'd done everything she could to forget him. Forget the way he'd rescued her. How he'd spent the night watching over her. The lethal look in his eyes when she'd begged him to leave. But nothing had worked. It was as if he'd been burned into her memory, surfacing whenever she lost the least bit of focus. That's why she'd come back to the bar—

against every instinct that told her it was dangerous. A part of her had hoped he'd be there. Waiting. Even though she knew she'd have to tell him to leave, again.

Russel's grip tightened, drawing her out of her thoughts. He narrowed his eyes, holding her down when she went to stand. "I know that look. If you leave here with me, you stay with me. No trying to run away. No lying to me. We're a team, and teammates have each other's back. That's the only option."

She glanced at where Thomas sat ogling the bartender and the blonde woman by the jukebox. "It's too dangerous. Russel—"

"With. Me. Take it or leave it."

"Can't we discuss this after we escape?"

He stared at her, green eyes fixed on her. His chin firmly set.

She huffed. "Fine. With you. But we have to go, now."

He kept his hold on her, motioning for her to wait as he glanced over his shoulder. He didn't seem the least bit worried that Thomas would see them. That he'd open fire in the middle of the bar. Christ, if he'd discovered what she was doing—and she had a bad feeling he had—she knew he wouldn't care how many people he hurt in order to get to her. But Russel didn't flinch as he switched his grip to her fingers, staying still one more second before standing and pulling her behind his back.

He didn't speak, using his hand to convey which way he was heading. He took her to the hallway that led to the washrooms, always keeping her body hidden behind his, then pressed them into the shadowed space along the wall. He didn't look at her, his focus on the room beyond.

She waited, heart pounding, her breath panting

painfully in and out of her chest. God, when had it become so hard to breathe? As if there were a series of bands cinched around her rib cage. She glanced at Russel, but he wasn't breathing hard. Wasn't standing there sweating, fidgeting in an effort not to run out of the bar screaming. She considered it a miracle she wasn't trying to drag him out of a bathroom window.

Time ticked by, each second stretching out until she wondered if an hour had passed. If Russel had somehow dozed off because they *should* be running, not standing there, waiting for Thomas to find them. She squeezed his hand, but he merely held up a finger on his other hand—the universal sign of "hold on". But she didn't want to hold on. She wanted to be outside, racing to her motorcycle. Disappearing into the darkness. She had evidence stashed inside, and if they could just get to it, maybe they'd live long enough to take down the organization.

Russel's shoulders lifted a moment before he was moving—pulling her along at a pace that nearly had her running behind him. He kept to one side, shifting left and right at a moment's notice. She wasn't sure why he didn't simply walk in a straight line, but she did her best to follow him. He passed the table Thomas had been sitting at—now empty—then continued to the other side of the bar. No one gave them a second glance as he veered toward a door at the end of a small hallway, stopping in front.

He motioned for her to wait, again, as he looked out the dirt-smeared window. "Shit. Can't see anything." He twisted to face her. "Here's how it's gonna play out. We go together. You keep your body low and behind mine. If there's anyone out there, you let me handle it. Chances are, they aren't expecting anyone other than maybe their buddies to come busting out. I'd leave you in here, but... Not chancing those assholes won't spot you or you'll try to ditch me. Are we clear?"

"I'm not going to try and ditch you." *Yet*.

He merely arched a brow. "Right. Are we clear?"

"Yes."

"Tell me what you're going to do."

"Keep low. Let you beat up the bad guys."

"Good girl."

Quinn's glared at his back as he turned around. *Good girl?* Seriously? But what bothered her more than him saying it was the way her damn heart quickened, as if the sentiment was hard-wired into her system. She didn't need his praise. Hadn't needed anyone's in a long time. Yet, there was no denying the warm sensation spreading through her chest and into her core. Independent or not, her body obviously reacted to the thought of pleasing him.

She groaned inwardly, moving with him when he opened the door and stepped out. Rain hid whatever moonlight there could have been, encasing the entire area in deep shadows. She tried to stay low but had only just turned when Russel shoved her to the ground before diving to his right. She managed to look up just as he rolled to his feet in front of another man. He knocked something out of the guy's hand, blocked a punch then advanced, tripping him onto the pavement. Two quick strikes and the guy went limp.

Russel looked at her, signaling her to join him. Quinn scrambled to her feet then darted over.

He lifted the guy up by his jacket, the man's head hanging limp. "Recognize him?"

"He's part of the security detail. Thomas hired him. Guy's probably a mercenary."

"Let's just hope he's the only—"

The door behind them swung open, and two of the men from inside barreled out.

"Down!" Russel shoved her to the ground, again, lifting the man he'd punched in front of him as one of the men from the bar raised his arm.

A series of dull pops sounded, the limp guy's body jerking in response. Russel shifted and flicked his wrist. The thug at the door went down, clutching his shoulder. His partner watched it happen, eyes wide, his gun half-removed from the holster. He looked back a second before his feet flew forward, and he landed hard on the wet asphalt beside his partner.

Quinn stood on shaky legs as Russel dashed forward, knocking both men out before grabbing something then hurrying back. She stared up at him, mouth slightly open, chest heaving, wishing she could ask him what the hell had just happened, but all that made it past her lips was an embarrassing squeak.

Russel grabbed her hand. "Answers later. Let's move."

Then, he was running, darting down the first alley then weaving his way across a few yards, over a fence then onto another road. She wasn't even sure if her feet were touching the ground, and he'd all but tossed her over the fence—vaulting it without even breaking a sweat. She was sweating. Sweating and breathing and barely keeping up with him as he made another turn then headed for a truck. God, she hoped it was his.

Russel didn't slow until he'd damn near run them into the tailgate. He opened the back, grabbed a bag, then went to one knee, rummaged through his kit until he removed a container. A minute later he was smearing dark paste across his plate.

"What are you doing? What is that?"

He didn't pause to face her as he wiped a bit more across the numbers then tossed the can back into his pack. "Camouflage paint. Might be enough to make it hard to read the plate. Toss your phone away, then get in."

Quinn rounded the truck, opening the door and sliding in. She dug through her purse for her phone, sighing as she tossed it out the window, watching it clatter onto the slick surface. She'd just finished paying the damn thing off. She yanked on the handle when something pinged off the back of the truck.

"Keep your head down, sweetheart."

Russel's fingers were in her hair, shoving her head below the dash as he spun the wheel with his other hand then peeled out, fish tailing across the slick road and around the next corner. A few more shots hit the truck, matching the slap of the window wipers, before they were clear, barreling down some alley, jumping across an intersection, then into another alley.

Quinn held on, buckling up as soon as Russel released his death grip on her. "Jesus, if Thomas doesn't kill us, you will."

He hit another intersection, cruising through at full speed, apparently confident the street was clear. "Nothing I can't handle." He looked over at her, winked. The fucker actually winked, full lips lifting into a killer smile.

She glared at him, the ass. He may have saved hers but

there was no denying the urge to smack his smug smile right off his rugged face. The one she'd been dreaming about whenever she managed to actually sleep. "I thought you weren't from here?"

"Grew up in LA." He glanced at her, skidding the truck around a corner then onto another street. "Sorry. Was that too personal for you?"

She ignored the remark. "So, how is it you don't seem worried that we'll get T-boned every time you hurtle us across four lanes of traffic?"

"There's only two, and I've done my homework. Each street is one-way. I only need to check that direction, and I can see it a few seconds before we emerge. I'd react accordingly if necessary. We're fine."

He might be fine, but she'd left her stomach somewhere back on one of the alleyways.

She sighed, releasing the breath she'd been holding before glancing behind them. "Think we lost them?"

"For now. But there're street cams all over the place. Hard to avoid all of them. If they're smart and have the right connections—or someone who can hack—they'll be able to search for us. And, seeing as we haven't passed another vehicle, yet…"

"They'll be able to follow, even if they don't your truck or can't see your plate to know it's us."

"Pretty much. At least until we get onto the interstate. Get lost in the crowd."

"Interstate?" She frowned at his stern look. The one that said she'd agreed to go with him. "My bike's back at the bar. It's pretty much all I had left, other than what's in my purse. I had some important stuff locked in it."

"Things can be replaced. People can't."

"I don't even have any clothes."

"I'll make sure you have clothes and other supplies, but first, we need to disappear."

"Disappear? How?"

"With a little help from a friend." He hit a button on his steering wheel. There was a slight hum, then ringing.

The line clicked, followed by some static. "I swear, Ice, if you're drunk dialing me…"

Ice?

Russel grinned. "Wouldn't dream of it Midnight. I need a favor."

"Can I send you the bail money wirelessly or do I have to drive all the way to Seattle?"

"Get hauled off to jail *once* in Paris, and that's all you remember."

The guy—Midnight—chuckled. "I happen to remember why they hauled your ass away, too."

"You would. No bail, just a number. Hank told me you've been talking to Rigs. Heard he's living…remotely not too far from here."

"If by remotely you mean the guy's become a hermit, yeah." Midnight sighed. "His injuries have healed but the scars, the flashbacks—he's having a pretty rough time. I was hoping to convince him to come out here. Stay with Bridg and me for a bit. Maybe talk to Hank. We could use an explosive's expert. And I swear he could shoot the balls off a mosquito."

Quinn snorted. Men.

Russel smiled at her. "Sounds like he needs a visit from the guy who dragged his ass out of that firefight. Tell him to stop wasting the chance I gave him."

"You're welcome to try. I'll text you his information.

Just... Tread lightly. And call, first, or he's liable to shoot you in the ass."

"Roger."

"Hey, Ice? Why didn't you call Hank? He's the one who got me the number."

"It's damn near midnight. He's got a family. That would be rude."

"You are such a jackass."

"I know. Thanks, buddy. Kiss Bridg for me. Tell her I'm sorry for calling so late."

"Right. Like she's not working."

The line disconnected, plunging the cabin into an odd silence. Quinn waited for Russel to say something—tell her who Midnight was or maybe call this Rigs he'd been asking about—but he seemed intent on the road, staring off toward the horizon.

She looked out the window for a while, watching the shadowed landscape blur past, until the endless hum of the tires got to her. She twisted to face him, staring at the hard beauty of his face until he acknowledged her with a slight shift of his eyes.

"Something on your mind, sweetheart?"

"What happened back there? That guy had a gun, then he was down, the other guy was down, and we were running."

His mouth twitched just a bit, enough to make her realize she might not like his answer before he sighed. "Unlike most of my buddies, I don't always walk around packing a gun. But I never go anywhere completely unarmed. I had a couple of knives and—"

"You threw knives at them? That's what that was?"

He glanced at her, brows furrowed, jaw set. "I didn't

really have much of a choice when that one asshole started shooting at us. If it's between us or them, I'll take us any day of the week."

She swallowed around the crest of fear. In all the commotion, the running, she'd forgotten she'd heard muffled shots.

"Having second thoughts about accepting my help, sweetheart?"

She smiled despite herself, remembering how he'd said something similar that first night. "Actually, I'm thinking it's the best decision I've made in a while."

He laughed, this time. "Touché." His smile fell. "You know I'd never hurt you, right? Despite what I might have to do to keep us safe."

He'd said "us" but she knew, without a doubt, that he meant "her". He'd do whatever was necessary to keep *her* safe. "I'm not afraid of you. Just remind me to hide the steak knives the next time we eat."

"I can live with that."

She rolled her shoulders, doing her best to stretch out the kinks in her back when another oddity struck her. "How did you know to park a few blocks off?"

He shrugged, merging onto the highway. "It pays to think seven steps ahead. I had a feeling that if you ever came back to the bar, it might go sideways before we got out of there. You were obviously frightened, so I took precautions. Plan for the worst. Hope for the best. That's how we do it in the Teams."

"The Teams?"

"Special Ops, but then you, knew that. You recognized my tattoo, didn't you? Which is why you weren't the least bit surprised by my conversation with Midnight."

She broke eye contact when he stared at her for a moment, weaving them through some light traffic. "I don't know what branch you were with. But I knew it was military. Hardcore military."

"And you still told me to go." He shook his head, clearly disappointed.

"Being a soldier doesn't mean you're prepared to take on an entire organization of criminals."

"Maybe not, but you could have given me a bit more to go on. Made it easier to find you."

"You weren't supposed to *find* me, Russel. That was the whole point of telling you to leave and not look back. I didn't want you to get hurt. Still don't."

She should have guessed he wouldn't simply disappear. But, after she'd made the decision to destroy her family's organization, she'd abandoned her new life and ventured back home. Given her father a story about her apartment being fumigated for rats and asking if he'd mind if she stayed in her old room. Needless to say, he'd agreed without hesitation. Why not? She was back under his roof. Under his watchful eye. Right where he wanted her. And, once she'd walked through those iron-wrought gates, no one was finding her, not even Russel.

"How did you know I'd be there tonight?"

He snorted. "I didn't. But, when every other lead went cold, I went back to the one place I thought I might get lucky. Didn't think it'd take a couple of weeks for you to show up, though."

"You've been going there for two weeks?"

"Paid off, didn't it?"

"Still."

Damn. What kind of man went to the same bar every

night for two weeks on the off-chance she might show up? It wasn't like he owed her anything. They'd hadn't even spent twenty-four hours together. And she couldn't claim it was because they'd had amazing sex. He'd spent the entire time sitting in the chair, watching her sleep off too many coolers. Waking her to check if she was medically compromised. Other than a couple of panty-melting kisses, he hadn't touched her.

Yet, here he was, driving through the rain, heading to god knew where after taking down three men—three armed men—as if it was normal. As if she were someone special.

She stared at him, again, seeing him from a new perspective—one that made her heart flutter and her skin feel tingly. She wanted to ask him why. Why he was risking his life to save hers. Why he hadn't just disappeared like she'd asked. Why he cared. But a part of her was scared. Afraid that he'd done it out of duty. That she was nothing more than a fucked-up obligation to him.

She'd felt like that most of her life. Not from her father. Criminal or not, he'd always told her he loved her. That she was his priority. He hadn't really succeeded in that department, though he'd tried. But the men who worked for him—they'd made it very clear that they only tolerated her because they were afraid of Henry. That they'd disappear like the couple of men who'd hit her. Now that she'd broken her agreement—was actively trying to send Thomas and his goons to jail—she was a target.

And, now, so was Russel.

Quinn closed her eyes. God, she was tired. Tired and scared and oddly aroused. Watching Russel best those men—armed with only a couple of knives... She'd be lying if she said it didn't connect with some ancient part of her DNA. The kind that took notice when an alpha male pounded on his chest. And, while it wasn't quite that simple, it had elicited the same response.

He'd fought for her. Had been willing to kill for her.

On some level, her body recognized that she was his.

She groaned and leaned against the seat rest. She was also apparently temporarily insane because that was the only explanation for the traitorous thoughts she was having. She was independent. Capable of taking care of herself. And, yet, she knew she'd be locked up in the trunk of Thomas' car if Russel hadn't been there. That's if Thomas hadn't killed her outright.

Russel's hand settled over hers, resting on her thigh. "Why don't you rest? We've got a few hours to go. Rigs' place is just outside Spokane. I'll wake you when we get there."

"It's okay. I'm not..." She stiffened a yawn. "Tired."

"It's a side-effect of the adrenaline dump. It's like crashing after eating nothing but sugar. A short nap will do you good."

Sooner or later, she'd have to ask him how he knew so much. She still didn't think he was a doctor, but... Maybe doctors traveled with SEALs and Rangers. Or maybe he was the military's version of a paramedic. She didn't really know that much about Special Ops. She'd always distanced herself from any form of policing, and soldiers were kind of along those lines.

And now... Now, she was apparently teammates with one.

He chuckled. "You are stubborn. Rest. Besides, I have a

shit ton of questions, and as soon as you wake up, you're giving me some straight answers. So, enjoy the rest while you can."

"And if I don't want to answer them?"

He smiled, sending the butterflies in her stomach into flight. "You will."

CHAPTER 7

RUSSEL DROVE THROUGH THE DARKNESS, wipers slapping out a beat as they worked to swish the rain to either side. After years in the desert, the endless rain made him antsy. Almost as if it was hiding danger that would pop out at him when he least expected it. Ready to wash away any evidence that he'd ever existed.

Of course, it could be the three weeks of little sleep and a lifetime's worth of stress. He'd have thought he'd be over worrying about anything after all his years in the service. But, sitting there, willing Quinn to walk through the door night after night because he literally had nothing else to go on—no other way to find her other than going back to the café and demanding answers—had taken more of a toll than most of his missions combined.

Overseas, he'd always had a concrete objective. That paired with reasonable intel had been enough to steady his nerves. After all, his end game was always the same—find his downed comrade and bring his ass back alive. Even if he was deployed with a team, it didn't change his directive. He was there to keep his brothers in one piece or patch them back up when things went sideways. It didn't matter if he was hurt. If there was heavy fire. If a teammate went down, Russel went in.

But that wasn't what Quinn required. She wasn't injured. She didn't need him to bandage her arm or keep pressure on an open wound. Her situation was the equivalent of cutting off half of him—the best half. The part that healed instead of killed. And that realization had made his heart race. He didn't question his ability to keep her safe—to eliminate any threat. That was a given. A reflex honed from years of training. He just hoped he didn't lose sight of who he really was in the process. Become worse than the monsters chasing her.

He glanced over at her. Though she'd fought it, she'd drifted off almost immediately, her body turned toward him, tucked against the seat. Her head rocked a bit from the motion of the truck, and her lips twitched as she whimpered quietly.

He frowned. She'd been restless for the last ten minutes, brow furrowing, fists clenching then releasing. Her eyes moved rapidly behind her lids, and he suspected the dream wasn't a good one. He reached for her hand, lightly holding it in his for a moment. Quinn shifted, squeezed her fingers, then settled, once again, drifting off. And Russel's heart kicked up.

He'd held lots of soldiers' hands. Used it as a means of reassuring them they weren't going to bleed out before he got them safely to the helicopter. It didn't matter how tough a man was. When he was lying there, barely conscious, blood sticky against his skin—holding Russel's hand was a sign he could relax. That someone else would watch over him. Have his back.

And Russel made a point of never letting a teammate die alone if he could help it. Knowing he couldn't do anything—working to save him just the same—those were the moments that had shaped the kind of man Russel had become. How he helped his brothers face death defined him more than all the lives he'd saved.

But he wasn't going to lose Quinn. He had no idea how she felt about him. If he was just a man she'd been forced to trust. Or if she felt as if she were falling without ever hitting the ground—the way he felt sitting there, holding her hand, wishing he could pull over to the side of the road, wrap her in his arms and just sleep.

Not that it mattered. She'd accepted his help—somewhat reluctantly—and failure was *not* an option. Whether she ever wanted more, he'd protect her with his life. See that she got whatever help she needed to get this Thomas guy and his thugs off her tail. But, for that, he needed answers—answers that would have to wait until she'd gotten some decent sleep.

Which meant he needed to get them someplace safe.

He glanced at the map displayed on his phone. He'd called Rigs, but the man hadn't picked up. Russel had left a detailed message—well, he'd told his buddy he needed a safe place for him and a friend to crash. One that wouldn't be easy to infiltrate. If that didn't clue Rigs in that Russel had possible tangos on his ass, then Russel had bigger problems.

Like what he'd do if Rigs didn't call him back. Midnight was right—Rigs definitely wasn't someone you just dropped in on. Especially since he'd left the service and was apparently dealing with some…residual issues. Russel wouldn't put it past the guy to have his entire place wired, and Russel preferred his body parts right where they were.

He huffed out a breath, wondering if he should try Rigs, again, or just plan on staying in a motel, when his phone jingled, the sudden sound making him jump. Damn, he was definitely losing it if he startled over his phone.

"Foster."

"You know, most people don't call after midnight. On account it's considered late."

Russel smiled. "We both know I'm not most people, and the fact you're calling me back at two…"

"Had a feeling you'd just keep ringing until I picked up. You're as bad as Midnight. Bastard won't stop calling. Keeps trying to get me to drive out to Montana. Says I should meet up with some ex-SEAL named Hank."

"Midnight's always been persistent. And Hank's a great guy. You definitely need to chat with him." Russel cleared his throat. "How ya been?"

Rigs snorted. "You've obviously talked to Midnight, so… He thinks I'm hiding."

"Are you?"

The line went silent, followed by a rough breath. "I'm…dealing. Adjusting."

"By living on the outskirts? Avoiding contact with anyone who might…what? React to how you look? Which is crazy, you know that, right? The scars really aren't that bad. Not the way you've worked them up to be inside your head."

"Right, says the guy who doesn't have one. *Anywhere*."

"Trust me. I've got lots on the inside. Besides, I didn't haul your ass out of that rubble just so you could play ostrich."

Silence. Not even the soft whisper of breath.

Russel sighed. "And that wasn't why I'd called. Guess I just can't tame that side of me."

A bemused snort. "That stubborn side is why I'm still breathing. I know you weren't supposed to come in. Zone wasn't clear. Heard you got bitched out for breaking ranks."

"Yeah, well, it wasn't the first time. Or the last."

"Heard about that, too. I'm sorry, Ice. I'm sure that was a tough one to swallow. Guys like you... You're the reason the rest of us could go in without worrying about getting hurt. We knew you PJs were just itching to come and drag us out. I have to say, you're a crazy bunch."

"Right, and setting explosives, defusing bombs is sane?"

"It's...complicated."

"I'm familiar with the term. Besides, you're not the only one who doesn't quite know how to adjust. Who knew it'd be so hard to integrate back? I always thought civilians had it easy. Now... Crap. Now, I just think they're all nuts."

"That's what happens when you're fresh out and already have a bunch of tangos on your ass. Want to fill me in on that?"

"I don't know much more than the fact that Quinn's in trouble. And the men chasing her have no issues about killing her or anyone who gets in their way."

"Quinn?"

"She's a..." Christ, Russel wasn't really sure what she

was, other than a source of frustration. The reason he felt so off-kilter. The girl was probably a witch. Had cast some kind of love spell that first night. He shook his head. "She's a friend."

"Sure. How's she doing?"

"Passed out. Too much adrenaline, too little sleep mixed with some alcohol… I doubt she'll wake up before morning."

"How far out are you?"

"About thirty minutes."

"I'll make up the spare bed. Just be sure you stay on the gravel drive, or you won't have to worry about those men chasing you, if you get my drift."

"You do realize civilians don't set charges around their property, right?"

"You just said they're all crazy. I'm just taking precautions."

"Right." Russel scrubbed his hand down his face. "You do know we're not done talking about how you really are hiding, right? Unlike Midnight, I don't care if I piss you off. He's far more…sensitive."

"Perhaps you should wait until you're actually here before you do that—bad guys on your ass, and all."

"Noted. We'll pretend we're both fine, for now. See you soon."

"Remember. Stay on the drive."

"Got it. And thanks, Rigs."

"Don't thank me until you get to my door without blowing up."

Russel smiled as the line cut off. It seems Rigs hadn't changed that much. Sure, Russel was pretty sure Midnight's assessment was right. That Rigs was hiding.

Afraid to face the world scarred from battle. And, if he was having flashbacks, suffering from PTSD... That complicated things.

Russel sighed. He'd have to wait until he was there to make a proper evaluation. See if he could talk Rigs into taking some positive steps forward. Russel knew firsthand how hard it was to be thrust into change. To find a new purpose. He was lucky. Hank had reached out to him and given him a lifeline even before he'd needed it. And Midnight had made a point of calling him damn near every night to ensure Russel wasn't going to disappear. Fall into some kind of depression.

Rigs... Once the Marine Corps had pieced him back together and stabilized his condition, he'd been shuttled off to Walter Reed then unceremoniously let loose. A decorated war hero left to fight his own demons in a world he'd abandoned a dozen years prior. To say it was daunting was an understatement. That coupled with injuries everyone could see—stamped across his face and chest—Russel understood why Rigs might choose to hide. Hell, Russel had considered it, himself. But he'd had friends that hadn't taken no for an answer. Who'd looked beyond his other-than-honorable discharge and accepted him. About time Russel gave that back.

Quinn stirred, groaning, again, until he took her hand back in his—gave it a squeeze. Knowing that his presence comforted her did funny things to his heart. Made it race, then skip, then fuck, he was sure it stopped, turned over, then started, again. And his stomach—it couldn't decide if there were a thousand butterflies living inside it or if it was just permanently stuck somewhere up by his throat. Either way, the feelings were new. Years of helping people, of facing gunfire and death without losing his cool, and her tiny hand resting in his made him break out in a cold sweat.

Man, he should have listened to his mother. She'd told him, repeatedly, that women had the power to unravel a man with nothing more than a smile. He'd never really put much stock in it. After all, she'd fled an abusive marriage. Had spent her life looking over her shoulder. Call him crazy, but that didn't sound like the kind of unraveling he wanted.

But, sitting there, holding Quinn's hand—Christ, he had a bad feeling *this* is what his mom had been talking about. Wanting to protect Quinn, he understood. It was bone deep. An integral part of his DNA. But wanting to hold her. Taste her mouth, her skin. Lose himself in those green eyes. *That...* It was foreign. Sure, he'd had a few short-term flings. A week, maybe a month. But, in his line of work, settling down hadn't made sense. He'd witnessed too many soldiers leave behind families. Wives. Children. People who were forever scarred by the loss. And he hadn't been able to bring himself to get attached.

Of course, it's not as if he'd ever met someone who had wanted him to change his mind. The women he'd dated had seemed to want the same from him—fun. Sex. Maybe a safe place to fall for a while. But they'd never asked for more and had left before he'd had a chance to realize it was time to move on.

But he wasn't a soldier, anymore. And, if he was honest, Midnight didn't seem too upset about how civilian life was turning out. In fact, Russel had never seen the man happier. Having Bridgette definitely made the difference. But it wasn't just Midnight. Hank. Swede. Taz.

They all had found a way to make it work. Had partners who made it worth the fight.

Russel looked at their joined hands, again. The way hers fit perfectly in his. Maybe he had something to fight for. Someone. He might not know how she felt, but damn if he wasn't falling for her. In fact, he was pretty sure he'd gotten in way over his head that first night. Sitting in the chair, watching her sleep—it had flicked some kind of switch. Made him long for more than just endless hookups. People breezing in and out of his life. The service had been his family. But he realized he had another one. Midnight and the guys at Brotherhood Protectors had made that clear. About time Russel found that special teammate. The one he hadn't thought existed until...

He snorted. Just his luck. He finally admitted he wanted a relationship—to be part of a couple—and the girl that grabbed him by the balls was involved in something dangerous enough to have a bunch of thugs on her tail, armed with guns and god knew what else. And she seemed as reluctant as he was to get involved. He sure knew how to pick 'em.

His GPS broke through his thoughts, rattling off the next set of directions. Russel focused on the road, on the steady downpour of rain—on anything other than the warm feel of Quinn's hand in his. The soft snuffling noises she made, or the subtle scent of her perfume that had slowly saturated every inch of his truck. Floral with a hint of something cool, he couldn't help but inhale it with every breath. And he knew it was permanently fused into his senses. That he could track it anywhere. Anytime.

He gave himself a mental shake, following the ghostly

voice as it continued to call out turns and distances. Another fifteen minutes and he was staring at the entrance to a small cabin set against some hills. Wire fencing ran out to either side, a couple of posts opening up a narrow gravel road. A few lights brightened the porch in the distance, a man's silhouette visible next to a railing.

Russel drove ahead, mindful not to venture even a hair off the gravel drive. Though, he suspected anything Rigs might have planted was mostly for show—a very mild charge to toss some dirt in the air and alert him to possible unwanted visitors—Russel wasn't about to test his theory. Rigs had been the best explosives ordinance soldier Russel had ever had the pleasure to work with, and his skills demanded respect.

The truck rocked to a halt as Russel shoved it in park. If nothing else, they had a few hours to rest—get their heads on straight. And get some damn answers. After that, they'd discuss their next move.

Quinn groaned when he lifted her against his chest, holding her close as he headed for the steps leading into the cabin. Rigs stood off to the side, half eclipsed in shadows.

He smiled—a flash of white amidst the darkness. "Glad you made it here in one piece."

Russel arched a brow. "I was hoping you were exaggerating on your defense strategy. But I'm not foolish enough to test you."

Rigs merely grinned. "Inside and down the hall. Second door on the right." He moved closer. "She okay?"

"Just exhausted. A good night's sleep might mean we get some answers in the morning. At least, I hope."

"I'll keep watch. Just in case. You two relax. I'll see you in the morning."

"Thanks, buddy. I owe ya."

Rigs waved it off, holding the door as Russel maneuvered them inside. He didn't miss the way Rigs seemed to avoid showing off the left side of his face, but that was a discussion better left for tomorrow. After Russel had gotten some sleep. And, with Rigs standing watch—nothing was getting past the man. Which meant Russel could actually let his guard down. For a few hours.

He headed for the room, placing Quinn on the bed before toeing off his boots then stripping down to a shirt and briefs. He removed Quinn's outer layer, leaving her in a shirt and panties, not wanting her to feel as if he'd violated too much of her privacy, then tucked her under the sheets, crawling in behind her.

He shuffled over, sliding one arm under her head and drawing her against his chest, letting the other wrap around her waist. She stirred, burrowed closer, then settled. Russel inhaled, drinking in her familiar fragrance coupled with a hint of coconut in her hair. God, she smelled incredible. He closed his eyes, his tension easing for the first time since he'd spotted her in the bar three weeks ago. Though, he knew it was only temporary. Tomorrow, she'd have to level with him about what she'd gotten herself into. Why those men were after her, and what it had to do with her family. Because he wasn't about to lose the first good thing to happen to him in a long time.

CHAPTER 8

RAIN PELTED AGAINST HER SKIN, dripping along her jaw to puddle on the pavement as Quinn got shoved down. Her hands connected with the asphalt, scraping a line across her palms. Voices rose around her, followed by a series of dull pops. The same sounds she'd heard in the café. Only these were directed at her—them. She wasn't alone. *He* was there. Somehow avoiding the bullets, eliminating the threats. One minute, she'd thought they'd both be killed. The next, he was grabbing her hand—spiriting her away.

And all she knew was his first name.

Quinn inhaled as she startled awake, remnants of the dream still playing in the background. She'd been crouched in the alley, watching as Russel saved her—again. Only this time, it wasn't from a bunch of guys who didn't want to take no for an answer. It was against armed men—Thomas' men. The ones he'd brought with him to deal with *her*. To deal with a traitor. That's what he obviously considered her. The only question was whether her father was involved.

The thought beaded her skin with goosebumps.

No. Her father might be a criminal. He might even turn a blind-eye to the violence going on around him. But she refused to believe he'd send men after her—men sent to *kill* her. It just wasn't...possible. Was it?

Another shiver raced down her spine, rousing her from the last vestiges of sleep. She blinked away the fuzziness, squinting to make sense of the shapes scattered around the room. Shadows still clung to every surface, only a hint of gray beyond the window across from her.

A warm hand palmed her stomach, drawing her against a wall of firm muscles. She inhaled, finally taking stock of her position. She was lying on a bed, Russel's left arm under her head, his right slung across her waist. Her head was nestled into the crook of his shoulder, his breath ruffling her hair with every easy exhalation. And the rest of her...

It felt as if every inch of her was snugged against him. Her back against his chest. Her legs interwoven with his. And her ass—it was pressed against his groin, the steely length of his cock—his semi-erect cock—notched between her buttocks.

She closed her eyes. There was no doubt the man was large. His hands, his shoulders, his chest, his feet. Though she'd assumed the rest of his anatomy matched, feeling the proof made the room spin slightly. And all she could think about was that if she hadn't been so damn drunk that first night, she'd know exactly what he felt like. Looming over her. Moving inside her. Pushing her into the bed.

She swallowed past the lump forming in her throat. She needed to think about something else. Anything but how good it felt in his arms. How right. It didn't matter that her heart raced whenever he looked at her. That her stomach flip-flopped if he so much as smiled. She'd given up on the dream of ever having a relationship when she'd discovered she was an heiress of sorts to a crime syndicate. That no matter how much she distanced herself, she would always be linked back to it—like a set of invisible chains shackled around her ankles. And she knew she'd never be able to drag someone else into that life. To put *their* life at risk. Last night was a perfect example of how dangerous situations could get. Sure, her actions since the café were largely to blame, but it could have happened regardless.

Thomas had made it clear in the conversation she'd overheard that he thought she was a liability unless she embraced her father's endeavors. And she knew, in her heart, Thomas would have eventually come after her. A preemptive strike to ensure he remained beyond the scope of the law. The last man standing.

Though, despite his attempts, he hadn't succeeded. And the reason was wrapped around her, his body warming hers, his scent infused into her senses. Russel had proven he could handle anything. And he hadn't even known what to expect. What he'd gotten himself into or the level of resistance he'd have to face. He'd just dealt with it. Taken out the threats then moved on, as if he hadn't just downed three men armed with guns and god knew what else.

Special Forces.

That's why she was alive. He was some form of Special Forces. He'd learned how to kill. How to survive, and he'd obviously been good at it. He'd said something about dragging his buddy, Rigs, out of a firefight. Then, there had been the comment about carrying men his size for miles. Maybe he wasn't at as much of a risk as she'd feared? Maybe he *could* stand against Thomas and his endless goons and not get himself killed?

His hold tightened, his lips curving against her head. "It's still early. You should rest some more."

God, that low raspy tone with a hint of sleep. She had no trouble imagining his voice sounding exactly like this after a night of sex—pounding her into the bed was how he'd phrased it. And damn if she didn't want him to do just that. Dissolve everything into nothing more than primal needs. Forget that they'd almost died. That they were on the run. That she'd eventually have to tell him *everything*. Because the chance of him wanting to have anything to do with her once he discovered her father, her fucking family, was dirty… To say it was unlikely was an understatement.

The guy was a war hero. Or at least, she suspected he was. Probably had a shoebox full of medals. Had honor shoved up his ass and oozing from every pore. She didn't know much about the Special Forces, but she knew men had to work hard to get there. Earn it through sweat and laser-focused determination. An unbeatable character. She'd grown up fed and dressed on blood money. Sure, she hadn't known it at the time and hadn't taken a dime since, but it didn't change the fact that her honor was tainted. Stained just like her DNA.

She shifted slightly, glancing at him over her shoulder. "Where are we?"

"Rigs' place. Got here a couple of hours ago."

"I…don't remember walking in."

He smiled, and her chest tightened painfully. God, how he turned from borderline scary thug to charming, sexy man with nothing more than a curve of his lips astounded her. The guy was pure sex appeal when he smiled. Or talked. Or fought off bad guys in the rain.

"You were exhausted. The adrenaline and all. I carried you in."

"You…picked me up out of the truck and carried me in, and I didn't wake up? I'm a light sleeper."

"Last night, you were pretty much dead to the world." He chuckled at her pout. "It's fine. I'd actually be more concerned if you hadn't passed out after all you went through. Would start me thinking you're some kind of spy."

Spy.

Yeah, she'd tried to be. Had made it her mission the past three weeks to gather as much evidence she could against Thomas and his men. While she realized there was little chance of her father escaping unscathed—that he'd likely end up in prison—she wasn't quite prepared to put him there herself. She knew it was stupid. Clinging to the image of the man who'd braided her hair and taken her to ballet lessons. But no matter how hard she tried, she couldn't shake it. Couldn't separate the dotting dad from the vicious villain.

So, she'd focused on Thomas. It seemed the man had been quietly taking over, one section at a time. First, it had been in acquisitions. Then delivery. Given another five years, and she had no doubt her dad would have been ousted or retired. Or killed.

Thomas would have been the new king. The head of the James' estate—the James multi-million-dollar company. The one that was a front for drugs and weapons and... The list went on. Other than actually trafficking people, her father had a hand in everything. And, now, Thomas was gradually worming his way in. One account after another.

Russel's hand opened, his huge palm splaying out across her stomach. God, it felt good. A couple of his fingers lightly grazing her skin as her shirt rode up. The tips were rough. Calloused. Much like his palms. Hands that had seen years of hard work. Years of serving. She didn't know how long he'd been a soldier. Didn't know what kind of soldier, other than he obviously had some medical knowledge, but she didn't doubt he'd earned every raised vein. Every muscle.

"Quinn? You okay?"

She turned into him, not quite crushing the moan as his hand slid across her stomach, coming to rest on her hip. Just a few more inches down and he'd be cupping her mound. Feeling the heat pulsing there as her breathing kicked up. The room had gotten warmer, the air thinner. It was a miracle she didn't have to focus on actually drawing oxygen in then pushing it out. But, somehow, her brain was still working. Still finding a way to function when every thought was on the shape of his lips. How they'd feel molded to hers.

He watched her, those green eyes staring at her. Looking as if they were seeing through to the girl she'd once been—the time before she'd virtually gone into hiding. Before she'd switched from Harlequin James to Quinn Scott. She'd thought about changing her first name, completely, but her father would have thrown a fit. Her mother had picked out her name—it had been just hours before she'd died. The name was sacred. Entrenched into Quinn's psych so much that all she'd been able to do was go by her shortened version.

But everything else—the person everyone knew as Quinn Scott—had been created for the sole purpose of escaping her heritage. Who knew she'd never get that far? That she'd lack the conviction—no, the balls—to shun her father. To turn her back on him. It was the right thing to do. The ethical thing. But she hadn't, and she wasn't quite sure what that made her.

Russel's brows furrowed. "Are you feeling sick? Did you get hurt?"

He went to push up onto his elbow when she lifted one hand and settled her palm on his cheek. His ever-present scruff abraded her skin, but she liked it. Liked the slight catch of the hairs against her fingers as she traced one cheekbone, ending at the corner of his mouth.

"I'm not hurt."

He frowned, still silently assessing her. "You sure?"

"Positive." She grinned, resting her other hand on his neck. "You really are handsome, you know that? Handsome and sexy and safe."

Russel's eyes darkened at the breathy quality of her voice, the small tinge of green she'd been able to distinguish in his eyes fading into black. His gaze traveled the length of her then up. The muscle in his jaw jumped, and his nostrils flared as he drew in a slow breath then let it out. "Quinn—"

She slid her finger over his mouth. "I'm not drunk, this time."

A smile, and bam, her heart kicked her hard. Made a sore spot in the middle of her chest.

He waited until she'd drawn her finger to his chin. "No, you're exhausted. And scared. And hopped up on adrenaline. That's a potent cocktail. One as strong as any cooler."

She quirked her lips. "Are you always this hard to get into bed? Or am I special?"

Another flare of his nostrils, only this breath sounded forced. As if it hurt to draw it in and push it out. "We're already in bed. And that's the point. You *are* special. I just didn't realize how much until you told me to leave and not come back."

Emotions clogged her throat. No one had ever looked at her the way Russel was right now. A thrilling combination of lust, respect, hunger. He wasn't holding back. Wasn't hiding behind some macho rule book. His feelings were staring down at her, daring her to look away. To deny that there had been something magical brewing between them since that first night. That behind the alcohol, the good deed, fate had been aligning the stars.

The perfect storm.

She'd never had someone special. Never *been* special. Never mattered to someone to the point they'd risk their life to get to her. And she wasn't quite sure how to deal with it. Sex, she could handle. Was familiar with. But what was looking at her in Russel's eyes was uncharted territory. Scary rapids that threatened to drown her with a single miscalculated turn. And what about her heritage? Would he still look at her like this once she told him the truth? Still think she was special?

Chances were, she knew the answer. Someone like him—how would she make him understand why she'd stood idly by when he'd spent his life running headlong into danger? How could she possibly measure up?

Better to make a lasting memory, now. Bleed as much out of her time with him as possible. Allow herself to get as close to love as she'd ever find.

Just. This. Once.

Quinn held his gaze, lifting her hand to join her other behind his head. "I told you before. I'd never regret making love to you. So, unless you're not interested…"

Russel's mouth firmed for a moment, then it was crushing against hers, sliding across her flesh and opening in invitation. She accepted, thrusting her tongue across his, tangling them until they either parted or passed out from lack of oxygen.

It was barely enough of a break before he was back, leading the assault, this time. Eating at her mouth then nipping and licking his way across her jaw. He continued over to her neck, biting at the muscle where it threaded into her shoulder. The small sting sent heat coursing through her veins, and she half wondered if her skin would spontaneously ignite. If she'd simply burn up before he'd done anything other than kiss her.

Her harsh pants cut through the darkness, every brush of his mouth drawing a low moan from deep in her chest. While she'd had her share of sexual encounters, nothing had ever felt like this. Uncontrolled hunger. Insatiable lust. One kiss, one touch, and she wanted more. *Needed* more. God, if he stopped…

Russel paused with his mouth next to her ear, his body pressing her into the bed. His erection jabbed her stomach, the long, stiff length stealing her breath. Damn, he was bigger. Harder. Deliciously warm, even through the layers of clothing.

A raspy breath caressed her lobe. "Why is it you always seem to think I'm not interested? That it's not using up every ounce of restraint, every tactic I learned in the service, to keep my hands off you? That I haven't spent the night holding you, wishing I could make love to you for hours?"

She arched into the next grind of his hips. "Then, what's stopping you, now?"

He eased back enough to stare down at her. "Like I said. You're different. And, yeah, I know that sounds crazy. We barely know each other. But that doesn't make it any less real. I don't pull punches, and I don't overthink things. When I make a decision, I go all-in. It's how I've been trained."

He brushed some hair back from her face. "I don't want a quick fuck, Quinn. So, if this is just a release of stress—a way to kill some time—I'll pass. Because I have this nagging feeling that once I get a taste of you, I won't settle for anything less than your full surrender. And that will take time. Weeks. Months. Years. If that possibility isn't on the table…"

She swallowed, wondering if she was secretly still dreaming. "Aren't you showing your hand a bit early? I thought guys were all about taking it slow? Waiting until the woman basically confessed her undying love before they admitted anything?"

"Guess I haven't heard about that rule. I'm not asking for a commitment. I'm just saying, if this is nothing more than a one-off…"

The inklings of fear shivered down her spine. "You

don't know me. You just had to rescue me from armed men. Aren't you the least bit worried I'm not worthy of anything more than a quick tumble?"

"You've got secrets. Serious ones that have you somehow in the crosshairs. But I'm an excellent judge of character. I'll take the chance."

"And if you're wrong about me?"

"I'm never wrong, sweetheart." He leaned down, brushing his mouth over hers. "So, what's it going to be? I'll climb out of this bed in a heartbeat. No hard feelings. And I'll still see you get whatever help you need. That's a given. Having sex, saying you're open to more than a one-night stand, isn't a prerequisite to my protection."

Warning bells went off in her head. Getting attached—that was dangerous territory. Soldier or not, Russel had no idea how dangerous Thomas was. He had the full resources of her father's empire. With how deeply the man had entrenched himself, Thomas could do virtually anything he wanted, and her dad would never know. Or maybe her father wanted her dead just as much. Either way, Russel would be a target.

Forever.

He chuckled. "I can practically hear you working through all the possible scenarios. Let me guess... You think because your family is dangerous—and no, I wasn't able to unearth what you meant by that—you don't get to have a life. To fall in love. Because we all know, love is a weakness people will use against you." He arched a brow. "Am I close?"

She knew her mouth had gaped open the moment he'd started talking, and she had to consciously close it. "They *are* dangerous. And I don't get the luxury of love."

"And if that wasn't the case? If you didn't have to worry about the danger?"

She palmed the back of his head, drawing him down to her. "Then, my answer would be yes. I'd want more. I'd *need* more."

His smile turned wicked. "Perfect, because you don't have to worry about the danger, anymore. That's my job. Mine, and my team's."

"Team?"

"I'll tell you more later, but first… I seem to recall promising to pound you into the bed."

CHAPTER 9

"But—"

Russel captured her mouth, swallowing what was undoubtedly a protest. Another excuse as to why she couldn't get involved. Why she didn't *deserve* to be more than a temporary lover. He'd had to hold back a growl, an actual animalistic growl, when she'd said she might not be worthy of more than a one-off.

Not. Fucking. Worthy?

It was absurd. True, he didn't know *her* story, but he recognized someone who'd grown up amidst violence. Who was trying to disappear, maybe distance herself, but hadn't been able to make a clean break. Maybe they had something over her, or maybe it ran blood deep. Family was family. He understood that. But he had no doubts that she was more than worthy of a guy like him. Hell, his own honor was in question. Who was he to judge?

So, her hesitations, her reservations. They had nothing to do with how she felt, and everything to do with fear.

Fear that her family would never stop chasing her. Fear that she wouldn't ever be free. But, mostly, fear that she'd get him killed.

She hadn't spoken those exact words, but it didn't take a mind reader to know that's what she'd meant. She didn't want to be responsible for his death. Didn't want to have his blood on her hands. Russel understood that, too. Respected it, even. But there was just one flaw.

He wasn't an easy guy to kill.

Countless enemy forces had tried. He'd gone up against some impossible numbers and had managed to drag his ass and his injured brothers' back in one piece. This bastard, Thomas, was welcome to come after him with as many reinforcements as he could find, but the asshole wouldn't get through. Russel. Rigs. The guys at Brotherhood Protectors—they were professionals. They'd dedicated their lives to learning how to fight. How to kill. They were the best of the best. The elite forces. No better friends, no worse enemies to have, and this Thomas prick had just become their number one nemesis. Guy was a dead man walking, and if he came close to Quinn, again…

Then, he'd be seriously dead. Dead and buried along with anyone else who tried. Because Russel was all about his mission. And his mission was Quinn.

He didn't care that it seemed irrational. That they were essentially still strangers. His instincts told him Quinn was special. That the spark that had instantly flared between them wasn't the kind that came along every day. More like once in a lifetime. Maybe it was Fate. Or thirty-odd years of shoving down every emotional need until it was stone cold ice in his gut. It didn't matter.

He trusted his instincts. And, once he committed, he didn't turn back. Didn't bail. He fought, long and hard, until the battle was won. Now that he was civilian, he had all the time in the world. Fifty years of time to battle against her doubts. And it all started with this kiss.

Quinn stayed a bit stiff against him for all of two heartbeats before sighing into his mouth and relaxing beneath him. He accepted her surrender, though it was hardly complete. This was just step one. Seduction and lust-dazed sex. The rest of the steps would come later. After they'd satisfied their physical needs. The first time was going to be fast. Fast and hard and, damn it, not nearly romantic enough to make her swoon. But... He'd spent the past three weeks fantasizing about her. Reliving the kiss in her kitchen, in his truck. Imagining how it would have been if she'd been able to stumble her way to her bedroom.

He wasn't one to dream. If he wanted something, he went out and got it. Sometimes, it was easy. Other times, it was a battle. But he'd never really had much trouble finding a willing bed partner. It had actually surprised him how many women were like their male counterparts —just looking for a hot night between the sheets. No strings, or at least only the kind that had slip knots in them. Easy to lose. And it hadn't ever bothered him before.

Then, he'd come to Quinn's aid—had driven her home, all the while reminding himself that he was just being a nice guy. That he had absolutely no business considering anything else. That she was off-limits.

Then, she'd called him out. Had made the first move,

and crap... He'd been lost. Had spent the night watching her sleep not simply because he was worried about her concussion or if she'd given herself a bout of alcohol poisoning. But because he hadn't been able to take his gaze off her. On the way her auburn hair pooled around her shoulders, the curly mess making her seem sexy and sultry. How her skin looked pale and smooth and utterly perfect. The soft snuffling sounds she'd made when she was dreaming. Or the way she'd smile up at him for one brief second, when he'd rouse her enough to see she was okay, before drifting off, again.

Then, after having to leave her—fucking abandon her to god knew what circumstances—she'd become an obsession. Not that he would admit that to her. But, damn, having her here, writhing beneath him from just a kiss... It was more than his brain could process. With so little blood left in the damn thing, he considered it a miracle he remembered to not simply rip off their clothes and sink inside her a few seconds later.

Romance was out, but foreplay. Surely, his lust-dazed brain could manage a few minutes of that. He'd just have to think about it as an op. He'd start at her mouth. Check. Mouths were connected, her tongue stroking his. In fact, he was far too close to shooting his load just from kissing her. From having her breasts flattened beneath his chest, her taut nipples poking incessantly at him. At the way she'd wrapped one of her legs around his as if trying to get him closer.

But, if he got any closer, he'd come. And he'd be damned if he'd do that. He usually had control. Ice wasn't just the way he was in the field. He was stone-cold focused with women, too. Was able to compartmentalize his needs and theirs. A bit of time dedicated to getting them off—a lick here, a finger there—and it was his turn. Long or short, it didn't seem to matter as long as he made it right, first.

But Quinn was different. Every inch of her begged to be touched. Kissed. Devoured. And he wanted to. He just wasn't sure if his dick would toe the line. It was hard—harder than it had ever been. He wouldn't be surprised if she gasped when she saw it. He was naturally large, but he suspected the damn thing looked like a pipe between his legs. It felt like a pipe. Hard. Thick. Unyielding.

And the last thing he wanted was to scare her. She'd already been scared, and sex wasn't supposed to be frightening. It was fun, and hot, and sweaty, and he wanted lightness and pleasure in their bed. Not her wondering if he'd swallowed a bottle of blue pills.

So, moving on to their clothes and managing to fist the hem of her sweater and lift it over her head without ripping it. That, was a fucking shining accomplishment. One of his finest achievements. Of course, her bra was next. Why did those things have so many tiny hooks? Were they designed specifically to give men blue balls? Because lying there on top of her, kissing her neck, trying to twist the damn clips open behind her back seemed harder than infiltrating an enemy compound. He could pick locks and extradite comrades easier than he could get those small metal clips to release.

Quinn laughed. Actually, laughed at him, then squirmed a few times, and bam—her bra was gone. Just gone. As if it hadn't existed. As if he hadn't just spent the last of his control trying to gently undo it. Not that it mattered. It could have vanished into thin air, been zapped away by an alien forces for all he cared. She was bare. From the waist up, nothing but an endless expanse of smooth, pale skin to run his fingers along.

He shifted his weight to his left elbow, using his right hand to slowly skim up her arm and across her shoulder. She had delicate collarbones. The kind that stood out. Christ, he could snap them without even trying. He must be double her weight, not that she was skinny. No, athletic and strong but still no match for him.

So, he kept his touch light, using the small fraction of his PJ side still firing to meter his touch. To caress and cherish. He couldn't imagine hurting her. Seeing even a flash of pain on her expression. He wanted her flushed. Gasping for air because he'd stolen hers. Wanted her body primed for him. Begging for his possession. And it was.

A circle of her nipple had it beading against her skin. Crinkling in on itself as small goosebumps rose around it then down her chest. He leaned in, blowing a heated breath across the hard nub before taking it in his mouth.

Quinn arched against him, his name a raspy whisper of air. He smiled. Yeah, this was how he needed her. Strung tight. Desperate. So when he mounted her, and damn, it was pretty much going to go down that way, she'd be ready for him. Would urge him on as he thrust inside then lost himself in a fast, hard rhythm that would end this first time far too quickly.

Her fingers dug into his back then tugged against his shirt. "Off."

Off. He understood that. Was on the same damn page.

Hell yeah, they still had too much on. His shirt and boxers, her panties. He lowered his head and rounded his shoulders so she could drag his shirt over his head. He would have sat up and taken it off, himself, but that meant losing contact with her skin. Not feeling the silky smoothness beneath him, and that order didn't seem to register with his brain.

Quinn muttered something then inhaled as he shifted to her other nipple, sipping it inside and sucking on it. God, she had beautiful breasts. Not overly large but full enough, with pretty pink nipples that glistened with his saliva. Made him want to paint her entire body with it. See it gleam in the dull light. Proof she was his.

He was thinking all wrong. Women didn't like possessive assholes, and he pretty much had that tattooed across his forehead, right now. But fuck it. On some cellular level, she was his. Right here. Right now. And he'd do whatever it took to see it stayed that way. Because tasting her skin—god, it was heaven. Sweet and salty with a hint of warmth.

He looked up at her as he lowered his hand, grabbing the edge of her panties. "Christ, you're so fucking beautiful."

She smiled, and his heart thumped. Hard. A painful thud that had him removing the last two pieces of their clothing in record time. He wasn't even sure if he'd moved or if he'd somehow willed them off. Used the *force* or some equivalent to make them vanish like the bra. Or maybe she'd done it. He'd suspected she was a witch. Had cast some kind of potent love spell on him. So, making their clothes disappear didn't seem that far-fetched.

Either way, now, she was bare. From head to toe, nothing but Quinn. And damn if she wasn't more beautiful. The way her hips flared out from her waist. The flex of muscles beneath her skin. And between her legs—fuck. A trimmed line of auburn-tipped hair that arrowed straight to glistening pink folds. They were puffy with arousal, leaving her slightly open—exposing the tiny hood of her clit.

He wanted to lick her there. No, needed to. Needed to know if the scent surrounding him tasted as good as it smelled. If she'd cream his tongue the way he'd envisioned in his dreams.

She snagged his arm when he went to move down her, locking her gaze on his. "I'm…close."

He reached for her hand and placed it over his dick. The damn thing pulsed against her palm. "Me, too. But this is just the first time. Once we take the edge off…"

Of course, he didn't say that taking the edge off might take the next twenty years, but she didn't need to know that. Didn't need to know the thoughts whirling through his head. The ones that would send her screaming from the bed, because he had absolutely no plans on letting her go.

Quinn moaned. "I could help you out with that. Give you the best damn blowjob of your life."

She squeezed, and he had to clench his butt cheeks together to stop from spilling into her hand.

He took a couple of calming breaths. "Let's save that for round two. Or four, because if I have to lay here, smelling your need for one more second without licking you…"

Her eyes widened then closed as he shuffled lower, opening her with one hand then licking a path along her cleft. Usually, he took his time. Drew patterns along the wet flesh. Teased the little nub with fleeting nips and kisses. But not this time. He dove right in. Face grinding against her sex, one hand sliding to her opening. He tested her readiness then slipped two fingers inside her.

She bucked against him, moaning his name as her muscles quivered. He kept licking, kept pumping his hand, wanting to slow down, but the signals weren't getting through. He was on full assault mode. Laser focused on making her come then pounding into her. He wasn't proud of it, but… She didn't seem unhappy with his approach. In fact, her walls were starting to ripple.

He added another finger just as he bit her clit, and she exploded. Hips rising to meet his fingers, body thrashing across the bed. It was so fucking hot he raised his head just enough to watch her unravel. See the flush move down her skin as a light sheen of sweat broke out.

She was still writhing when he climbed on top. Thankfully, some distant part of his brain had him reaching for his pants on the floor beside the bed. Removing a condom and sheathing himself before he slid into her bareback. Because he wanted to. Wanted to feel her skin give around his, her juices hot against his shaft. But he wouldn't do that until they'd discussed it. Until she believed in him half as much as he did in her.

He gathered her close, sliding his arms underneath her and locking his hands around her shoulders. First time had to be missionary. Gazes locked. Her body beneath his. Surrounded by him. He wanted to look down at her as he entered her. Wanted to watch every tiny reaction as he finally possessed her.

"Quinn. Open your eyes."

She was still descending. A deep red flush colored her skin, and she looked slightly dazed when she finally managed to stare up at him. Her chest heaved against his, each press grazing her nipples across his flesh like hot brands. She didn't talk, just lifted her arms and wrapped them around his back, tugging him closer as her legs encircled his hips, placing her hot, wet sex directly against his dick.

Russel clawed for control. He was trained. Surely, he could hold out one more minute. Long enough to enter her slowly. She tilted her pelvis, rubbing her folds along her length.

Her lips caressed his ear. "More. I need more."

He pressed forward, sinking a few inches inside her, when her head pushed into the pillow as her heels drove into his ass, thrusting him the rest of the way in.

Searing heat engulfed his shaft, even through the thin barrier, and he had to stiffen every muscle to keep his release at bay. "Christ, sweetheart. I'm trying to go slow. I don't want to hurt you."

She moaned, and he froze, afraid he'd done just that, when a series of contractions worked down his length. He snapped his gaze to hers, inhaling at her clenched jaw and rolled eyes.

"Are you coming, again? Fuck. Hold on."

She managed to tighten her grasp a second before he reared back then surged forward. Hard. Demanding. Setting up a punishing rhythm. The bed squeaked in the background as he pounded into her. He vaguely remembered not to use all his weight. To meter his stokes just enough he wouldn't hurt her. But it wasn't gentle. Wasn't the kind of loving she'd probably expected. He hadn't missed her choice of words. Asking him to make love to her, as opposed to fuck her like she had that first night.

But he wasn't doing a great job of it. Ramming into her, thrust after thrust, lost in the heat of her sex, the sound of her coming. It was primal. A merging of bodies that went on and on until the fire in his sac spilled over, and he came in long, hard spurts. Emptying into the condom and praying he didn't punch right through it.

Quinn clung to him, arms and legs trembling as he stayed rigid above her until the last of his release had been spent, and he collapsed on top of her. His heavy breathing echoed through the room when he finally had the strength to lift his head. He went to shift his weight, aware he was probably crushing her, when she gripped him harder.

Her tiny fingers bit into his back, her head pressed against his shoulder. "Don't go. Not, yet."

He managed to get his hand to move—cup her chin until she was gazing up at him. "Not going anywhere. Promise. I just thought it might be hard for you to breathe."

She shook her head, a stray tear leaking out of one eye. She cringed, but he smiled. He knew physiology. Stress was released via the tear ducts. So were other emotions. Intense pleasure often resulted in a complete breakdown of barriers, similar to the release of stress. So, tears after orgasming—it wasn't unusual. Though, it also meant she'd had a strong emotional reaction. Good. He didn't want to be the only one invested. The only one already thinking about the next fifty years.

He smiled at her. "You okay?"

She laughed, but it was for show. "Perfect."

"Yes. You are." He dropped a slow, sensuous kiss on her mouth, feeling himself starting to harden. "Though, I do suggest you take this moment to breathe, because I promised you the night, and it's only just begun."

CHAPTER 10

Sunlight bathed the room when Quinn finally managed to open her eyes. It was obviously well past sunrise and, judging by the shadows stretching out across the floor, closer to noon.

She groaned, still trying to shake the fuzzy feeling from her head, when she realized what felt off. Russel was gone, his side of the bed cold. She bolted upright, grabbing at the covers as they slid to her waist. The room was cool, and she was naked.

Naked. She'd slept with Russel. Or, not slept.

She lifted her knees and braced her elbows on them, palming her face in her hands. When she'd woken last night, having sex with him had sounded like a great idea. They'd nearly died. Had been dancing around the attraction between them every second they were together. So, blowing off some steam—having a few orgasms—had seemed a reasonable recourse to all they'd been through. A small celebration of life.

But then, Russel had shifted gears. Had gotten...

personal. Christ, he'd basically said that, if she agreed to have sex with him, she was agreeing to be in a relationship with him. A relationship.

The guy was nuts!

He'd just fought off armed men—men sent to *kill* her. And he thought getting involved was wise? Was anything other than completely insane, because she thought it was insane. Who signed up to have a bullseye put on their back over a tumble in the sheets?

Crazy people.

And ex-soldiers, it seemed.

But what was crazier—what blew her mind—was that she wanted one, too. Wanted to think in terms beyond the next sunrise. Beyond the end of the weekend. That's as far as any "relationship" had ever gone. Two days then done. Over. Nothing but a ghost.

Russel seemed to think two years was equivalent to a first date. Twenty to celebrating a few months. It was as if he lived by a different time scale. The Russel scale. Like dog years only longer. Twenty to one. Like a bet at the race track.

She should have told him no. Sorry. Can't do it. Can't put your life on the line. Because she'd forgotten to mention the part where her father was a crime lord. One who apparently had holdings in her name. Her name. Harlequin James, photographer and heiress to a crime empire. Which meant she might go down with the ship when it finally took on water—through the hole she'd been trying to blast in the hull. The reason Thomas was gunning for her.

But, instead of shoving him away, taking the initiative and going to sleep on the couch, she'd surrendered. Actually surrendered. She might as well have waved a damn white flag in the air because she hadn't put up any kind of a fight. Hadn't remembered all the reasons she'd pushed him away. Nothing had registered beyond the hot, wet press of his mouth on hers, and the white-hot need that had sparked inside her.

Heat billowed up from her core, increasing her breath. God, the things he'd done to her. After they'd gotten the first round over—the one that had been better than any other sex she'd ever had—he'd gotten serious. Had mounted her, again, pushing her through several more orgasms before pumping his body weight of sperm into her. Then, he'd carried her to the shower. Naked, but she'd just clung to his shoulders, trying to kiss him the entire way.

They'd showered, fucked, then showered some more.

Then, after carrying her back, he'd settled between her thighs and tasted every inch of her. She couldn't even remember how their last encounter had ended, fairly certain she'd passed out before he'd climaxed. But, judging on the stiffness in her joints, it had been just as mind-blowing as the other times.

Quinn took a deep breath, scrubbed her hands down her face then sat upright. The situation was definitely screwed up. And she wasn't sure how she felt about putting not only Russel, but this "team" he'd mentioned, in the line of fire. But it didn't seem to matter what she thought. Russel had made it clear he was hell bent on protecting her. Period. Arguing now, *after* he'd saved her life, seemed pointless.

Instead, she lifted the covers and swung her feet over the edge. She hoped the fact Russel hadn't stayed in bed with her wasn't an indication that he'd changed his mind. He'd be wise to. And she'd tell him to get out while he still could a dozen more times given the chance. But a part of her didn't want him to go. Didn't want to face this alone. Face the future alone.

After pushing anyone and everyone away—limiting herself to mostly acquaintances instead of friends—to never allowing herself to care about anyone more than idle friendship... Having Russel open the door to new possibilities—to a bonafide relationship—had cracked through the tough shell she'd built around her. And, like it or not, her damn heart had started pouring out. Seeping through the fissures until it was sitting there, exposed. Raw. Ready to be broken. She just hoped it was broken because he'd walked away and not because she'd gotten him killed.

The thought had her moving, reaching for her clothes, which Russel had folded on a chair at the end of the bed. She lifted her shirt and a note fluttered to the floor. Quinn bent over, unfolding the paper then reading the oddly neat handwriting.

GONE OUT FOR SUPPLIES. *Rigs is here. The guy's top notch. Ex-Marine. If things go sideways, glue yourself to his ass. And it would be wise not to venture off alone. He's got the place...secured.*

Russel.

P.S. You're damn cute lying there, snuffling, hair a perfect mess. Especially since I was the one who messed it up. Be back soon.

. . .

THE GUY WAS SMUG. Smug and pushy, and it made her heart beat faster because, beneath it all, he cared. He wasn't just tagging along out of a sense of duty. Every look, every touch, was a display of how deeply he felt for her. He'd willingly put himself between her and bullets. Bullets! And he hadn't even insisted she talk, yet. Had spent the night making her feel as if she was the center of his world. Even now, he'd left a note so she wouldn't worry. Wouldn't assume he'd just left.

Which she would have. Because that's what she'd always done. Left. Escaped before anyone could figure out who she was or get caught in the crossfire.

She folded the note and shoved it in her pants' pocket then quickly dressed. He'd left another towel for her, and she took a quick shower before tentatively heading for the main living area. Other than their room and the bathroom, she wasn't sure what to expect. Hadn't met this Rigs guy.

She reran what Russel and his buddy, Midnight, had said in the truck the night before. Something about a firefight. About him having scars and what she assumed was PTSD. Which, hell, she understood. Just one round of having someone shoot at her, and she felt like she was losing her mind. She couldn't imagine what it would be like to face that day in, day out. Always putting your life on the line.

So, he likely had visible scars—the kind that some people wouldn't understand. Would gawk at. Maybe had experienced some kind of amputation. She could deal with that. Had taken photographs of burn victims for an exposé and had seen her share of war veterans when she'd done the calendar spread. As long as he didn't try to kill her, she'd manage.

The smell of coffee led her to the kitchen. A large pot was brewing in the far corner, a couple of mugs set out in preparation. She walked over, inhaling the rich scent, when a hand landed on her shoulder.

She screamed, grabbed the person's wrist, locking it against her, then pivoted, ducking under the guy's arm and successfully exchanging places. She turned to face the man, hands in the ready position, her weight shifted forward onto her toes.

A bemused smile greeted her before the guy crossed his arms over his chest and leaned against the counter, his right side in silhouette. "Not bad, Red. I wasn't expecting you to counter."

Her breath heaved in her chest, the frantic sound echoing around them. She took a step back when he groaned and shook his head.

"Easy, I'm not going to hurt you." He extended his hand. "The name's Rigs. Ice's buddy."

Of course. This was his house, so obviously he was her host of sorts. She should have guessed that, but after all she'd been through, her body was primed to fight, first, ask questions, later.

Quinn stared at his outstretched hand for a few moments before shaking it as she dragged her gaze up to his face. Rigs was handsome—with piercing blue eyes and symmetrical features. His hair was longer than Russel's but a similar shade of brown with hints of blonde running through it. His skin had a healthy tan to it, as if he'd spent a lot of time out in the sun. Though she suspected it was most likely from his career in the military. Ex-Marine, Russel's note had said. Which translated into badass. Rigs had probably spent the past few years overseas in one desert camp after another.

He took a deep breath then turned to fully face her, exposing two large scars crossing his left side—from his temple, through his eyebrow, then down past the corner of his mouth. The lines were raised, with a few ladder-type stitch marks visible. God, he must have had the lacerations closed in the field. No self-respecting plastic surgeon at a hospital would have left that kind of damage behind. She couldn't imagine how much it had hurt, and not just physically. While they'd most likely fade a bit with time, they'd be a permanent feature for the rest of his life. Not that she thought they detracted from his appearance, but she understood why he'd be sensitive about them.

She met his gaze, thankful she hadn't flinched and that any flush on her cheeks would be attributed to their brief interaction. "You're Rigs? Then why the hell did you sneak up on me like that?"

He watched her, eyes narrowed, his hand still holding hers. He seemed to be waiting for her to react, which she wouldn't. She's just hoped it didn't mean they'd be standing there all day. Because he could search her face until sunset, and he wouldn't find the kind of rejection she believed he was looking for. The kind that made him feel like less of a man. Less human. She thought the opposite. That the scars were badges of honor. Proof he'd had the balls to face the unthinkable without fear. Unlike her. She'd spent a decade running away from it. Hiding under another name so no one would figure out her secret. Her scars were invisible, but far uglier.

He sighed then chuckled, finally releasing her hand. "I wasn't sneaking. Walked up to you like I would anyone."

"Except where you didn't make a sound. Most people would have called out or at least cleared their throat. I'm not used to people touching me out of the blue."

He shrugged. "Old habits. I was just trying to get your attention."

"You could try saying my name, next time. And it's Quinn, not Red."

"Quinn. Right. So, *Quinn*, how long have you studied jujitsu?"

"How did you know that's what it was?"

Another shrug.

Damn, what was it about military guys and being able to read her? "A few years. It became obvious one day that it would be wise to be able to defend myself."

"Smart. Women still tend to be targets for violence, however unfair that is. It's unfortunate those moves won't stop a bullet."

No, but Russel had. Christ, she bet Rigs could, too. Like *Superman* or *Wonder Woman*. Just deflect them off his bare hands without sweating. She was sweating, again. Standing there, the weight of his stare pressing in on her, made her nervous. As if he knew who she really was but wasn't letting on.

Could he? She'd had the odd person give her a second glance, as if they were trying to place her face, but she knew she'd never met Rigs before. She wouldn't forget a guy like him. Like Russel. They were unforgettable. The kind of men who stood out in a crowd. Like a spot of color in a black and white photo.

She pushed away the thought. She hadn't been

Harlequin James for ten years. And she'd changed a lot in that time. She no longer resembled the mousy, skinny teenager she'd been. So, the chances Rigs knew who she was…

Still.

She took a few steps back, sinking into a chair next to a small round table. "I was more concerned with being able to knock the odd drunken guy on his ass than anything else. Though, I guess I'll have to up my training. Learn how to avoid getting shot."

Rigs snorted. "That's easy. Don't put yourself in the position where it can happen."

She cocked her head off to the side. "It's not like I went looking for trouble." Well, in a way she had. She'd been snooping around. Gathering evidence. So, yeah, she had been looking for trouble, and it had definitely found her.

Another snort. The kind that told her Rigs didn't believe her. "Doesn't matter. You've got Ice, now. And he's very good at avoiding bullets. Stopping them, too."

That name, again. Ice.

"I keep hearing people call Russel that. Ice. Is it his nickname or something?"

"He didn't tell you?"

She tried not to cringe, hating the way her face heated. The man had spent the better part of the night inside her, and she still only knew his first name. God, she was pathetic.

"To be honest, we haven't really talked about anything personal."

"Right. You wouldn't want to accidentally blow your cover." He smiled at her sharp intake of air, continuing without making another remark about her past. "So, what do you know about Russel?"

She crossed her arms over her chest. "Enough."

"Then, you know he's a PJ. Or was a PJ."

"PJ? What's a PJ?"

Rigs shook his head. "Please tell me you at least knew he was military."

"I saw his tattoo. I know he's former Special Forces. I just…didn't dig any further. So, what's a PJ?"

"Pararescue. They're the crazy sons of bitches who go in when Special Forces get ambushed or shot down. They rescue *our* asses. Usually in the worst possible conditions. Russel's the reason a few hundred soldiers aren't lying in a pine box."

God, Russel was even more heroic than she'd thought. She didn't need to look up his vocation. She knew what pararescue meant. He jumped out of planes. Went wherever he was needed, which according to Rigs was behind enemy lines. That's what he meant by worst possible conditions. That's why Russel carried guys for miles. Why he hadn't seemed fazed at all by three men trying to kill him, compliments of her. He'd faced worse and lived.

She met Rigs' gaze. "That explains his medical knowledge. And how he evaded those armed men."

It explained everything, except why he was risking his life for her. She wasn't a soldier. A *brother* as he'd put it. In fact, she doubted she deserved being rescued after sitting idly by for so long.

She glanced at her hands, doing her best to stop them from trembling. She wasn't sure she wanted to know any more. Hearing how great Russel was, how honorable, only made her loathe herself more.

"Anyway, you're right. Ice is his nickname. Most of the guys in the Teams either get labeled due to their personality or end up getting called by their rank or last name."

She lifted her gaze to his. "So, why Ice?"

"Because of how he is under fire. Nothing gets to him. Nothing. Bombs going off, bullets kicking up the dirt next to his foot or ricocheting off the wall beside his head, and he's stone cold. Always focused. Always steady. I don't think I've ever seen the guy's hand shake. Seen him let his emotions show." Rigs' lips quirked. "Until this morning, just before he went out. Standing here, talking about your safety. Just the thought of leaving you… Never seen the guy so nervous. I think he was actually sweating."

She stared at Rigs, unable to answer. How could she?

Rigs shrugged. "Guess it has to happen to most of us, sooner or later. Ice held out a long time. He deserves to be happy." He leaned in. "You *will* keep him happy, right?"

She swallowed, half choking in the process. "I—"

"Oh, for fuck's sake, Rigs. Back the fuck off."

Quinn gasped, jumping up and turning—practically falling against Russel as he moved in behind her, catching her elbow when she tripped on one of the chair's legs. He had a couple of bags in his other hand, the scent of freshly baked bread wafting out of one of them.

He sighed, placing them on the table before pulling her gently against him. "Ignore him, sweetheart. He enjoys making people sweat."

She nodded, still unsure how to respond.

Russel glared at Rigs—who looked more than pleased with himself—then cupped her chin, lifting her gaze to his. "Hungry?"

Her stomach growled before she could reply.

He laughed. "I'll take that as a yes. Good. I brought fresh bagels, some cheese, a fruit bowl and coffee that won't peel paint."

Rigs grunted. "I welcome you into my home, and you insult my coffee? That's harsh, bro."

"You'll live. Longer, now, that I brought real coffee." Russel laughed at Rigs' scowl, focusing on her, again. "Why don't you sit? I'll grab some plates."

Quinn sank into the chair, again, eyeing Rigs suspiciously. While she suspected Russel was right, and Rigs had wanted to get a reaction out of her, she couldn't help but feel that part of it was his way of protecting Russel. Maybe paying the man back for saving his life.

She thanked Russel for the coffee he placed in front of her, looking over at her host. "So, what about Rigs? Is that your name or…"

Russel snorted. "It's more what he used to do. Explosives. Best ordinance specialist I've ever met. There isn't a problem Rigs can't fix with some wire and some well-placed C4. His real name's Kent. Kent Walker."

Great, now, she knew Rigs' last name, but she still didn't have a clue what Russel's was. Maybe she could sneak a peek at his driver's license because asking him, now, was beyond embarrassing. "I thought your buddy, Midnight, said he was a crack shot? Something about shooting the balls off a mosquito."

Rigs laughed. Not a fake one for show, but one that shook through him from deep inside his chest. "Wow, is Midnight still sore I beat him that one time in sniper practice?"

Russel sat down beside her, laying one arm across the back of her chair as he piled some food on his plate with his other hand. "If by once, you mean every single shot, then yeah. You know he hates to lose."

"The guy can track tangos like no one I've ever seen before. I swear he can smell them or see their trail as a colored mist in the air. Trust me. He didn't need to be the best at everything."

"You try telling him that. You know Rangers are touchy." Russel took a swig of his coffee, looking over at her. "Sleep okay?"

She coughed, nearly spitting the liquid across the table at Rigs. Had Russel seriously just asked how she'd slept? Because she was pretty sure he was the reason she hadn't gotten nearly as much as she probably should have.

She wiped her mouth with a napkin, mumbling an apology to Rigs. "Great. Thanks."

Rigs chuckled.

Russel arched a brow. "You got something to add, buddy?"

The man's mouth lifted then pressed into a line. "Nope. Nothing."

Quinn groaned inwardly, heat burning a line through his cheeks then down to her chest. She vaguely recalled the bed squeaking—had the headboard hit the wall? Obviously, Rigs had heard them. Which wouldn't necessarily bother her, but he knew they were virtually strangers. She hadn't even known what Russel did in the military. Yet, she'd spent the night making love to him.

She didn't make love. She had sex. Got off. But last night—it had been so much more. The way he'd held her. Touched her. Tasted her as if he'd die otherwise. It didn't matter that it hadn't been gentle. Romantic. *He'd* made it intimate.

Russel leaned in close. "Like I said. He's an ass."

"And *he's* sitting at the table, jackass."

Russel glanced at Rigs. "I know. My eyesight's fine."

Rigs huffed then stood. "And to think I actually invited you here. I'll go do a quick recon. Give you both some time to eat. Give Red, here, a chance to get her story straight, because when I get back, I'd like some answers."

Quinn inhaled, watching Rigs disappear out a side door. She wanted some answers, too, only her questions involved the alien feeling in the pit of her stomach. The one making it hard to eat. To breathe. That had her longing to trust Russel. To tell him everything. Something she wasn't sure she was willing to risk, just yet.

CHAPTER 11

RUSSEL BIT back the angry reply directed at Rigs as the man walked across the kitchen then slipped out the door. While Russel realized his buddy was only stating the obvious—Russel wanted some fucking answers, too—Rigs' tone could have been better. The one that said he clearly didn't trust Quinn. Though, Rigs didn't seem to trust anyone, lately.

Quinn stiffened beside him, glancing at the closed door then back to her plate. She hadn't really eaten anything, just moved the pieces around. Of course, eating when your stomach was tied in knots wasn't easy. And there was no doubt in Russel's mind she was scared.

Not about who was after her. That was a tangible fear—one she'd obviously been dealing with for some time. It was talking to them that had her skin blanched white, her breathing shallow—as if she was planning on running at any second. Providing these "answers" Rigs had mentioned had sent her from nervous to freaked out in record time.

Russel eased his arm forward, laying it across her shoulder with his hand resting on her arm. He gave her a squeeze, smiling when she looked at him. Damn, all that beautiful green looked as if it had been swallowed by the enormous whites—the same color as her skin. She looked on the verge of passing out.

The medic in him kicked in. He lifted her coffee and held it out to her. "Drink."

She blinked a few times, frowning before finally taking the cup and putting it to her lips. He tried to ignore the way her tongue darted forward to test the temperature before she took a small sip. It seemed silly to be jealous of coffee, but damn, he was. Wishing she was putting her lips on him like that. Tasting him.

She'd gone down on him in the shower. Had knelt amidst the spray and worshipped his dick until he'd come across her chest. Long ropy white strands splashed against her skin—some dripping from her mouth. God, it had driven him wild. He'd been pretty unrelenting after that. Taking her against the shower wall once he'd regained enough blood. Then spending the better part of an hour licking her to the brink before easing off. She'd finally come hard—he had tiny scratches at the base of his neck from where she'd dug in her fingers as she'd unraveled around his tongue—and he'd taken her one last time.

She'd passed out on her next orgasm, lying limp beneath him as he'd emptied inside her one more time. They'd forgone condoms. He'd only had the one, and when he'd offered to ransack Rigs' place to find more, she'd calmly stated she was on birth control and was clean—got tested at her yearly physical. That she'd never gone without and hadn't had a lover in over a year.

She'd said more, but Russel hadn't heard anything after it had clicked in that he could go bareback. Bare-fucking-back. His skin against hers, her juice hot and slick against his dick. God, he almost hadn't waited until she'd stopped talking before driving into her. He'd never gone without and just imagining how it would feel…

It had been even better, but now wasn't the time to be reliving their night. Now, was the time for action. The kind that had been beaten into him. There was a threat—a nasty one aimed at the woman sitting next to him. The one he was pretty damn sure he wanted to spend the next fifty years getting to know. The one looking at him as if talking about the men who were after her was scarier than facing them alone.

But she was going to have to talk because Russel wasn't letting them get to her. It didn't matter why they were after her, how many were coming. He just needed enough intel to know what steps to take. How to keep her alive. She could be a criminal mastermind on the run, and he'd still feel the same. Still itch to touch her. To have her lean on him. He was strong. He could shoulder her weight. Be her foundation. He knew she wasn't helpless, but this was his area of expertise. He'd trained for it. Lived it. She was going to have to trust him.

And his team. No way he was facing this alone. He could. Over half of his missions had been solo. One guy sent in to retrieve a downed soldier. But Russel wasn't stupid, and taking on unknown forces, alone, to prove his manhood was beyond stupid. He didn't go into battle without his team, and this was war. He wasn't sure what kind, yet, but he'd use every resource he had. And that meant having the guys from Brotherhood Protectors at his side.

He picked up a piece of bagel and held it out to her. "You need to eat something before you pass out on me. And not the good kind of passing out, like last night."

Her eyes widened as a pretty pink blush rose along her cheeks then down her neck to settle on the upper swell of her breasts. He remembered tasting those breasts. Tugging on the tight, hard nipples. Licking the soft underside around to where it disappeared under her arm. The woman was pure desire.

Quinn recovered then leaned forward enough to take a small bite. Not as much as he would have liked but at least it was something. He nodded, waited until she'd swallowed then offered it, again. She gave him a raise of one eyebrow but took another bite, this one a bit larger than the last.

He grunted, put down the bagel then picked up the coffee, again. Quinn shook her head but accepted it, relaxing a bit as she drank. A bit of color returned to her face as the blush faded.

Good. She didn't look about to fall out of the chair, which meant it was time to talk. He knew she'd fight him. She'd made it clear she didn't want to get anyone else involved. Didn't want to endanger others. But, he wasn't easy to kill, and danger was his territory.

He also suspected that the fact it involved her family complicated things. He knew all about dysfunctional families. Had been raised in one then escaped because his mother had mustered the courage to leave. To give him a life beyond violence. But he also knew that, despite how terrible families could be, they were still blood. And turning your back on that wasn't always easy. There was an invisible bond that made it hard to break free.

He waited until she'd downed half the coffee before reaching for her hand. It was so damn small compared to his. Pale and soft and delicate. He could break it simply by squeezing his fingers around hers. He wouldn't, but it made him realize how vulnerable she was. She was a fighter, no question, but she wasn't equipped to face armed men. That had been obvious in the alleyway. The stunned look on her face, the enormously wide eyes. She'd been in a state of shock, which meant she hadn't faced that form of violence before.

But he had. For fifteen years, and he'd face it, again. For her. He'd do just about anything for her.

Russel smiled. "Better?"

She sighed, her breath fluttering some stray wisps of hair around her face. They settled next to her chin—a glint of red in the morning light. "Call me crazy, but I don't think your buddy, Rigs, likes me."

"Actually, it's quite the opposite. He wouldn't be this… intense if he didn't already feel a pull towards you. He's just a bit lacking in social graces, right now. It's been hard for him. It's much easier for him to deal with the physical side of a situation. You're in danger. He can deal with that. It's tangible. Emotions…" Russel shook his head. "I get the feeling Rigs is avoiding those at all cost."

Quinn glanced at the door, again. "If that's him caring, I'm not sure I want to see what he does if he's passionate about a person."

"He'd probably start blowing shit up. But he's right. We do need answers, and you're the only one who can provide them."

The color faded, again. Shit. She wet her lips then pulled free of his hold, standing and walking over to the counter. She put her back to it, allowing the edge to brace some of her weight.

She looked over at him, and his damn chest did that hard thump. The kind that left an ache right in the center. "It's not that simple. Not to mention the fact that you might not like what you hear."

He stood and made his way over to her. He wanted to touch her. Hold her close and reassure her that it didn't matter. That he wasn't a quitter, and nothing she said was going to sway him. Because he was a damn good judge of character, and he knew she wasn't evil. That whatever trouble she was in was the by-product of loyalties to her family.

Instead, he fisted his hands to keep them glued to his side. "It doesn't matter if I'll like it or not. I can't keep you safe if I don't know what I'm up against. You knew those men last night. Now, I need to know why they're after you. Why they were there to kill you, because if you think for one second that wasn't their objective…"

She groaned, spearing her fingers through her hair. "I know why they were there. It's just… How can I tell you everything and not betray *him*? Despite everything, he was always there for me. Protected me. I can't just turn my back on that. I know I should. That it's morally right. That I'm basically as guilty as he is simply by remaining quiet. But…"

Tears welled in her eyes, and he ignored the voice in his head. The one that told him he was in PJ mode. That this was a mission, and missions didn't have time for feelings. For comfort. They were all about getting the job done. He needed answers, and she had them. Simple. So, holding her, stroking her hair, whispering it was going to be okay, wasn't part of his line of thinking.

Except, the side of him she'd awakened. The man he wanted to be for *her*—had seeped through. And that guy couldn't stand there, watching her tears slowly fall to the floor. That man needed to take away her pain. Even if it was only temporary.

Quinn rested her head against his chest, drawing in a series of choppy breaths. "This isn't like me. I never break down."

He chuckled. "Then, that makes two of us. I usually don't cave when I want answers."

"It's not that I don't trust you. It's—"

"Complicated."

She smiled against his shirt, a watery laugh breaking free. "Yeah."

"Then, we'll take our time. Work through it. You're not on trial, here, Quinn. I'm not going to crucify you because you're having a hard time betraying your family. We can start off with the easy stuff." He pulled back, staring down at her. "Okay?"

Her chin quivered, and a few more tears leaked out, but she nodded, wrapping her arms around her when he stepped back. Released her.

He motioned to the table, and she walked back over, pretty much falling into the seat. She looked tired. Beaten. And he had to fight the urge to pick her up and take her to bed. Love the sadness out of her eyes.

The door opened, and Rigs shuffled in, eyes wary, mouth pinched tight. Russel noticed the man didn't shield his scars from her, facing them both straight on. Russel made a mental note to ask Quinn about it, later, then took a step forward.

He looked pointedly at Quinn. "You ready?"

A shiver shook through her, but she nodded, again. He gave her a reassuring smile then removed the burner cell he'd picked up in town, punching in Hank's number. The guy answered on the first ring.

"Ice. Update. And why the fuck didn't you call me last night?"

"Hey, Montana. We're fine. Thanks. And I didn't call because it was late, and you have a family. Besides, I had it all under control."

"You get jumped outside a bar by armed men—men you sent to hospital—but it's nothing I should be concerned about? Is that what I'm hearing?"

"You know, Midnight needs to keep his damn mouth shut."

"Midnight didn't tell me shit. I heard it come over the scanner. I've been…keeping tabs since you've been there. And, when I heard three men were found, unconscious with knife wounds behind that bar you'd been staking out, it wasn't hard to put it all together. I know how good you are with a knife."

"I didn't have much of a choice. They started firing, and—"

"I'm just glad you and your friend are okay. Though, I hope this means we're about to get some concrete answers, because I hate going into an op blind. And, right now, I can't see a damn thing."

"That's why I'm calling. Hey, can you get Midnight in on this? And Bridgette? We could definitely use her expertise in this."

"Give me a second."

The line clicked, was silent for a few minutes, before a small burst of static crackled through, followed by a few voices. Russel moved back to the table, placing the phone in the middle. He put it on speaker.

Hank breathed over the line. "Okay, you're on speaker. First, some introductions. Quinn, I'm Hank Patterson, also known as Montana. I'm not sure if Ice mentioned anything, but I head up Brotherhood Protectors. It's a security company made up of ex-veterans. Ice had just joined up, but it seems he got one hell of a first assignment all by himself. I've got Axel Swenson or Swede here with me, and I've patched in Sam Montgomery, aka Midnight, and his fiancé Bridgette Hayward. She's a lawyer. They're at her clinic, but they're alone. Ice is using a burner cell, and I routed this through a few VPN servers, so… We should be secure."

Russel nodded at her then addressed the crowd. "Great. Sam, Bridg? Can you hear me okay?"

"Loud and clear, buddy."

Russel glanced at Quinn, ignoring the sheer panic on her face. This was obviously far more than she'd bargained for. He nodded. "Okay, I've got you on speaker, too. Rigs is here with Quinn and me. This is all a bit overwhelming for her, so I thought we'd start off simple. Get some basic intel and go from there."

A series of "yeahs" sounded over the cell, then silence. They were waiting for him to take lead. Rigs didn't sit, electing to stay over by the counter, his arms crossed over his chest, his face somewhere between a scowl and a grimace.

Russel took a deep breath. This was it. Go time. Only,

it didn't feel like it usually did. His stomach was in knots, and a cold sweat had broken across his skin. Whether it was Quinn's fear transferring over to him, or just his own —that she'd refuse to talk to them. Find a way to run—he wasn't sure. But he didn't like it. Hated it, in fact. Nothing got to him. Nothing. Except her.

"Like I said. We'll start off easy. You told me earlier that your family is dangerous, and the word criminal has come up a few times, though I don't know what you mean by that. Then, last night, those men showed up—men you knew—armed and out for blood. We need to know why they were after you."

She swallowed. Hard. As if it was the most difficult thing she'd ever done. Her hands twisted on top of the table, and her feet scuffed at the floor beneath the seat.

He put his large hand over hers. "I know this isn't easy. That you don't want to betray your family, but we can't help you, sweetheart, if we don't know what we're fighting. I can dodge attempts on your life until we're old and gray, but that won't eliminate the threat. And that's what I do. What we all do. We eliminate threats. So, take a deep breath, and start wherever you think is best."

Quinn stared at him, all pouty pink lips and big green eyes. She didn't speak for the longest time, just kept looking at him as if she was searching for something. She must have found it because she finally released a weary breath and broke eye contact, staring at his hand covering hers. "My family is…different."

"How so?" Hank's voice echoed through the room.

She glanced at the phone. "I'm not sure I even know how to answer that. It's so far from the norm, it's absurd. To put it bluntly, they're criminals. My father is head of a multimillion dollar company. He's respected. Envied. Revered, even. But it's all a lie. A front for one of the largest criminal organizations on the west coast."

"What kind of activities?" It was Bridgette. Always thinking about the lawyer side of things.

Quinn closed in on herself. Right there, just hunched her shoulders as if trying to shield herself from the fallout she obviously thought was coming her way. "You name it, they do it. Everything from drugs to weapons to simple stolen goods. Except human trafficking. I wasn't able to find any evidence of that. A small mercy, I guess, in a shitload of horrible things. But it's also a front for money laundering. From an even bigger syndicate operating out of LA. They run millions of dollars through the company every week—make it impossible for the government to track. I think that's become the bulk of the business. It's the part my father's in charge of. He doesn't let anyone else touch the laundering aspects. But the other stuff. The drugs and weapons. That's controlled by his associate."

"You mean Thomas." Russel hedged his bet. "That was the guy's name you said last night. The one you were afraid of."

"Yeah. Thomas Carlson. He's...evil. As in Satan, himself." She stood and paced away from the table. "This is crazy. Once I tell you this, you'll all be at risk. You can't even begin to imagine the resources Thomas has at his disposal. The money. The men. It's virtually endless. The best course of action is for me to just disappear. Alone. They won't know you're involved. Well, maybe you, Russel, but they might not know your name, yet. Please, I'll just leave. I know how to disappear. I won't be the reason you all get killed."

A chorus of sighs.

"Ice, man, please explain to the lady how we operate." It was Midnight.

Russel walked over to her, taking her hands in his. "What the rest of the team is trying to say is… We're already involved. And we're not backing down. We don't care about the odds. About his endless resources, and his petty gang thugs. This is about more than just your safety. If the guy's hurting people, we want his ass in jail. So, no, Quinn. You're not running off, alone, and you're not putting us at risk. We're choosing to fight."

He raised one hand to tuck some unruly strands of hair behind her ear, smiling at her slightly opened mouth and wide eyes. "Take your time. Get it all straight, then tell us what this bastard is guilty of, and how we can help you. Which means, you need to come clean."

He took a deep breath, held it, then slowly let it go. "And that starts by you telling us your real name. Because Quinn Scott didn't exist prior to ten years ago. And I'll bet my ass, that's where this story really begins."

CHAPTER 12

And you start by telling us your real name.

Quinn stared at Russel as his words looped inside her head. Damn. Not only had he unearthed her identity, he knew it was fake. Not that she'd ever believed it was failsafe, but she'd paid a hefty sum to make it convincing. No one had uncovered that, before. But, even more astounding, he'd known, and he'd still helped her. Still...made love to her. Had stated he wanted her in his life.

God, he really was crazy.

Russel smiled, and just like that, some of the fear bled from her system. Her muscles eased slightly, and the gagging feeling in her throat diminished. He wasn't scared. Not an ouch of fear. He wasn't even breathing hard. *She* was wheezing. She was sure of it. Her heart rate was probably over two hundred, and she was pretty sure her blood pressure was beyond medical help. And yet, he was standing there, calm. Collected.

Ice.

She closed her eyes, fighting the instinct to run. He

was right. It really was too late. These men—they wouldn't give up. They'd track her down. Force her to accept their help. Better to get it all out in the open.

Lips caressed her eyelids, and she opened them to find Russel nothing more than an inch away. Green eyes shining in the sunlight. Lips curved into the kind of smile that dropped her stomach and spun the room. He motioned to the table, and she allowed him to lead her over—plunk her ass back in the seat.

Quinn gathered her composure. This was it. The point of no return. Either they stuck with her, or they jumped ship. Though, she knew they wouldn't. They were warriors. They'd spent their lives fighting for justice. They wouldn't bail once they learned how much was at stake.

She cleared her throat, glancing at him then Rigs. The other man was unreadable—face firmly set. Arms still crossed over his chest. She focused on the phone, on getting her tongue to form the words, because right now, it felt large and sluggish. Too big to fit.

Another deep breath, and the tight feeling eased. Not completely, but enough she might be able to get out more than just a squeak. "Before I tell you that, you should know something outright. I won't give you any evidence that will clearly implicate my father. I know that might be wrong. Trust me. I've spent years agonizing over it. But…"

God, more tears clogged her throat. She hadn't cried this much in ten years. "In his own way, I know he loves me. And he's never, once, raised a hand to me. Never done anything other than try to raise me on his own. I realize, looking back, that it wasn't the kind of home to have a kid in, but… He did his best. And I…I can't hurt him that way.

Not directly. I know there isn't much hope he'll escape, but it won't be by my hand."

Silence. Nothing but utter silence.

Then a hushed breath. "Quinn, this is Bridgette. I know we haven't met, but I understand why you'd feel that way. Up until a few months ago, I worked for the US Attorney's office in Seattle. Oddly, it was in the Organized Crimes division. I know the kind of courage it takes to break out of that environment. How much it's cost you. And I give you my word that I'll do whatever I can to help you. So, if you'd let me know what I'm up against, I can start."

A US Attorney?

Shit. This was either really great news, because she had a flash drive full of documents and photos that would put Thomas on death row or it was her worst nightmare, and she'd be putting her father in a cell right along beside the bastard.

Russel's hand covered hers, again. Strong. Warm. Unyielding. He was telling her he was there for her. She didn't know why. What she'd done to earn his trust. Hell, what looked like his love. But she was happy for it. It made everything seem a bit less vast. Up until now, she'd been lost in an ocean with nothing concrete in sight. But, with his hand over hers, it grounded her. Gave her something to focus on.

She smiled at Russel. "You're right. Quinn Scott was my attempt to distance myself. Growing up, I hadn't really realized my life wasn't typical. That everyone didn't have armed men covering every inch of their property or that their fathers didn't have meetings in the middle of the night. It wasn't until I was eighteen that I learned the truth. That my dad wasn't a successful businessman, and that my uncles and their sons weren't part of a thriving corporate venture. That they were all…criminals. My father had gone to great lengths to hide it from me. So, when I discovered the truth, I left."

She collapsed against the back of the chair, her strength flowing out and into the floor. God, she was tired. Tired of looking over her back. Of being someone else.

"But I knew I couldn't go far. I'd confronted my father, and he'd admitted that he wasn't what he appeared to be. He said I was free to go. All he asked was that I didn't question him about his business, and that I agreed to meet him for lunch once a month."

Russel grunted. "That's what you were doing when you made me leave you. You were having your regular meeting with him."

"That's why I couldn't ask you to stay. My dad's very protective. If he'd discovered who you were—that you were ex-military—he would have had Thomas come after you. Prevented you from unearthing the truth."

"So, what happened? Obviously, something did, because those men were there to hurt you, Quinn."

She shuddered, memories of that day filtering through her mind. "While I was in the café, I saw something I shouldn't have. A man. He was tied to a chair, all beaten and bloody. I was convinced it was all Thomas. That he was doing this behind my father's back, but then… Then, my dad went into the office with Thomas, and they…they…"

Russel sighed. "They killed the guy, didn't they?"

She nodded, a few tears running down her cheeks.

"I'm sure it was Thomas who pulled the trigger, but that's when I realized I couldn't turn a blind-eye, anymore. That by saying nothing, I was just as guilty of killing that man as they were. That I was every bit the criminal my father was."

"Quinn—"

"No. I can reason it away, but we all know it's true. That's when I decided I was going to take it all down. But I couldn't gather any evidence without going back to the estate. I made up a story so my dad would let me stay in my old room for a couple of weeks—one he was more than happy to believe—and spent every moment I could going through files and reports. I took photos of everything. It seems Thomas had taken over most of the company—everything but the money laundering side of it. I'm not sure my father even knows that he's been overrun. That's when I decided to focus on Thomas. But I must have screwed up. Somehow, he discovered what I was doing."

She looked up at Russel. "Last night. I don't know why I went back to that bar. I think I was secretly hoping you'd be there. That maybe I could have one last night before everything changed. I had planned on turning myself over to the FBI the next morning. Showing them everything I had saved onto a flash drive. Enough to put Thomas away. But then, he showed up, and…"

"And things went sideways."

"If you hadn't been there…" She'd be dead. Or tied to a chair with pieces of her bones sticking through her jeans.

"Do you still have the flash drive?" Bridgette's voice was tight. Slightly higher than it had been a minute ago.

"Not…with me." Quinn groaned and slumped onto the

table, her elbow bridging most of her weight. "I taped it to the inside cowling of my motorcycle."

Russel cursed. "Shit. The one we abandoned."

"You didn't know. And it wasn't like we were in a position to get it. I also hadn't planned on telling you any of this. If I'd insisted, you would have questioned me until I'd spilled it all. But I put an encrypted backup on my cloud server. It's under lockdown. I programmed it to allow one hour of access every forty-eight hours. If I don't input my code during that window, it stays in lockdown, regardless of anything I do. The first opportunity is tomorrow afternoon. So, I can get it all back."

"That was smart thinking." Did the other woman sound proud? "Though, I don't want you doing that until you're here. Where these guys can keep you safe, and I have access to more resources. I'll have a better idea what you're truly facing once I go through those files."

"There's just one small problem." Quinn locked her gaze on Russel's. "When I was in the café, I also overheard my dad say that he had properties and accounts in my name. I swear, I didn't know about them, but... It'll be my word against theirs. I'm the daughter of a crime boss. That's not going to carry much weight. Not that it matters. I don't care what it takes. If I have to spend the rest of my life in jail, I want it gone. The whole fucking thing. Burned to the ground."

"Why don't you let me worry about that? But...I need to know your name. So, I can start doing some very careful probing of my own."

She swallowed, again. Christ, saying her name shouldn't be this hard. Russel squeezed her hand, and just like that, the band around her chest loosened.

"I didn't venture far from the truth. My mother picked out my name just hours before she died. And I…I couldn't completely give it up. So, I shortened it."

Russel frowned. "What is Quinn short for?"

"Harlequin. My name is Harlequin James."

"Holy shit." Bridgette's voice reverberated through the room. "As in daughter to Henry James? Seriously?"

"What?" Russel was looking around as if he could uncover whatever had Bridgette agitated. "Why holy shit? Who's Henry James?"

"Just the man at the top of everyone's watch list. You remember how long the Bureau had been trying to take down Alexander Stevens? That case that nearly got me killed?"

Russel's face hardened. There was obviously a story there. "I'm familiar."

"Double that time. Or triple it. Henry James…the man's a legend. I knew he had a daughter but… He kept your existence very hushed. I don't think I've ever seen a photo of you. Then, about ten years ago, there was a death certificate. A drowning accident."

Quinn nodded. "That was his way of trying to give me an out. He let me become Quinn Scott as long as I remained loyal to him as a daughter. I guess it was part of the excuse I made for not coming clean. Turning him in."

"No." Bridgette's voice was stern. "Do you have any idea what would have happened if you'd tried to turn him in without proof? You'd be dead. For real. And an eighteen-year old isn't supposed to be gathering evidence against her family. Christ, I can't believe you've managed to stay alive and out of it this long on your own. Russel."

He sat up a bit straighter. "Yeah. Still here."

"I am personally holding you responsible for her safety. If she gets so much as a scratch, I'll send Sam after you."

He chuckled. "I believe I was the one who rescued *his* ass, but don't worry. Not going to happen. Period."

"Okay, it sounds like we have enough to go on." The guy, Hank. "Rigs, have you got alternate transportation they can borrow?"

Rigs took a step closer. "I'm picking up a vehicle this afternoon that can't be traced. Russel can leave his truck here until this is dealt with. I suggest we leave first thing tomorrow. They should be safe here, until then, and I have a few contacts I can call in Seattle. Find out more about this Thomas Carlson guy, and what we might be facing. I'd hate to go back out on the road without any kind of intel. He could have an entire army amassed and looking for them. Better we know ahead of time if his connections end at the state line."

"Agreed. Okay, we'll expect you at Bridgette's office tomorrow before that window of Quinn's opens. We'll make further plans from there. But…should the circumstances change, I expect a call. Regardless of what time it is. Understood?"

"Crystal clear." Russel picked up the phone then clicked it off. He turned to Rigs. "You need backup getting this vehicle?"

"Got it covered. No one's looking for me. Besides, it's riskier to have you both leave here before we're ready." He headed for the door, again. "Just hang tight. I'll be back sometime tonight. The place is yours, but…don't go walking about. I haven't had time to disarm any of the security measures."

Quinn sat in the chair, heart pounding, mouth dry, as the door clicked shut. She'd done it. Told them who she was, and somehow, they hadn't run away screaming. She knew what Bridgette was talking about. After digging for evidence, she'd unearthed far more than she'd wanted to. The only saving grace was that her dad had always been more of an administrator. A figure head of sorts. Yes, he laundered money, and he was well aware of what Thomas did—of the violence—but she hadn't found anything to suggest he'd ever been involved in it.

Of course, she hadn't proven that he wasn't, either. Or that he hadn't sent Thomas after her. She didn't want to believe it, but until she knew, one way or the other, she'd have to at least be open to the possibility.

A hand settled on her shoulder, and she turned. Russel was watching her, eyes narrowed, nostrils flaring with every whispered breath. He didn't look shocked or angry, but there was a fierceness about him that made her squirm under the weight of his stare.

He leaned forward, stopping with his nose nearly touching hers. "You could have told me. In my truck that day. I would have understood. But I also would have had your back. Could have been there, in the café, with you."

"Right, up until my father realized you were a threat. Then, you would have been the next guy tied to a chair with his knee shattered and blood…"

The images came rushing back. The whiteness of the bone against the denim. The blood collecting in pools on the plastic sheet—the one Thomas had put underneath the guy so the blood wouldn't get on the rug. So, he'd be able to clean it up fast. No bleach, no residual DNA. God, how many times had he done that? How many sheets of plastic had he gone through? And had her father watched every time?

"Quinn?"

It was too much. The blood. The guns. The acrid smell of fear and sweat—the sound of Thomas' fists connecting with bone. The hollow pops, the ones that had sounded through the door. The ones that could have killed Russel. She could see it. Him lying on the ground, blood washing away with the rain. And Thomas would have been standing over Russel's body, thankful he didn't have to clean it up. God, he probably had more of that plastic in his car.

"Fuck. Hold on."

Arms wrapped around her, then she was against Russel's chest, moving through the house. She didn't see where he was taking her—the walls a dull wash of the images still playing inside her head—when something sounded in the background. Tinkling sounds that penetrated the hazy blur. She blinked as Russel removed the last of her clothes and lifted her into the shower.

Hot water splashed across her skin, finally cutting through the nightmare. Russel had her on his lap, sitting on a small ledge at the back of the large enclosure, his arms like steel bands around her. Holding her tight. Keeping her safe. She took a few gasping breaths, then leaned into him, gripping his forearms with both her hands. He couldn't let go. If he did, she'd fly apart.

He nuzzled her neck, dropping a kiss on the shell of her ear. "Easy, sweetheart. Just breathe. You're safe, and I'll keep you that way. So, let it go."

To her horror, tears welled in her eyes and spilled over onto her cheeks, mixing with the water cascading down his arms. She didn't try to stop herself, just laid against him, letting the past slowly fade. The water was starting to cool by the time he finally eased up on his hold. But he didn't let go, managing to stand with her in his arms.

She wrapped her hands around his neck, still leaning into his chest as he exited the shower, turned off the taps, grabbed some towels then took them back to the room they'd shared the night before. He settled her on the bed, wrapping a huge length of terry around her. She shivered, not sure why she was cold, when the bed dipped from his weight. He shuffled against the headboard then bodily lifted her and placed her between his thighs, again.

She burrowed against him, her head in the crook of his shoulder, her hands over his as he held her tight. Not as firmly as in the shower, but enough it soothed the jumpy feeling in her stomach. The one that threatened to toss what little food she'd eaten across the bed.

He brought his cheek next to hers. "Just keep breathing."

Breathing. He said it as if it was easy. Natural. Not the labored effort it took her to draw air in then push it out. But, slowly, the burning sensation in her lungs faded, each breath a bit easier than the last. Russel didn't move, didn't talk. Just sat there, wrapped around her, listening to her gasping pants.

When she'd finally regained some modicum of composure, he released one hand to tuck her hair behind her ear.

"Feeling better? Chest still tight?"

She shook her head.

"Words, Quinn. I'd like you to tell me you're okay."

She swallowed, nearly gagged, then twisted enough to look at him. "Better."

There. She'd managed a word without puking. Without passing out. Surely, that was enough? A Herculean effort.

He smiled, and her stomach fluttered. Not the nauseous feeling like before. This was warm and tingling. The way she felt when she realized she was about to capture the perfect shot. Only *this* made *that* feel colorless. Two-dimensional.

"Not quite the declaration I was hoping for, but it's better than nothing. Do you need to rest? Or have some more food? Maybe a shot of whiskey?"

"You."

He frowned. "Me?"

"It's what I want. What I need. Just you."

His eyes narrowed, the green color slowly darkening as the skin over his cheekbones tightened. "Quinn—"

"Are you always going to try and talk me out of making love to you?"

"Are you always going to want sex when you're on the edge?"

"You're describing every moment of every day of my life for the past ten years. I'm always looking over my shoulder. Wondering if someone's watching me. Following me. If I'm putting friends or co-workers at risk simply by agreeing to meet them for a drink or collaborate on a project. It's never a perfect time, and I've never been safe. So, if you're waiting for that moment—it doesn't exist."

"Not yet. But it will. We'll figure this out. But even if we don't. If Thomas is untouchable. If there isn't a way to bring him down, no one is ever going to hurt you, again.

Not as long as I'm breathing. That's not a promise. It's a fact."

She twisted in his arms, losing the towel in the process. "Then, here's another fact. I want you. No, *need* you. On the edge. After the fallout. Doesn't matter what's happening around me, I can't get you off of my mind. Can't focus. I've never felt like this. Like I'm careening out of control. Stuck on a Ferris wheel that won't stop turning. But what's crazier is that I don't want to get off. I want to stay on it. With you. So, unless we're back to you not being interested…"

Russel's mouth twitched a moment before his hand slipped to the back of her neck and his mouth crushed down hard on hers. A brief meeting of flesh, then he twisted her mouth open and licked his way inside. He tasted like coffee. Like spicy man and strength. A potent combination that was somehow linked to her DNA. One taste, and she was ready. As if he'd inserted a code and unlocked her defenses. No need to scale her walls or knock them down, he just opened the door and walked inside.

She gave him control, wrapping herself around him, trying to climb onto his lap without letting go. She couldn't let go. Couldn't get her fingers to release their death grip on his neck. They were glued to his skin. Stuck in place as she returned his kiss, eating at his mouth when he paused for a quick breath.

Russel chuckled, lifted her up as he straightened his legs, then set her back down—directly above his erection. The head was hot and wet, pulsing with every brush of her skin against it. She balanced her weight, hands still digging into his flesh, her tongue still tangling with his, and rubbed the flared crown the length of her cleft.

A guttural moan rumbled through Russel's chest. Low. Throaty. Like the growl of a wild animal just before it struck. She grinned and repeated the motion, teasing him with a hint of penetration.

An actual growl surfaced, this time. It was deeper. More of a warning, now. He was declaring his dominance. Giving her time to accept it before he lost control.

Good. She wanted him to lose control. Wanted to see him sweat. Shake. She didn't want Ice, the calm, cool soldier who faced death and didn't blink. She wanted Russel. The man who'd swept her off her feet. Who was willing to stand by her, despite the fact she came from poisonous stock. The apples that fell from her family's trees were like the ones in Eden. Tempting but deadly.

He nipped at her bottom lip, licking the small hurt as he grasped her hips and held her still. She wiggled, gasping when he tightened his hold then thrust up, plunging inside her in one forceful stroke.

Colors danced across her vision, dimming the edges as the coil inside her core whirled inward, tightening painfully then shattering. She arched back, bending over one of his arms as he stayed still inside her, her walls contracting around his length.

Heat poured off her body, coating it with sweat as her orgasm pounded through her. Her head fell backwards, her neck muscles cording until the searing pleasure receded, and she collapsed forward, her forehead on his, her hands now gripping his shoulders.

"Fuck, yeah, sweetheart. Again."

He pulled out then pushed back in. Harder. Deeper. He

didn't stop, each punishing stroke more forceful than the last. The bed squeaked, the headboard banged, joined by their joint grunts. It was primal. Raw. And she didn't want it to stop.

Russel quickened his pace, shafting her hard, holding her captive as he claimed her. His mouth, his hands, his cock. Over and over, kissing, touching, thrusting. Every inch felt possessed. Every breath shared as he pushed to the edge, again.

She held on. Clung to him in desperation, wanting to go over but not wanting it to stop. She'd never been taken before. That was the only way to describe it. Even during their rambunctious play last night, she hadn't felt this owned. But not in a suffocating way. He was cherishing her. Showing her how much she mattered. That she was special.

Her climax hit her hard, stealing her breath, dragging her under while shattering her into a thousand pieces. Russel shouted her name, drove up into her and came—emptying in a series of jerking half thrusts. Quinn floated in a numbing haze, finally coming back to herself—minutes, hours, days—later.

Russel held her close, his breath hot and spicy across her cheek. He gave her a squeeze, moving one hand to pinch her chin—raise her gaze to his. She lifted heavy eyelids, smiling up at him as he stared down at her.

He nuzzled her nose. "You okay?"

"Mmm."

"You are a woman of many words."

She laughed. "Perfect. Tired."

"How tired?"

And just like that, her muscles flexed. Gathered back

strength she swore was gone. Drained out of her like her tears in the shower. Even her sex heated, clamping down around Russel's semi-erect shaft. God, how was he still even remotely hard?

She tilted her head a bit, giving him a playful smile. "With you? Never *that* tired."

CHAPTER 13

Her words took a few moments to penetrate Russel's skull—most of the blood quickly rerouting to his dick. He'd just come inside her. Had felt as if he'd drained himself dry. Wondered if he'd even be able to come, again, sometime in the next few months. Surely, between last night and this encounter, he'd ejaculated a year's worth of sperm. Maybe two.

But, as her voice replayed in his head—*with you, never that tired*—his body reacted. Blood poured into his shaft, and his sac felt heavy. Nearly busting with need.

He didn't understand it. They were still essentially strangers. Or were they? That first morning, she'd said she knew him, and he'd doubted it, but her observations had been spot on. As if she'd climbed inside her head, watched his memories in fast forward, then given him the abridged version of his personality.

And he definitely knew her. Not the regular stuff. He didn't know her favorite color or if she liked Italian food. Had no idea when her real birthday was or if she wanted to travel. But he knew she was brave. Was willing to face a life on the run—a life in jail, if need be—to stop some very dangerous men from continuing their spread of evil. She'd begged him and his buddies numerous times to leave—to save themselves—because she couldn't stomach someone getting hurt because of her. She'd isolated herself, lived in a virtual prison, all in an effort to keep trouble away from anyone she cared about.

And he knew she'd never been in love.

That's what she'd meant when she'd said she'd never felt this way. She'd used different terminology, but it meant the same thing. She was out of her element. But so was he.

He wasn't used to letting his emotions dictate his behavior. He controlled them, not the other way 'round. He'd spent fifteen years alone—content. Focused. Dedicated to his job. To the service. And all it had taken was one night watching her sleep, and he'd fallen off the deep end. Had tossed out his old rule book and allowed a new one to take its place. One whose only purpose was to keep her safe. Find ways to make her smile.

He didn't have a lot of experience with love. His mother had loved him, but she'd spent most of her time working three jobs just to put food on the table, a roof over their heads. His teammates loved him, in a brotherly way that transcended blood. But romantic love—the kind that grabbed him by something far more sensitive than his balls—that grabbed his heart... He didn't have a clue what that was.

Was it this unrelenting need to hold her? Touch her? Feel her safe and warm in his arms? Or the cold slither of fear that curled around his spine whenever he thought about her getting hurt? Running off alone and ending up dead on the side of some two-bit country road?

Whatever it was, he had it. Bad. And he didn't see it letting up in the near future. Maybe in fifty years. Seventy. But not now. He didn't care that her father led a questionable life. She wasn't her family, and not wanting to turn her father in, to put him in jail, didn't make her guilty of sin. It made her compassionate. Loyal. Both of which he understood. He'd had his honor questioned, too. But he'd had friends who had been willing to overlook it. To have his back. Who had she had?

No one.

Well, she did, now. He wasn't going anywhere unless she physically kicked his ass out. Until then, he'd watch over her. Be her first line of defense.

Quinn inhaled as he gathered her in his arms then spun them around, laying her down on the bed. He usually wasn't a fan of missionary. Sure, it had its place, generally the first time. A quick one-off to take off the edge then on to more interesting positions. On their knees, against the wall. Any way that made it feel less—personal. Intimate.

But not with Quinn. He wanted to savor her. Watch her. Breathe through her. Quinn welcomed him down, sliding her arms beneath his and across his back as her legs wrapped around her thighs. She was wet. Sticky from their combined releases. But he didn't care. He'd bathe her, again, after. But, first, he needed to make her his. Bind her to him. Make it impossible for her to see her future without him in it. At her side. Teammates.

He went to his elbows, brushing as much of his skin against hers as he nudged her sex. She smiled, and he slid home, slowly inching inside her until his sac slapped her flesh. God, it was heaven. Hot. Wet. So tight it prickled tears along his eyes. He couldn't remember ever being inside a woman that had felt this right.

He paused, fully seated, sweat beading his skin, his breath short and rough. "See what you reduce me to? You touch me or smile, and all I can think about is holding you. Loving you. Feeling you unravel in my arms."

Her eyes softened, her mouth lifting into a smile. The same kind as in the bar that first night. The one where a spotlight had shone down on her from above. Just like it was shining on her, now. "You're shaking."

He froze. He never shook. Not under fire and never with a woman. Yet, she was right. His hands rested across her collarbones, his fingers lightly brushing her skin, the slight tremble in them impossible to miss.

He should be scared at how much power she held over him. She was half his size. No match for him. And yet, she broke through his usual barriers, reducing him to bedrock.

Her small hand cupped his jaw. "It's okay. I'm scared, too. You…" She levered up—touched her lips to his. "Love me."

His mouth settled on hers, kissing, lifting, repositioning then settling, again. Long, wet kisses that matched the gentle way he moved inside her. Full strokes instead of the short jabs he'd made as he'd emptied inside her. She was hot. Incredibly wet, and it took his years of training to keep his pace steady. Loving. Because that's what she needed.

He prided himself at reading women. Speaking their body language. She'd been right there with him last night.

Hot. Rough. Dispelling some tension. Some fear. Even their previous encounter had been tailored to her needs. But now... Every inch of her begged to be cherished. Worshipped. The way she slid her hands over his back, kneading his muscles. How her heels pressed against his ass. The needy moans she made as he kissed her neck, tilting it to give him better access. She didn't want him to pound her into the bed, this time.

She wanted his love. And fuck if he didn't want to give it to her.

Time blurred into the background, nothing more than passing shadows across the floor. He didn't rush, didn't do anything other than feel every second of every pass inside her. Slowly building her up until her fingers dug into his skin as her legs tightened around him. Small fleeting contractions prickled his shaft, and he knew she was close.

He leaned down. "You're not alone, anymore, sweetheart. So, let go."

Her eyes widened, the glassy depths holding his gaze before they rolled, and she broke. He watched her climax, still slowly pumping her until her head lolled to one side as her grip loosened.

Russel gave her one more kiss then followed her lead. Thrusting into her until the fire burning just behind his balls shot forward, taking him with it. Strong pulses moved along his cock, once again, emptying his seed inside her.

He hung his head, resting it on her collarbone until he realized he was probably crushing her into the bed. He shifted, but she tightened her hold.

"Not ready, yet." Her voice was raspy and low. As if she hadn't been sure she'd be able to speak.

"Not going anywhere. But I'd rather not have to deal with any crushing injuries."

She laughed. God, it sounded like heaven. "You're not crushing me. In fact, it makes me feel…safe."

Safe. When he knew she hadn't felt that way since leaving her home. Escaping.

He shuffled back, braced a bit more of his weight on his elbows and waited until she was ready for him to move. He didn't care how long it took. If his damn arms went numb in the process. He'd lie there the rest of the day if she needed. Eternity seemed reasonable.

Because she was his mission. And he wasn't failing this one.

"Ice."

Russel bolted awake. After spending the afternoon in bed with Quinn, they'd gotten up, showered, again, and made dinner. Rigs had texted, informing Russel that he was doing some more recon. That something felt…off. That's all Russel had needed to know. He'd ended the call then gathered together anything he thought they'd need for the trip to Montana and stacked it beside the door where they'd be accessible in a moment's notice. Supplies he'd bought. Weapons from Rigs' arsenal. The man could have fought off a small country with the amount of firepower he'd stashed away in a locked vault.

Soldiers weren't supposed to keep their equipment.

But most ended up with a smattering of what had kept them alive. And what they didn't bring home, they usually reacquired. Which Rigs had done and then some. And that wasn't including the charges he'd set up around his place.

So, the hard, low rasp of the man's voice next to Russel's ear put him on full alert. Man to PJ in half a second, flat. He glanced around, his Beretta in his hand. He'd tucked it under his pillow when it had become obvious Rigs might be spending the night out. Russel had just hoped he wouldn't need it.

He scanned the room then focused on Rigs. "Update."

"Men. Lots of them. Some from the road, others closing in on ATVs. Not sure how they found you, though, I'm betting that Thomas fucker has someone on the inside. Checking weather and traffic cams. Damn near impossible to avoid them. Wouldn't take much to track you to the turnoff. And, when you didn't show up on any cams closer to town…" Rigs sighed. "Not many places out this way. A quick scan from an overhead satellite would show your truck. Should have hidden the damn thing in the shed. I'm slipping."

"Then, we both are. Call me crazy, but I didn't think they'd get that information so quickly. How many?"

"Twenty. Maybe twenty-five. They're moving slow. Waiting until all their backup is in place." He grinned. "That's gonna be hard when things start exploding."

Russel nodded, rousing Quinn. He placed his finger over his mouth, smiling when her wide eyes narrowed and she nodded, quietly getting out of the bed and into her clothes.

He followed suit, motioning for Rigs to lead the way. "How much damage will your countermeasures do?"

Rigs stopped in the kitchen. "Not nearly as much as they could. I wanted it to be more of a warning system. Something to throw any intruders off. They don't know if the next one will only toss dirt in the air or blow their legs off. I'm hoping they think the latter."

"Where's the vehicle?"

"Out back. There's a small two-track just south of here. We can take that until it crosses back over the highway. I've already loaded your bags. Was waiting until I had a clear picture of how they were setting up before waking you. Didn't want to miss something important."

Russel nodded. Rigs was fastidious about intel. Didn't compromise a second's worth, especially when he knew Russel would be ready to leave within a couple of minutes. That Rigs wouldn't be risking their safety by watching for a few extra minutes.

Russel kept his palm on the small of Quinn's back as they headed for the backdoor. It opened silently. A rusty jalopy waited in shadows, the chassis raised higher than normal. "Armored?"

Rigs snorted, his sideways glance saying, *of course, jackass.*

Russel let it go, helping Quinn into the back. "Stay down. I don't want you getting clipped by a stray shot."

She opened her mouth then closed it, climbing in without questioning him.

Rigs grabbed Russel's hand when he went to push the seat back. "You, too, Ice. And you'll keep your head down right next to hers."

"Fuck that. You can't drive and see all the threats. I'm riding shotgun."

"Not this time." He pointed a finger at Russel. "You're a

medic. You know the score. We need you in one piece in case we end up in more than one. Besides, if you ride up front with me, they could take us both out. I don't think this fucker has truly skilled snipers in his ranks, but I can't swear on it. A good marksman could kill us with the same bullet. I sure as hell could. If that happens, who would protect Harlequin?"

Russel pursed his lips.

"I know you hate this. Trust me. You PJs are a rare breed. But…you also know that I'm right. So, get your ass in the back, keep both your heads down, and don't fucking die on me."

Russel held back his retort—fuck he hated that Rigs was right—and shuffled in beside Quinn. He didn't ask if she wanted him to hold her, just drew her into his arms then reclined on the seat. He kept his back to the rear in case any bullets managed to pierce the vehicle. It wasn't as good as giving her a Kevlar vest, but he was thick, and chances were a bullet wouldn't get all the way through him then into her.

She instinctively drew in on herself, virtually disappearing within his arms, and he couldn't help but wonder if she'd huddled for safety before. If her father's colleagues had ever come after her before she'd escaped out on her own. He had a bad feeling they had.

The old SUV rumbled to life, the engine quieter than he'd expected. Count on Rigs to have a damn armored Jeep made on a moment's notice. That, or he'd been planning for this kind of event. Either worked for Russel.

Rigs started off slow, weaving the car through an invisible slalom course. Russel didn't need to ask to know Rigs was circumventing explosives he'd buried in his yard.

Mines. Tripwires. Russel suspected the man had cast a wide net of charges across the property—a pattern guaranteed to catch even the most observant intruder.

He didn't know how skilled these men were. Had Thomas hired ex-military men to do his bidding? Had he found veterans whose loyalties only registered in dollar amounts to come after Quinn? If he'd figured out who Russel was—and if the man had people in law enforcement or hackers of any worth, it wouldn't be hard to puzzle it out. Russel's face would be on the security footage from the bar. There was a chance the bastard had sought out people he thought would have what it takes to kill him, not just Quinn.

The thought soured his gut. He hated hiding. Waiting to see what came his way. He preferred to go on the offensive. As soon as they got to Montana, he was learning everything thing there was about Thomas Carlson—right down to the type of briefs the creep wore—then he was taking the fight to him. He didn't care if Bridgette wanted to do this the legal way. Quinn was in danger as long as the bastard was alive, so, Russel would see he didn't stay that way for long.

The vehicle surged ahead, gaining a bit of speed when a ball of light exploded behind them, filling the darkness with a blinding yellow glow that Russel was sure set the Jeep off in sharp contrast. Dirt shot into the air, raining down on the roof as Rigs hit the accelerator, still swinging the SUV right and left. Russel watched through the rearview as a line of men appeared behind them, more charges lighting up the night. Loud pops broke the silence —short, sharp bursts that tossed heavy fire their way.

Fuckers had automatic rifles—AK47s and M4s by the

sound of it. The average mercenary's pick of deadly weapons. The bullets pinged off the back of the jalopy, occasionally giving the vehicle a shove. Rigs countered, but he didn't have enough room to properly swerve. Glass cracked then broke above the seat, showering Russel and Quinn with tiny shards.

He shifted over her. "Stay under me."

She moved with him as he took them to the footwell, crushing her beneath him. But, if the belly was armored, she'd have less of a chance of getting hurt by stray fire.

More thumps, then a hole appeared above his shoulder—right through the passenger seat. He wanted to check on Rigs, but the man had hit the gas, all but tipping them on two wheels as he raced across the ground.

"Stay down. Just another few seconds, and we'll be clear of the charges. Then, we can fly." Rigs cursed when the vehicle skidded to the left. "Fuckers hit the wheel. I've got run flats, but damn, they're determined. There's another line of them closing in on the left."

Russel chanced a quick peek. "You need another set of eyes."

"And you need to not get shot."

Rigs floored it, knocking Russel against the seat. His head hit the side as the SUV veered sharply to the left, then picked up more speed. Another engine roared nearby, the sound getting louder. Rigs headed right, must have hit some kind of ridge because the damn Jeep left the ground. Russel's stomach lurched up then crashed to the floor as the SUV slammed into the ground, bouncing a few times before gaining enough traction to propel them forward, again.

Shouts rose around them, then more high-pitched

pings off the back and sides of the vehicle. Russel glanced up in time to see Rigs remove his gun then shoot out the driver's side window. Either the glass had been shattered or Rigs had lowered it because there was nothing but the loud report of the gun filling the air.

There was some screaming, several more rounds, then the world descended into an eerie quiet. The vehicle charged ahead, occasionally skidding on gravel. Rigs didn't talk, his attention on a revolving pattern of road, mirrors, road, mirrors.

The engine droned in the background, then the tires hit something smooth, the sound of crunching gravel changing to a steady hum.

Rigs sighed, then his hand clamped around Russel's shoulder. "Looks like we lost them. For now."

Russel pushed off the floorboards, muscles stiff from the cramped space. He glanced out the back. Deserted blacktop stretched toward the horizon, the dull surface just visible in the hint of moonlight. Glass covered the seats, the tiny pieces fanning out in every direction. So much for staying in the back. He couldn't guarantee he'd get rid of all the glass, and the last thing he needed was either of them slicing a leg open.

He helped Quinn up, motioning for her to stay put as he maneuvered into the front passenger seat. She could ride the rest of the way on his lap, where he'd have tangible proof she was all right.

Quinn crawled over the carnage of glass and bits of upholstery, settling between his thighs without making a sound. He wrapped his arms around her, wishing he could encase her in a bulletproof bubble before looking over at Rigs. More glass covered his lap, a collection of cuts along his left arm.

Russel leaned over then froze.

Rigs huffed, giving him a sideways glance. "Don't look at me like that. It's a fucking graze."

"A graze?" Blood stained the man's right shoulder, slowly moving downward. "I know what a fucking graze looks like, and that isn't one. Pull over."

"No."

"I'm not asking you, Rigs. Pull the fucking car over. Now."

Rigs set his jaw, then twisted to look directly at Russel. "We stop, and they catch up. Or there's a new batch waiting ten miles ahead, and you're still playing nursemaid on the side of the road when they show up. I'm fine. You can patch it as we drive, but I'm not pulling this damn jalopy over until we reach Montana. And don't even worry about gas because I had an extended tank put in her. She can go for eight hours straight."

"Or I just wait until you pass out from blood loss."

He snorted, the fucker. "Didn't black out when that wall collapsed on me. When you dragged my ass out of there. Not even for the two days you spent carrying me to the LZ after stitching me up. I think I can muscle through a small cut on my shoulder."

"You are some piece of work." He huffed. "Where's my bag?"

"The main stuff is in the back, but I put your kit under your chair. Had a feeling you'd bust my ass if it wasn't within reach."

"Damn straight."

Russel thanked Quinn when she pulled the bag out

from under her legs and handed it to him. He didn't even have to ask her to shift, she just lifted and moved toward the window, making herself as small as possible. He took a moment to look at her. He was pretty damn sure she hadn't gotten hurt, other than maybe some cuts from the glass, but he didn't like to make assumptions.

Her skin was pale, her eyes still overly wide. Her pulse fluttered beneath her skin at the base of her neck. Elevated. Maybe a bit erratic, but not life threatening. He narrowed his eyes, but she shook her head, motioning to Rigs.

She was a trooper. Though obviously scared, she wasn't complaining. Wasn't freaking out. Other than the minor breakdown this afternoon, she'd held it together. Had followed his instructions flawlessly, never wasting time by asking him to explain. He knew he'd been essentially barking out orders, but this was his wheelhouse. His territory—something she understood on an intrinsic level. He admired that. Admired her.

He focused on the injury—on what he had control over right now. Right here, because the horizon was a vast expanse of unknown threats. A condition he planned on changing as soon as they rendezvoused with the rest of the team. Thomas and his men would be held accountable. He vowed it. One way or another, they'd pay.

CHAPTER 14

THE NICELY APPOINTED office was full of people. Five men. One woman. All of them staring at her. Watching Quinn's every movement as if they'd never seen another person breathe before. She coughed, and two of the men palmed their weapons. It was overwhelming.

After a lifetime spent of blending into the background. Making herself invisible. Doing everything she could *not* to attract attention to herself, being at the center of an immense amount of focused energy made her pulse race. Despite the comfortable temperature in the room, a cold sweat beaded her skin, and it was taking all her strength to hold her ground. Not run for the door and disappear.

She didn't think it was a conscious decision on their part. But, with Rigs waking them in the middle of the night, then the race to get to Montana before another group of mercenaries or thugs closed in on them, they'd arrived early. And, now, it seemed that everyone was content to just stand around and wait until she was able to download the evidence from her server.

She glanced at a clock—thank god there was an old-fashioned one on the wall and she didn't have to ask one of them. Five more minutes.

She forced herself to swallow, to gaze around the room. Do anything other than look at the expectant faces fanned out in a semi-circle around her. She was at Bridgette's desk, hands resting beside the keyboard, as they gathered behind her. Soft whispered breaths that made the hair on her neck prickle.

Four minutes.

She fisted her hands, finally twisting to face them. "Ya know, hovering behind me isn't helping any."

The guy on the left—Hank—sighed. "We're all just a bit…anxious."

"Understood. But all this tension is making my hands shake. I might mess up the code, and I only get one chance to get it right."

And, just like that, they disbanded. Hank and Swede walking over to check the doors and windows as Midnight led Bridgette back to the coffeemaker. Only Rigs and Russel remained behind her. Russel had insisted on redressing Rigs' shoulder. The bullet had left a long, jagged crater across his flesh, which she knew would scar. Not that he didn't already have lots. It hadn't been apparent until he'd removed his shirt that the scars on his face weren't the only ones he'd suffered during that incident.

Long, raised keloids ran across his chest and down his ribs, ending a few inches above his waist. She couldn't imagine how he'd survived for two days, or how Russel had managed to carry him *and* keep him from bleeding out. It seemed so obvious to her, now, that she was the weak link in the group. They were soldiers. Hardened. Able to bend steel and chew on bullets. Rigs was shot and hadn't so much as flinched. Then, there was what Russel called "situational awareness".

She'd always considered herself to be acutely aware of her surroundings. Above average when it came to reading a room. But these men...

They'd made it into an art form. It was obvious by the way they endlessly scanned the area, as if expecting trouble to jump out at any second, that they wouldn't get caught unaware. Even Bridgette had her strengths. She was a lawyer. A previous US Attorney. That took hard work. Dedication and the kind of intelligence most peopled envied.

What did Quinn have? A few years of self-defense training and an eye for symmetry. Colors. Not the kind of qualities that would keep her alive or out of jail based on her current circumstances. She'd never fired a gun in her life, and if she tried to throw a knife, it would most likely just bounce off and clatter to the floor.

And, of course, there was the part where her family were criminals. Not petty thieves. How had Bridgette phrased it? At the top of everyone's watch list? Yeah, that was her contribution. The daughter of a mobster.

She jumped when a hand landed on her shoulder, nearly tumbling out of the chair as she tried to scramble to her feet. Everyone turned to look at her, the metallic squeak of the springs just now fading.

Russel frowned. "You okay?"

She pretended to smooth out her shirt. "Guess I'm a bit edgy."

"You're not the only one."

Except she was the only one who *looked* edgy.

He placed his hand on her arm. "I just wanted to tell you that it's time."

Time?

The files.

She reclaimed her seat then clicked on the computer. The hard drive spun for a few moments then flashed to life. She hunched over the desk then set to work—accessing her remote server, imputing the correct code then initiating the download. In under twenty minutes, she had the files unencrypted and sitting on Bridgette's desktop.

Quinn worried her bottom lip, aware this was another point of no return. Once she showed the other woman the files, there'd be no going back. No way to save her father if—when—he got caught in the crossfire. All those years of taking care of her, and she was essentially stabbing him in the back. It didn't matter that she'd concentrated her efforts on Thomas, on *his* crimes, it all led back to Henry James.

Russel squeezed her shoulder. "Quinn?"

She choked back the bile burning her throat then turned. Everyone had gathered, again, but she focused on Russel. On the green of his eyes, the soft skin of his lips. On the way his mouth lifted ever so slightly as he watched her closely.

She cleared her throat then stood. "That's all of it. Copies of ledgers, manifests. Lists of inventories and suppliers. I also tried to photograph as many of the men as I could so they could be identified. I only know a few of them by name. Some of the information is still in code, but I can translate it for you if you need me to."

Bridgette's eyes widened. "You know their code?"

Quinn shrugged. "I was pretty much confined to the property until I was sixteen. Not much to do, so I'd play spy. Try to sneak around without getting caught. I used to hide in my dad's study and see if he noticed. Sometimes, I overheard stuff. I didn't really understand what it was at the time, but… When I saw the codes, I thought they were puzzles. And I spent weeks going over whatever I could get my hands on until I figured it out. I didn't realize what they implicated. I just enjoyed the challenge."

Midnight stepped in beside Bridgette. "Is that how you managed to get all of this? You played spy, again?"

"I was…motivated."

"Christ." The man shoved his hand through his hair. "What the hell would you have done if you'd gotten caught?"

"I didn't."

Russel spun her slightly to face him. "But you could have. Damn it, these men are killers. And you snuck around the house, taking photographs?"

"I did what I had to do to get concrete proof. My word against theirs wasn't going to cut it. Quinn Scott doesn't even exist. How was that going to look? How credible can I be when I'm a fake? I needed proof. And not just for the authorities. I needed it for me."

His mouth pinched tight. "You wanted to know how deep your father was in it. If he'd always been a part of the violence."

Her chin quivered, but she held on. "He looked me in the eyes when I was eighteen and swore he'd never killed anyone. Never resorted to violence. That all he did was move money around. Sell a few things some people frowned upon. And I believed him. I agreed to look the other way if he let me have a life outside of his. So, yeah, I wanted to know if he'd stood there that day and lied to my face. If every person that's died as a result of my family's business still being functional is more blood on my hands."

"Quinn—" Russel's face reddened, but he seemed to bite back the rest of his reply. "You didn't find anything, did you."

It wasn't a question.

"No. Trust me, if I had…" She swallowed with effort. "But I didn't find anything to prove he hadn't, either. And, now, men from that organization—my family's business— are trying to kill me. So… You tell me the answer."

Russel sighed, glanced at his buddies, then headed off to grab a cup of coffee.

Quinn watched his back for a few moments, the obvious disconnect tightening her chest, then turned to Bridgette. "Like I said. That's everything I have. I don't even know if it's enough."

Bridgette smiled at her, gave her hand a squeeze, then sat down. She stared at the screen, moving the mouse as she flipped through some of the pages. She hadn't gotten more than several images in before she reached for her cell then turned. "These files… God, Quinn. You've single-handedly just crippled one of the largest criminal organizations to date."

She couldn't smile. Didn't really feel anything other than numb. "Can you put Thomas in jail for the rest of his life?"

"I can put the bastard on death row if the prosecution wants it."

"Good."

Bridgette's smile faltered. "Quinn. Harlequin. You should know—"

"Don't. I'd rather not. I know it probably doesn't make sense to you. Any of you. You've all spent your lives fighting for justice. Running into the line of fire, never thinking about your own safety. So, loving a man who the rest of the world sees as a monster? It doesn't make much sense."

Hank stepped forward. "No one's judging you."

"I am." She pursed her lips, hoping it would keep the tears at bay, because she wouldn't cry, again, damn it. "When I look at Henry James, I see the man who read me stories every night. Who checked for monsters under my bed. Who never once blamed me for my mother's death. He said he'd never let anyone hurt me, and for as long as I lived there, he did his best to keep that promise. And now…now, I'm breaking mine. I know it's the right thing to do. I just wish it *felt* right."

She wrapped her arms around her chest. "I don't suppose there's somewhere I can wash up? That doesn't require you to call in the rest of your men?"

Bridgette stood and pointed to the back of the room. "There's a small shower through there. It's stocked with toiletries and some spare clothes. I'm not sure how well they'll fit, but you're welcome to anything you find. A lot of the women I help leave with nothing more than the clothes on their backs, so… I like to have a few comfort items for them. Please, take your time. There's not much you can do until I've gone through these files and noted anything I might need your help on. I'm going to call a colleague of mine. Pick his brain a bit. Then, we'll talk."

Quinn nodded then turned, walking as quickly as she could to the back room. Knowing the others were watching her, feeling sorry for her, just made everything worse. She didn't want their pity. Didn't want them to make excuses for her. Grant her forgiveness because there wasn't any. She'd made her choice, and she'd have to live with the fallout. Good or bad.

The washroom door creaked as she closed it, shutting out the rest of the world. Maybe she could pretend for a few minutes that it didn't exist. That she hadn't just handed her father over to the authorities. That she hadn't betrayed him.

Steam filled the small space as she stepped beneath the spray. It wasn't overly strong, but enough to chase away the chill that had settled in her bones. It was the first time she'd been cold since the bar. Up until now, Russel had been her source of heat. Her foundation. He'd sensed when she'd needed his strength and had offered it without her asking.

Pain flared in her chest. He'd looked so...lost, when he'd turned away to grab coffee. She hadn't meant to make a scene. To put her fears, her failures on him. If it wasn't for him and his teammates, she'd be dead. A dozen times over. So, spiraling into self-pity was the last thing he deserved.

Quinn closed her eyes. Maybe, with time, she'd learn to forgive herself. To see it the way others did. But, right now. Right this moment, she was damned. Guilty for not stepping up sooner, and guilty of abandoning blood.

The pain blossomed, creeping through her chest and up to her throat, making it hard to breathe. To swallow. Water poured over her shoulders, but all she felt was the oppressive weight slowly suffocating her. Edging her toward darkness. She palmed the tiles, wondering if she might throw up, when the shower door opened, and a swirl of cold air curled around her.

She jumped, trying to turn, when Russel's large calloused hands slid across her waist then settled on her rib cage. They tugged her against a wall of hard male flesh, his shaft long and stiff against her back. Tears threatened, but she refused to cry, leaning into him. Trusting him to bear her weight.

His lips caressed the side of her jaw, smoothing up to her ear. "It's going to be okay."

She placed her hands over his, clinging to him. "Say it, again."

"It's going to be okay. *We're* going to be okay. Promise."

"I thought maybe you'd changed your mind. I wouldn't blame you. I'm not like your friends."

Russel's raspy breath swept across her neck. "Do you remember when you asked me why I was at the bar that first night?"

She tensed. "You said something about a change in career."

His fingers flexed against her skin, digging in slightly then flattening. "I didn't quit the Air Force because I was done. I was discharged. But not the normal way." He exhaled. "My last mission—I disobeyed direct orders. Went after a teammate who'd been captured. In the process of freeing him, I killed a very important informant. My punishment was getting an other-than-honorable discharge."

"Other than honorable?"

"It means everything good I did has been virtually

erased. Replaced by this…black mark. It might as well be a scarlet letter. I lose my pension. My dignity. My honor. There're lots of people who can't see past it. Who only see the words and not the actions behind them. I got lucky. I have brothers who look beyond it. Who have my back. But there'll always be those who judge and assume based on those four words. So, no, Quinn. I'm not going to walk away over sins your father committed. For not wanting to betray your only family."

He took another breath, holding for a few heartbeats before slowly exhaling. "I know this is all happening quickly. But I don't care about that. I care about you. But, if what I told you changes whatever you feel for me…"

She stood there for a moment, listening to him breathe. Feeling his muscles clench and release against her skin, before spinning inside his embrace. She tilted back her head, staring up at his face. At his shadowed jaw and green eyes. He wasn't pretty like some men. Probably wouldn't get a spot on the cover of a magazine, but every time she looked at him, he became more captivating. More handsome.

She laid one arm across his shoulder, smoothing her other hand along his chin. "I was right."

His lips quirked, a hint of a smile showing through. "About choosing to let me give you a lift home? Of course, you were, sweetheart."

"About you being the kind of man I'd always dreamed of being with. I'm falling for you."

His eyes widened then darkened. He shuffled her back, pressing her against the wall of the shower. A light mist sprayed across them as he leaned forward, dropping his forehead to hers. "That's okay. I'm already there, so, I'll catch you."

His mouth settled over hers, and everything else faded. The sound of the water. The hum of the overhead fan. There was just Russel and his lips on hers, his tongue dipping into her mouth. He didn't rush. Took his time tasting and licking, easing up enough to catch a breath, reposition his mouth, then kissed her, again.

Quinn wrapped her arms around him, palming his head and kneading the bulging muscles in his back. She wanted to get closer. Touch every inch of his skin. Feel him pressed against her. Moving inside her.

The kisses deepened, lengthened, then he was lifting her up, spreading her thighs and driving into her. Long, steady thrusts. Hips grinding, her ankles crossed behind his back. He ate at her mouth, one hand palming her breast, the other squeezing her ass cheek.

She held on, gasping in breaths as pleasure coiled in her core. She dug her fingers into his flesh, bit at his lips. Anything to keep from screaming out his name.

Russel moaned against her ear, tilting her hips, changing the angle. His pace increased. Each stroke longer. Harder. His breath grew raspy, his heart rate pounding in time with hers. She felt each forceful beat. Felt her body respond in kind. His cock swelled every time he bottomed out, his sac slapping her cleft, his muscles clenching beneath her touch. He was on the verge of coming, but so was she.

Quinn nipped at his ear. "Now. God, Russel. Please."

She wasn't sure which word set him off. If hearing her growl out his name made him pound into her or the way she'd all but begged. She didn't care. All she needed was

Russel. Consumed with his need for her. Claiming her. Binding them together.

The air thickened. Heavy with steam. With their panting breaths. She pressed her heels against his ass, levering up, trying to meet each stroke, when he released her breast, wedged his hand between them and rubbed her clit.

She exploded. Eyes squeezed shut, her fingers clamped around his neck and head. Her body contracted around him, rhythmic pulses that locked around his shaft. He drove into her, using all his weight, crushing her against the wall until his cock swelled even more.

"Fuck, Quinn."

His control shattered. The long strokes replaced by sharp jerking thrusts. He moaned against her ear, locked his mouth on her shoulder then stiffened. Then, he was coming, his cock emptying inside her, his fingers digging almost painfully into her ass. Over and over, hips pressed together, the water spraying across his back, misting into her face.

It was perfect.

Russel held her tight, his weight holding them up as the tremors slowly subsided. She tucked her head into his shoulder, allowing herself to drift, to lose herself in the warmth of his skin, the feel of his breath against her neck when someone knocked on the door. She managed to lift her head slightly as a creak echoed through the room.

"Ice."

Russel clenched his jaw, squeezing her closer before barely turning his head. "What's up, Sam?"

"There's been a...development."

"Roger. We'll be right out."

The door clicked shut. Quinn closed her eyes. She didn't want to let go. Didn't want to slip from this bubble outside reality. Where there was just the two of them. Just heat, and skin, and tangled limbs. Where she wasn't Harlequin James, whistleblower and crime heiress. Where she could pretend that everything would turn out okay.

Russel sighed. He dropped a kiss on her shoulder, then her neck, working his way to her lips. He didn't possess her like before. Didn't twist her mouth open and delve inside. It was just a brushing of flesh on flesh. Soft. Gentle. Tears threatened, but she choked them back.

He eased away, letting her feet fall to the floor, as he slipped free. One large hand cupped her jaw, tilting it up. "Whatever it is, you're not alone. Teammates, remember?"

She nodded, afraid her voice would crack if she answered. If she breathed. He smiled, quickly washed them both then twisted off the taps. Her skin beaded with goosebumps as the air immediately cooled. He handed her a towel, stepping out without one. He didn't seem to feel the cold. To be anxious, at all.

That's when she realized—Russel was gone. Ice was back.

It only took a couple of minutes to dry off and dress. Bridgette had a variety of yoga pants and soft long-sleeved shirts. Quinn found a set that fit well enough, taking a moment to run a brush through her hair. God, even combed out it looked unruly, curls going in every direction.

Russel appeared behind her in the mirror. He looked perfect. Skin still nicely tanned, eyes bright. Alert. The creases feathering out from them might have been a bit deeper, a bit more noticeable. And his five-o'clock shadow was nearly a beard, again. But he didn't look like a man who'd avoided an army's worth of hired thugs in the past twenty-four hours.

He smiled, lightly brushing his fingers over the mark he'd left on her neck. "You're beautiful."

She snorted. "If you like the pasty, nervous wreck look."

His hands moved to her shoulders. "If that's what this is, then you pull it off. Ready?"

She swallowed but nodded. She wasn't ready. Not to face the others—especially when she knew they were all aware of what she and Russel had been doing in the shower. And definitely not ready to hear this "development". She knew the code for bad news when she heard it.

Russel took her hand in his then led them back into the office. Everyone turned to watch them as they walked toward Bridgette's desk. Quinn's heart rate kicked up, and despite the cold shiver that beaded her skin with another round of goosebumps, her face heated. She hadn't been thinking clearly when she'd jumped in the shower—when she'd jumped Russel. She'd needed the comfort. To reduce her world from complicated to binary. It had been more than sex. More than getting off. It had been reassurance. A promise that she hadn't just lost everything with one act of bravery.

They stopped just back from the desk, Russel behind her, his strong hands braced on her waist. He pulled her against him slightly—just enough for her to lean into his chest. She felt his heartbeat through her back—slow and steady. One for every second. It soothed some of the restless energy strumming through her. Regardless of what she discovered, she could handle it as long as he was there. Calm. Ready to react on a moment's notice.

Bridgette stood, immediately joined by Midnight. Her fiancé took a position similar to Russel's—a visible show of support and strength.

Bridgette glanced at the other men, looked directly at Russel then sighed. "I just got off the phone with a colleague from the US Attorney's office. I wanted to get a sense of how this would play out. What options we had before doing anything official. Like I said. They're aware of your father's activities. As soon as I mentioned his name…"

Quinn forced herself not to shake. Not to show any emotion. She'd knew this was coming. The fallout. And she knew she'd have to live with the consequences of her actions. And not just her father's. She had no idea what accounts or properties he'd been talking about. Hadn't unearthed information on them. That meant she could end up in a cell right alongside him.

She forced in a shallow breath. "And?"

Bridgette pursed her lips. "I'm not sure how else to tell you. Jeremy just heard from the feds. Your father was rushed to the hospital late last night. He's in critical condition from gunshot wounds."

CHAPTER 15

SHIT.

Russel clenched his jaw to hide his surprise. He'd been expecting a number of responses. That Quinn's father had fled the country. That he was secretly orchestrating the attempts on her life. That the mysterious accounts the man had in Quinn's name were going to be far more trouble than they'd anticipated.

And Russel was ready. He'd already worked out a number of different responses. How to comfort her if her father had turned out to be a monster. How Russel was going to escape with her if it looked as if she'd end up on the wrong side of the investigation. He didn't care what went down. How the rest of the group thought it should play out. Quinn was his. Period. And, if that meant running, abandoning his life. Reappearing somewhere else, as someone else—he was ready.

Her father shot. It hadn't made the list.

He tightened his hold, pulling her more firmly against him. She was stiff. Unyielding. He listened for her breath then realized she was holding it. Not even a whisper of sound.

Russel lifted one hand to span her rib cage. Her pulse tapped against his palm. Choppy and quick. She was going to pass out if she didn't get her lungs working.

He bent over her, keeping his voice low. "Breathe for me, sweetheart."

She hiccupped then drew in a few shaky gasps.

He drew her even closer. "Slower. Try to match mine."

He made a point of exaggerating his breathing, letting his chest expand fully before expelling it. It took a few moments, but she managed to pick up the rhythm, her heart rate finally slowing beneath his hand.

Bridgette sighed. "I'm so sorry, Quinn."

She managed a nod.

Russel gave her a squeeze. "Do they know what happened? Who shot him?"

Bridgette glanced at Sam.

Midnight moved to her side. "Jeremy said Henry's housekeeper, Gladys, found him around midnight. He was unconscious but breathing. She called 9-1-1, and they rushed him to Harborview. He was in surgery most of the night and is currently in critical condition in their ICU ward. He had his cellphone in his hand." Sam looked directly at Quinn. "Apparently, he'd tried to call you. A few times."

Quinn made a strangled sound deep in her throat before her head bowed forward. "I tossed my phone away after they attacked us at the bar. So, they couldn't track it."

Russel leaned in closer. "I'm so sorry, sweetheart. If I hadn't asked you to do that—"

"They would have found us even quicker." She glanced

back at him, eyes glassy, chin quivering slightly. "You've saved my life more times than I can count. You and Rigs. This isn't your fault."

"It's not yours, either."

She snorted and pulled out of his hold, marching over to the window. She didn't stand in front it, obviously remembering their instructions to stay clear of the windows and doors. Instead, she glanced out from the side, staring at something up the street. "Is he going to make it?"

Bridgette patted Sam's hand, signaling she'd answer. "Jeremy didn't know. Since it's gun related, the hospital was obligated to call the police. When your father's name came up, they called the feds, who notified the attorney's office shortly after. But the doctors would only say that he was still critical."

Quinn nodded, still looking out the window. "I think we all know who shot him."

Hank moved forward. "You think it was this Thomas Carlson guy."

"I know it was."

"Quinn—"

"It was Thomas. He's the only one who would benefit. He knows I have evidence—that it's all over if I get away. But, if he can kill me—kill my father… He'll get it all. The entire organization."

Hank glanced over at Russel, motioning to Quinn with his head. Russel sighed then slowly picked his way over. He didn't touch her, even though his fingers itched to hold her. Comfort her. Her life was falling apart around her, and she didn't have any one else to turn to. God, she must have feel alone. Alone and guilty and pretty much like shit.

He stopped just shy of her. "What do you need?"

She stiffened then turned to face him. "Excuse me?"

"Nothing I say can make this better. So, tell me what you need, and if I can give it to you, I will."

Her jaw clenched, the muscles in her temple throbbing before she drew herself up. "I need Thomas' soul burning in hell."

"Okay. Then, let's figure out how to capture this son of a bitch."

No. Not going to happen. No fucking way. Over Russel's dead body. Absolutely not going down like this because it was crazy. *She* was crazy.

But there they all were. Standing around talking—planning how it was going to happen. As if it was viable. Reasonable. Well, they were going to burn Plan A. In fact, Russel was going to obliterate Plan B, too. Probably Plan C. He was going to move them straight to Plan W—whatever was as far away as possible from having Quinn be bait.

Hank had aerial shots of the Blue Moose Tavern spread out across Bridgette's desk. Had dots spread out—locations he'd have the team setup. The sheriff was nodding away, adding the odd suggestion. They even had a fed—Mark Springer—off to one side, watching. Listening. He'd flown in from Seattle—had apparently been heading the James investigation for the past year. Was eager to take the entire syndicate down, especially Thomas Carlson.

Except for the part where to take it down, Quinn was right square in the crosshairs. She wasn't on the front line. She *was* the front line.

Russel clenched his jaw. They were soldiers. They were the ones who went into battle. Who took chances. Yet, no one else seemed to see it. Seemed at all worried about sending her in. Alone. Because Quinn insisted that Thomas wouldn't come close to her if he could place any of them.

Hank paused, looking around the room. "Okay, we all clear? Quinn?"

Hank didn't need to ask. He'd gone over the plan half a dozen times. But Russel knew Quinn had committed it to memory the very first time. Her back was rigid, her muscles flexed and primed for battle. And her eyes—shit, they were laser focused. Brimming with fire and determination. Any hint of doubt, or fear, had bled out of her the moment she'd realized she had a chance to take Thomas down. Permanently.

Quinn nodded. "Clear."

Hank grinned. "Good." He scanned everyone, again, pausing on Russel. "Now, we should… Shit. Ice? It looks like you have something to add."

Russel took a step forward, hands fisted at his sides. He tensed every muscle. Anything to keep from marching across the room, punching a hole through their stupid maps then hiking Quinn up on his shoulder and leaving.

He took a deep breath, repeating to himself that he wouldn't yell. Wouldn't make a scene. "I'm just curious when everyone decided that sending a *civilian* in alone to face an armed man—a serial killing sociopath at that—was a good idea? Because, the last time I checked, *we* were the fucking soldiers. We're the ones trained to fight and kill."

He spun on Midnight when the man touched his arm. "Don't even start with me, Sam, because I know damn well you *never* would have backed a plan where Bridgette walked out into the open and invited the men after her to take a few pot shots."

Sam pressed his lips together, glancing at the woman in question before sighing. "You're right. I wouldn't have. Would have fought it like a damn banshee. Would have torn everyone in here a new one for even suggesting it. But I also know she would have vetoed my vote if she'd gotten it into her head that going out there was the only way to bring those men down. And there wouldn't have been a damn thing I could have done about it."

"Thankfully, we have other options. Like capping the mother fucker the moment he drives into town."

The fed—Springer—stepped forward. "You know we need Carlson alive. We've been over this. Ms. James—"

"Scott. Her name is Quinn Scott, and I don't give a rat's ass how many times we've been over this. I didn't just spend the past forty-eight hours keeping her alive so you could hand her over to the bastard who wants her dead! The same man we're pretty sure put her father in the hospital. She gave you all the evidence she has. That'll have to be enough."

Hank cleared his throat. "Let's all take a deep breath and remember we're on the same team."

"I don't need a deep breath. I need a fucking plan that

doesn't have us all standing around while Quinn puts her life on the line."

Springer pointed to the maps. "She'll have protection. Men stationed outside."

"And if Thomas decides to just pull a gun and shoot her point blank? In the middle of the bar? Then, what? Because I can promise you that he would have done it back in Seattle if I hadn't gotten her out of there, first."

"As good as the evidence is, we need Thomas to implicate himself and confirm *Ms. James* hasn't been a part of any of it, in case we find those accounts and properties she said her father mentioned. Thomas doesn't know she's already turned the files over. He believes she's still on the run. Probably thinks he killed Henry, too. That's why he jumped at the opportunity when Quinn called him—offered to hand it all over tonight if he agreed to take it and walk away."

He grinned at Quinn. "You were very convincing, Ms. James. And, if I bought it, Thomas did, too. Opening fire in a crowded bar. Blowing it up. Even shooting her would be a stupid move. There's no way he could guarantee he wouldn't be caught on film by a cell phone or a security cam." He crossed his arms. "I've been studying this man for a while. He wants to be king of the James' empire more than he wants *Harlequin James* dead."

"You're betting her life on your...assumption. That's not a risk I'm willing to take."

The rest of the men stood there, mouths pinched tight, backs stiff. They weren't backing Russel, but they weren't arguing with him, either. He firmed his stance. He could be just as stubborn.

"Russel."

He stilled as Quinn's voice drew his attention. She'd moved over to him, one hand lifting to rest on his forearm. She gave him a squeeze, and his chest followed suit. Closing in tight, making it hard to breathe, as his heart punched him hard in the ribs.

He brushed some hair back, keeping his touch light. Gentle. Completely at odds to how he felt. "I know you think I've been overly protective. Or paranoid. Or that I'm overstepping my bounds, but… Quinn."

She smiled at him, and that spotlight appeared. Beaming down from heaven. Lighting up her face like the Fourth of July or Christmas. She was so beautiful. So strong and determined, and he couldn't lose her. Not now. Not after coming to terms with the fact he'd fallen in love with her. He didn't care that it was quick. That people would say he was crazy. He felt the rightness of it in his bones. His soul.

She glanced at the others. "Can we have a moment?"

His teammates seemed to vanish. Just disappeared into the walls or maybe Quinn had snapped her fingers and done it for them. He wouldn't be surprised. Only Springer stood glaring at them for a minute before grunting then taking a few steps away.

Russel looked around then focused on Quinn. He knew she was going to try and talk him down. Convince him that this was a completely reasonable plan. But he wasn't being swayed that easily.

"Look, Quinn, I know I don't have the right to make decisions for you, but—"

"Do you know how many times anyone has ever stood up for me?"

He frowned. That wasn't what he'd thought she'd say. "No."

"Once. And that was you in that bar weeks ago. Sure, my dad dealt with any of the men who stepped out of line after the fact, but not like this. Just when I think you can't impress me more, you do something that blows me away."

"Then, you understand why this is a horrible idea. The worst in the history of bad ideas."

She stared up at him for a long time, eyes searching his, her hand still resting on his forearm, before looking down. "What I know is that I spent ten years hiding. Pretending my father wasn't destroying lives because I was afraid. Not just that Thomas or men like him would come after me. Hurt me. But that people would find out. Discover who I was. That they'd know I wasn't brave enough—strong enough—to take a stand."

She raised her other hand and stroked his jaw. "Then, I met you. One of the last truly good men in this world. And everything changed. You were willing to risk your life without even knowing what you were facing. In the truck, when you turned to me and said you'd come into the café with me… That's when I realized I couldn't pretend any longer. That if I ever wanted to have a real life—one that allowed me to be with a guy like you—I had to make a choice. I'm not saying it's been easy. And, if you weren't so damn stubborn, I'd be dead. But this is my chance. To step up. To do the right thing. To quiet those voices in my head."

He placed his hand over hers. "You don't have anything to prove."

"Maybe not to you. But I do to myself. I know it's dangerous. And I'll admit. I'm scared. You're absolutely right. I'm not like you or Hank or Midnight. I'm not a warrior. But I know Thomas, and I *can* do this."

"Quinn. Please."

"Teammates, right? That's what you said. That we're teammates, and teammates have each other's back. I'm not alone, Russel. I've got your team backing me up."

"And if Thomas decides to simply pull a gun and pop you in the head? If he doesn't care about security cameras or that you might have backup? Then, what?"

Rigs appeared at their side. "Then, I take the bastard down. I swear, if he so much as twitches, he'll be dead before he draws."

Russel flexed his jaw. Fuck, he hated this. "How am I supposed to just let you walk in there?"

Quinn smiled. "Rigs told me yesterday that *you're* the reason he and the other Special Ops soldiers could go in without being afraid of what would happen. Because they knew, if the mission went sideways, you'd be there to get them out. So, you see? I don't have to be afraid because I have this kickass PJ on my side, just itching to ride in and save the day."

"I can't raise the dead, sweetheart."

"You won't have to. Because I have an even better weapon."

Russel arched his brow.

She tiptoed up and wrapped her arms around his neck. "I have you. Not the soldier, Ice, but the man. And I'm pretty sure Russel's fallen in love with me. So, I know he won't let anything happen to me, because he needs me to come back, so I can tell him I love him, too."

Then, she kissed him. Not all tongues and teeth like when they'd made love in the shower. Just a delicate press of her lips on his. A soft brushing of skin. And he felt it down to his toes.

Russel rested his forehead on hers. "You don't fight fair."

She chuckled. "Pretty sure you started it. I'll be okay. And you, Rigs, Midnight, Hank, and Swede will be there to back me up. Thomas won't know what hit him. I need to do this, Russel. And I need to know you'll be part of it."

"Damn straight because there's no way I'm letting you go, now." He forced himself to step back—release his fingers one by one then tuck his arms at his side. Hardest damn thing he'd ever done.

He turned to Springer. "I swear to god, if anything happens to her, I'll hold you personally responsible. And I can assure you, that won't end well for you."

Hank sighed. "Down, Ice. We don't need you threatening a federal officer."

"Not a threat, Montana. Just a fact. Fine. Let's get this insanity started before I change my mind and take Thomas out the second I see his lying face."

CHAPTER 16

Nine fifty-five. Five minutes to showtime.

That's what Quinn told herself as she sat at the table off to the right side of the bar. The one her "team" had specifically chosen for her. They'd talked about sight lines. About emergency egress points and target analysis. She'd nodded. Acted as if she had a clue what most of it meant because all she really needed to know was that Thomas would walk through that front door in under five minutes, and she'd finally get a chance to send his murderous ass to jail.

Or better yet, the asshole would try to hurt her or abduct her, and Rigs or one of the other men would put a bullet between his beady little eyes. She knew Russel was itching to. That letting Thomas live wasn't part of Russel's end game—not when they all knew the man could still get to her. Hire someone from within prison to kill her.

But they could worry about that later. After they'd successfully executed their plan because, while she wouldn't admit it, especially to Russel, she wasn't convinced this was going to be as smooth as they thought —despite the caliber of men backing her up. Thomas might not be a soldier. He hadn't trained for brutal missions in dangerous places. But he wasn't some low-level gang member, either. He was part of a highly successful criminal organization that had managed to evade federal prosecution for over thirty years. He was smart. Efficient. And Quinn knew he'd have a backup plan. Several, maybe.

He'd anticipate she wouldn't come alone, and just thinking that she might get one of Russel's friends hurt— or, god, killed—ate at her. That wasn't even considering anything happening to Russel, because that... That messed with her brain too much. Made it impossible to think. To focus. To breathe. She'd chosen this path, knowing she might not make it out the other side alive. And she'd accepted it. But losing Russel...

She couldn't go there. Couldn't imagine continuing on without him. He was right. It had been insanely quick—a month, in technical terms, but only days, really. Days spent by his side, under his protection. But it didn't alter the fact she'd fallen in love with him. Had known, from the moment he'd held her in his truck, begging her to let him help her, that she'd stumbled upon the kind of connection that happened once in a lifetime. And, after living like a ghost, she wasn't going to waste another moment worrying about whether anyone else would understand their feelings.

All she needed was Russel. Which meant taking this fucker, Thomas, down.

Four minutes.

She folded her hands on the table as she scanned the

crowd. She had a feeling Thomas would send some of his men in ahead. Have them scout out the bar—see if they could place anyone she'd brought with her as backup. They wouldn't. Hank's team was too good. Rigs and Swede had ventured into the bar an hour before her. She'd caught one glimpse of them when she'd walked in, then they'd just disappeared. Rigs was supposed to be playing pool in the corner behind her, and she knew he was there, somewhere. But damn if she could spot him.

And Swede. She half wondered if he'd gotten himself painted to blend in with the wall paneling—like those dancers sometimes did. Their entire bodies done up to resemble part of the scenery—because he was just…gone.

According to their "plan", Midnight would be up on one of the rooftops. He'd tried to argue that Rigs should be there—something about him being a better shot—but Rigs had shaken his head and calmly stated that Midnight was equally skilled and the best fit. That he would blend in with the biker crowd on account of his scars. Also, that Midnight had been there before, and they couldn't chance someone might recognize him and somehow out him.

That had sealed the deal. Hank was also perched up high, watching the other direction. They were coordinating with the sheriff and Springer. Arranging it so the outliers of Thomas' gang could be rounded up by a contingency of cops waiting in the wings. Nothing was going to get past them.

Three minutes.

Quinn looked around, pausing on a man at the bar. Leather jacket. Some kind of numbered tat on the side of his neck. He was one. No doubt. She kept scanning, settling on another guy near the hall to the washrooms.

He'd been standing there, leaning against the wall since she'd first entered. Originally, she'd pegged him as a predator. The kind Russel had scared away that first night. But, now... He was part of this. No question.

Two minutes.

There were another two men by the pool table—gazes constantly drifting toward her—which made four. A few other guys raised the hairs on the back of her neck, but she suspected they were just creeps. Men looking for a good time, whether a woman was willing or not. Guys she'd usually avoid. But compared to Thomas' thugs—they hardly registered.

One minute.

Quinn took a deep breath. Springer had wanted her to wear one of his wires, but she'd refused. Thomas wasn't a fool. He knew what to look for. Would somehow make the nearly invisible device in her ear or see the tiny mic that Springer thought looked like a button. Instead, she'd hidden a device in her camera, which she'd put right out in the open. Just placed it on the table beside her because Thomas wouldn't question that. She always had it in her purse, and she'd already worked up a story.

Ten pm.

She leaned back, steadying her nerves as the door to the bar swung inward. And there he was. Dark hair slicked back, casual designer clothes fitted perfectly to his six-foot-two frame. He wasn't muscular, but he was tall and lean. Fit enough to be agile and quick in his movements. She knew lots of women found him attractive. Sought his company.

He made her skin crawl.

Thomas didn't stop at the threshold, walking confidently over to her as if he knew where she was before entering. He had. His men had no doubt told him everything she'd done for the past fifteen minutes while she'd been waiting for him. From the kind of drink she'd ordered to whether she'd talked to anyone. Looked suspiciously at one of the patrons who might be an inside man.

She hadn't.

He grinned as he stopped next to the chair, ogling her for a minute before kicking out the wooden seat then sliding into it. He took a quick glance under the table—looking for a wire taped to the underside, she suspected—then relaxed back in the chair.

His gaze dropped to her camera then up to her face. "Planning on taking my photo, Harlequin? Want something to remember me by when you're holed up in some shit-poor town in Mexico?"

"Consider it my insurance policy. It's angled so I was able to snap one of you the moment you walked in without lifting it." She removed a cell and held it up. "It's linked to this phone. You so much as look at me wrong, and it, along with all the data, will be sent to some very interesting people. The kind that want your ass on a spit."

He stared at her for a few heartbeats then tipped back his head and laughed. "Oh, my dear. If only your father had properly groomed you. You would have made one hell of an addition to the business. But I assure you. As long as you hold up your end of the bargain, I won't lay a finger on you. Not here."

"Not anywhere. That's the deal. I give you the flash drive, and then, I get to disappear."

He shrugged. "Does anyone truly disappear? There's

always a trail. But fine. You hand over the flash drive, and I'll get up and leave. Let you do your best vanishing act."

She eyed him, noting the smug tilt of his lips. The way he watched her as if he was privy to a secret. "Like you said. I would have made one hell of a business partner for my dad. If that had been my thing. Which it wasn't. But it also means I'm not stupid, either. So, why don't you just tell me what your contingency plan is? Save us both the hassle of having to sit together for any longer than necessary. Because I know you don't trust me. You must have something you think will persuade me not to double cross you. Something better than physical threats. Or you never would have agreed to come out here and meet me in the first place."

"Touché. You definitely are Henry's daughter. Fine, let's cut through the bullshit." He reached into his pocket, and Quinn had a brief moment of panic—imagining Rigs or Swede mistaking the man's actions and killing him—but Thomas' brains were still intact when he placed a similar drive to the one in her pocket on the table.

She arched a brow. "What's that?"

"That is your ticket to death row. You see, your father really did want to protect you. He'd never approved of the…messier side of the business. Wasn't one to ever get his hands dirty. But even he realized that you were a commodity he just couldn't pass up. So, over the years, he's amassed a fortune in your name. True, it's blood money but…what isn't these days? I'm afraid it won't look too good to the authorities. And the best part is, I had nothing to do with it."

He slid the drive over to her. "Go ahead. You can keep that one. I have more."

"You're assuming I want my freedom more than I want you to pay."

"I'm assuming you want to disappear. Otherwise, you wouldn't have called me." He motioned to her with his fingers. "Your turn."

She stuffed her hand in her pocket then removed a flash drive Bridgette had made for her and tossed it at him. "There. That's everything."

He held it up, turning it over a few times before staring at her.

"Go ahead. Have one of the men you sent in here ahead of you take it out and check. It's all in there. Enough evidence to put you on death row."

He cracked a smile. "You always were good at reading a room. I had hoped you wouldn't pick up on my guys—not in a bar full of dangerous men, but I wasn't convinced."

He held up his hand, and the guy in the leather jacket sitting at the counter slipped off his seat and walked over. He took the drive then headed straight for the door.

Thomas grinned. "Darryl will just verify everything, and then, we can part ways."

"Fine."

Thomas watched her for a while, still smiling. "Oh, and those men you undoubtedly have stationed around here—the snipers and backup shadowing you in here—I suggest you call them off. Otherwise, daddy dearest won't see the sun rise."

She bit the inside of her lip to keep herself in check. "Who says I care?"

"You haven't missed a lunch with the man in ten years. You care. That was always your downfall, Harlequin. You care too much for a man who isn't worth the tears you'll cry once he's dead."

He paused when Darryl came back in, moving over to him then whispering in his ear. Thomas nodded, waving the man off.

He cocked his head to the side. "Seems you're far smarter than I thought. I hadn't realized you'd taken that many photos. Well done. And none of it directed at your father. Guess my assumption was correct. So, I'm going to sweeten the deal. I'll assume that you've heard that your father had a rather unfortunate collision with a bullet—or three. But...I made sure he's still very much alive. In fact, he's on the fourth floor in room 409 as we speak. Being carefully...guarded by men I trust far more than the ones in here. Unless you want your father's IV to acquire some nasty air bubbles, I suggest you call your men off."

He stood. "And, if you double cross me, if I even think you've given any of this to the feds, your father and everyone you've ever known—that geek journalist you worked with. Those friends you occasionally go drinking with. Your uncle, cousins. That man who dropped you off at the café. Everyone will meet with a very painful, very bloody death. So, you choose. Snap your fingers, and I'm sure I'll be taken into custody. And your father dies. Or let me go, rat me out, and everyone else dies. I don't have to be free, or even alive, for that to happen. How's that for a contingency plan?"

Quinn stared at him. He wasn't bluffing—the tight press of his mouth, the narrowed eyes. The easy rasp of his breath, and the way his hands remained lax. He was calm. Confident. And unless she was willing to kill her father, he'd won.

"Fine. You're free to go." She pushed quickly to her feet and leaned over the table. "But know this. You so much as breathe in my direction, and you'll be dead. The men I have—they can't be bought. Unlike yours. I bet, for the right price, they'd shoot you, themselves."

"I don't need loyalty because I have more money than you could dream of. But, more importantly, I have your father. All this time, you've been so careful to avoid any kind of attachments, and you didn't even realize you already had one I could use. And I'll see he burns long before I do. In fact, I'll be keeping him really close."

He gave her a mock salute then turned. Pain and anger boiled inside her, and in that instant, she knew. Had known all along it would come down to this. She only hoped she'd be able to look at her reflection in the mirror once it was done.

"Thomas."

He stopped, looking at her over his shoulder. "Yes, Harlequin?"

"You're just forgetting one thing."

"Oh?"

"I'm Harlequin James. Henry James' daughter. And my father taught me well, including the part where I don't make deals with scum like you, no matter the cost. You were wrong. I want you to burn in hell more than I want anything. You can kill my father. Kill me. But, in the end, you're going to spend what's left of your miserable life knowing I took you down. Me. How's that for a rebuttal?" She lifted her hand. "That's the signal in case you were at all confused. There's a man over by the pool table. He's got your beady little eyes in his crosshairs. And he *never* misses. You can thank the Marine Corps for that. Move, and you die."

The smile fell from Thomas' face as Swede and Rigs appeared out of nowhere, along with Springer. He glanced at the men then laughed. "Finally. A move worthy of a true James. I just hope they'll let you out of jail long enough to attend your father's funeral. Because he's as good as dead. And you'll be next."

Springer gave Thomas a shove, bending him over the table as he read him his rights. The creep was still smiling as Springer mumbled his thanks and that he'd contact them, shortly, then carted him away.

Quinn stood there, shaking, watching Thomas disappear out the door before being spun then enveloped in a nearly crushing embrace. Russel's scent filled her senses, the frantic beating of his heart soothing her. This wasn't Ice. The soldier who never lost his cool, never shook. This was Russel. The man she'd fallen in love with. And he was hers.

She relaxed against him, fighting against the tears that threatened. She couldn't think about what she'd done. The lives she might have just put at risk. All she could do was hold onto Russel.

He held firm for what felt like forever before finally easing back. "You just aged me ten years. A thousand missions, and I've never been that fucking scared."

"I wasn't worried. I have a pretty kickass team."

"Right. Not worried." He snorted. "You took one hell of a risk. You okay?"

"I just signed my dad's death warrant. Ask me, again, in fifty years. Maybe, by then, I'll have found forgiveness. That's if I don't end up in jail."

"It'll be okay. Bridgette. Tell her. They can't come after her, now, right? Not with everything Thomas said."

Russel moved back, allowing her to turn and face the people standing behind her. She'd been so focused on holding onto Russel, she hadn't realized they'd gathered around the table.

Bridgette worried her lip. "First of all, your father's had an officer outside his door since I contacted Jeremey this morning. He's already called over. Notified the man that there might be an attempt on your father's life. To double check all the staff. He's safe."

Safe. It didn't exist. Not as long as Thomas was still alive. Still able to wield his power. But Quinn nodded. "Thanks. I appreciate that. But what about this flash drive? Thomas wasn't bluffing. I'm sure whatever is on it is more than damning."

Bridgette frowned, staring at her hand when Quinn placed it in her palm. "I've been known to work the odd magic, legally speaking. I'll do whatever I can. Like Russel said, taping the meeting will definitely help your cause, though it sounds as if Thomas wasn't involved in this aspect. That could…complicate things, depending on how incriminating this information is."

Russel huffed. "So, she risked her life for nothing? Is that what you're telling me, because it sure as hell sounds like it."

Bridgette pursed her lips. "I…I can't answer that until I've gone over everything. In the end, her father might be the only one who can exonerate her."

Quinn straightened. "I've been thinking about that. Assuming Thomas doesn't manage to kill my father—"

"He won't. Jeremy gave his word the officer there is first class."

"Either way, what if I could convince my dad to give up the LA branch? The one he launders money for? He has records. It looked like they went back over twenty years. I just decided not to copy them. But, knowing my dad, he's got copies stashed someplace in case Thomas decides to get rid of them. Surely, that would be worth something."

Bridgette's eyes widened, and she's glanced at Sam, barely holding back her excitement. "Do you really think you could do that? Because…" She whistled. "I might be able to swing a deal. Get him into Wit Sec. You, too—"

"No. Not me. I… Not me. But it would help?"

"It would change the entire scope of this case. Your father's empire is huge, but he'd be giving us that *and* the men behind an organization that encompasses the entire West Coast. That we suspect has ties to Columbia and China. I… I can't even begin to think of the lateral fallout. This could bring down drug and weapons dealers we've been hunting for years."

"So, I guess that means we're heading back to Seattle."

Russel frowned. "I hate to be a buzzkill but… It's not safe. Thomas has too many men. Even I might not be able to watch every angle."

"I have to go back. I have to see him, again. Even if I wasn't trying to convince him to testify, I need to explain. To have the guts to tell him to his face. I was willing to let him die. I've turned over evidence that will put him in jail for the rest of his life if he doesn't agree to cooperate. Whether he helps me or not, the least I can do is be there when he wakes up. Come clean. Please."

He stared at her, and she saw the internal battle. Ice didn't want to acquiesce. He was all about safety. About not putting her in harm's way. This went against his training. Against his instincts. But Russel... He wanted to please her. Wanted to take away the pain she knew radiated off her in waves. Wanted to give her closure and maybe, just maybe, a fraction of peace.

She waited. She couldn't force him. He had an unyielding will once he'd set his mind to something. So, all she could do was stand there and let him decide. Sure, she could run, but—after all he'd done. All his teammates had done—she'd never betray him like that. She'd had enough betrayal to last two lifetimes.

Midnight appeared at their side. "I understand your reservations, Ice, and normally, I'd be right there. No way she's going into a viper's nest full of possible tangos. But, if Bridgette can get Quinn a pass—maybe keep her dad out of prison, not to mention take down a global crime syndicate... It's worth the risk. And you won't be alone. I'm accompanying Bridgette to the US Attorney's office. I can have your back every step of the way."

Rigs knocked shoulders with Russel. "I've got nothing better to do. Midnight can watch over Bridgette. You and me can keep Red safe. No way this can be worse than Somalia in '08."

She thought about smacking Rigs for the Red comment, again, until he winked at her, the bastard. It looked as if Russel had been right. His buddy seemed to have a soft spot for her. Or he was still trying to pay Russel back. Probably the latter.

"Need I remind you that we nearly got our asses capped in Somalia? Not to mention that I couldn't get that stink off me for weeks." Russel blew out an exasperated breath. "And I'll never win a fucking argument if you guys side with her... Every. Single. Time."

Rigs shrugged. "What can we say? She's easier to look at."

Russel eyed Rigs. "You know something, brother? I'm starting to regret saving your ass."

Rigs simply stood there, smiling smugly.

"Fine. We'll load up and head out." Russel stared down at her, pointing one long, calloused finger at her. "But don't even think of going anywhere alone until Thomas is serving ten life sentences on death row. Got me?"

Quinn nodded. "Yup. I got ya. Right where I need you most."

He shook his head, taking her hand. "You're always going to use my feelings against me, aren't you? And, no, don't answer that. Okay. Stay behind me, just in case. We'll trade out the tires then jump in Rigs' rusty piece of metal and head out with Sam and Bridgette. We can stop and pick up my truck, on the way. But be prepared. After you've done this, we're coming back here, and you're staying in one of the safe houses with round-the-clock bodyguards until we get a handle on how much of what Thomas said was coming out of his ass, and how much he can make good on."

"Deal. As long as you're the one guarding my body."

He tripped a step then chuckled. "Guess this is what I get for driving you home, huh?"

"I did warn you."

He stopped and pulled her in for a quick kiss just shy of walking out the door. "Yes, you did. And I'm glad I didn't listen."

"Me, too."

Rigs groaned, pushing past them. "I swear, if you two make goo-goo eyes at each other the entire trip, I'm gonna go with Bridgette and make Midnight ride with you."

CHAPTER 17

SEATTLE. Harborview Medical Center...

RUSSEL WAS READY. In addition to his two knives, he had his Beretta stashed in a shoulder harness. A Walther PPK in an ankle holster, and several extra clips in his pockets. He didn't normally go out in public armed for bear, but... Quinn's life might be on the line. And he'd prepared accordingly.

Of course, Rigs most likely had even more weapons stashed on him. The guy elevated paranoia to an art form, not that Russel was complaining. There was comfort in knowing Rigs probably had some sort of explosive hidden on his body, and that the man wouldn't hesitate to step in front of a bullet meant for Quinn. He'd have done it for strangers. So, for his buddy's girl...

Russel still couldn't get over that. Quinn was *his*. It sounded archaic, and he had a feeling if he ever actually voiced it that way—off-handedly let the words "you're my woman" slip—Quinn would catch him on the jaw with a left hook. Or maybe she'd go straight for his balls. And he wouldn't blame her. It was a dick thing to say. But it didn't stop the thought from looping through his head.

He wasn't the kind of guy that thought women had a place. He'd served with them. Respected them. And yet, there it was. A big ugly truth staring back at him. Quinn was his, and he wasn't the least bit sorry for seeing it that way. Because he was just as much hers. If she still wanted him.

When she'd stood in Bridgette's office, her gaze locked on his, and told him that she knew he'd fallen in love with her, and that he'd see she made it back so she could tell him she loved him, too… Christ, he thought his damn heart was going to jump clean out of his chest. Just burst through his ribcage and into her hand. Because that's where it stayed. Tied around her finger and beating inside her tiny palm.

But they'd been so focused on gathering a few supplies then heading back to Seattle—to meeting with Bridgette's colleague, Jeremey, briefly to discuss a few aspects of the case—that they hadn't enjoyed a moment alone. Couldn't. It wasn't safe, and Russel wasn't compromising her safety just so she could tell him she loved him.

Even if he was dying to hear the words. True, he hadn't told her that he loved her, either. Not with his own voice. But she knew. And, now, he needed the same in return.

"Damn it, Ice, get your head out of the damn clouds. This is an op."

Russel gave himself a mental shake, flipping off Rigs. "I'm in the game, asshole."

"Are you? What color was the hat of the guy who just passed us?"

Shit. Busted.

"Black."

"Lucky fucking guess. Okay, you take Quinn up to the room. There should be a cop outside the door. One inside, I'll linger behind. Watch for tangos on your back. But don't fucking leave the room before I get there. I'll be monitoring it the whole time, but if trouble comes knocking, you're safer in there until I can eliminate the threat."

Quinn leaned forward between the seats. "Do you really think they'll risk making a scene inside a hospital? There are bound to be security cameras everywhere. They'd never get away with it."

Russel placed his hand over hers, still marveling at the difference in size. "From what we've learned, most of Thomas' hired contracts are either gang members or mercenaries. Not the kind to worry about making a scene. They'd probably just shoot out the cameras if they even thought about it. Plan for the worst—"

"Hope for the best. I remember." She drew a deep breath. "I'm ready whenever you guys are."

Russel nodded. "Stick close. If anyone starts firing…"

"Hit the ground and let you deal with the bad guys. We've done this before."

"Doesn't mean we get complacent. Okay, let's go."

He stepped out of the truck, noting everything. The woman with the carriage—diaper bag and bottle. Echoes of a wailing kid, so probably not a cover. The man talking on the phone up the street. Gaze slipping to his watch. Possible, though no obvious bulges under his arms. A few more people were walking on the sidewalks, their focus turned inward—on their way home, oblivious to their surroundings.

It was late, and the wind had picked up. It wasn't raining, but the air was cold and damp for March. They'd waited until nearly sunset—taken turns casing the area all afternoon. Judging the best route. Russel had elected to go in through the Eighth Street entrance. Decrease the possible slight lines for snipers. Though, fuck, there were still far too many for a rifle in the hands of the right man. Rigs could have taken them all out from one of the tall skyscrapers in the distance. Russel prayed Thomas didn't have that kind of skill on his payroll.

They put Quinn between them, using their body mass to block as much of her as they could, until they reached the doors, then Rigs nodded and turned. In the space of two heartbeats, the guy was gone. Out of sight. Behind a bush, or maybe he'd scaled the damn walls. He was capable of anything. Russel was going to have to make it up to him, somehow. He knew Rigs wasn't fond of being out in public, but he'd endured the stares and occasional gasps as if he'd never heard them. As if the scars on his face weren't a source of pain that never went away.

Russel cupped Quinn's elbow. "Okay, you focus on what's ahead. We'll head to the stairwell, go up to the fourth floor then make our way over. We won't rush. Nothing to draw attention to ourselves. Just a happy couple visiting family."

"At least I don't have to fake the happy couple part."

He glanced at her then resumed his scan. Damn, he couldn't afford to get distracted. It was likely Thomas had people in the system. Or dressed up to play the part. No one was above suspicion. So, having his chest tighten at the thought that she considered them a couple…

Fuck. He was starting to wish they'd covered this in his training. How to function while in the vicinity of the woman you love. Because, for the first time in his life, he didn't know how to separate the man from the soldier. How to shut that side down. He was great at compartmentalizing his brain. Locking away stuff that didn't help with the success of the mission.

Pissed about not being assigned to an op? No problem. Gone. Worried about a friend he'd pulled out of rubble two days ago and who was still critical? Slap it in a box, close the lid, and it was gone, too. Safe to look at another time. But Quinn…

It didn't matter how hard he tried. How many boxes he tried to put her into. Seal away his feelings for her. One sound, one smile, one fucking stray thought, and they were front and center. Taking up valuable hard disk space he needed for tactics. For seeing seven steps ahead or anticipating which way a bullet would ricochet. A wall would fall. All of it compromised because he couldn't seem to get past what would happen if he failed.

A fucking catch-22 if ever there was one. For all he knew, the hospital was clean. Thomas had been bluffing—at least the part about having men ready to kill Henry James. The officers standing watch hadn't been challenged. So, hopefully, this was all overkill.

The heavy fire doors clicked shut behind them as they slowly made their way up the stairs, Russel ready for things to get ugly. Now, would be a great time. Send in one from above, another from below. Hell, send in a whole damn gang. Toss some tear gas into the mix, and they'd be screwed.

But they made it up all three flights without incident. Down the hall and across to the other ward, too. Even as they zeroed in on the correct room, nothing jumped out at them. No men carrying semi-automatics. No spy-types with knives or shivs made out of plastic. In fact, the halls were fairly empty, with only the occasional nurse or orderly passing them. None of which bore the markings of a killer in hiding.

The cop at the door greeted them, checking their IDs then waving them on. The door whooshed closed behind them, the pungent aroma of antiseptic and formaldehyde thick in the air. Russel kept Quinn close, nodding at the other cop before heading for the bed. He let Quinn go ahead, taking his spot beside her.

Henry James wasn't what Russel had expected. Though definitely pale, with deep smudges beneath his eyes, the man looked—human. He had neatly trimmed hair and a slight graying scruff over his chin. His face was more delicate than most of the men Russel had worked with, and he didn't see any evidence of callouses on the man's hand. But there was no denying the resemblance. The same high cheekbones, the same nose. Based on the man's coloring, he'd bet money they had the same green eyes.

It was like looking at a male version of Quinn. And it freaked him the hell out. Men like Henry were supposed to be monsters. They were supposed to look their part—sallow skin, riddled with evidence of over-indulgence. Have hard, if not unappealing features that made it easy to hate them. Henry James looked every bit the CEO he pretended to be. It wasn't difficult to imagine him in Armani suits talking before a board of directors.

Except for the part where it was all a lie, and his very existence put Quinn in the line of fire.

Quinn touched his cheek. Softly. As if she was afraid she'd either hurt him or wake him. Russel wasn't sure which. But that one tiny caress had Henry opening his eyes. He blinked, focused, then blinked some more. Then, his eyes widened, and the man's face lit up. Much like Quinn's did whenever she looked at Russel.

Fuck. Her father really did love her. Not that Russel was hoping for something else, but it definitely made this harder. If the man refused to testify, to help her…

Quinn gave her dad a watery smile. "Hey."

Henry lifted one weak arm, tugging at his oxygen mask.

Quinn tsked him, holding it firmly in place. "Sorry, Dad. You need to keep that on." She took his hand in hers. "I…I don't have much time. Thomas…"

Henry scowled. He obviously knew exactly what Thomas had done. What the man was truly capable of.

She nodded. "I know. But… We got him. My friend and I. He's in custody."

Henry shook his head. "Not…safe."

The words were muffled and nothing more than a harsh whisper, but they packed a punch.

"I know. That's why I'm here. There's something I have to tell you. I…I lied to you earlier. I didn't come back to the house because of rats. I came to gather evidence. I…I saw Thomas in the café. I saw that man. I heard…"

Henry's pale face bleached white, and the blip of his heartbeat kicked up.

"It's okay. I know it wasn't you. That somewhere along the way, it turned into far more than you'd bargained for. But after that, I couldn't…"

She swallowed hard. "I didn't give them anything about you, but…"

He smiled. "It's…okay."

"No. No, it's not. Thomas. He had a stack of files. Accounts and properties in my name. But, worse than that…he tried to kill you. Kill me. He needs to pay. So, this is what you're going to do. If you're still the man that raised me, that kissed my skinned knees and took me for ice cream on Mom's birthday, then you'll take a stand. I've made a deal. If you're willing to tell the feds all about the money laundering—help them bring down Thomas and that organization in LA—they'll put you into Witness Security. You'll get a second chance. A new start. But you have to cooperate, Dad. No more secrets. No more lying. It's time to end this. Please."

He stared at her, heartbeat a steady ping in the distance, before closing his eyes and nodding.

Quinn choked back a sob but gave his hand a squeeze. She turned to Russel. "Can you call Bridgette? Tell her to send some Marshals over? They might have to wait until he's stronger, but… He's a man of his word."

The officer stepped forward. "The nurses prefer it if you don't use your cell phone in here. Something about the machines. I don't get it but…"

Russel nodded. "Sure. I'll call them once we're done." Once he had Quinn out of there. No way was he leaving her alone, not even in a room with a cop where Russel was standing outside the door. Too bad if no one liked it. That was just how it was going down.

Quinn gave him a guarded nod, focusing back on her father. The man was trying to keep his eyes open—speak to her—but he didn't seem to be able to form the words.

Russel stayed close, giving her some privacy without leaving her side. She was talking quietly to her father, when the door opened. Russel had his gun in his hand and his body covering hers before he realized it was Rigs.

His buddy nodded, sliding in beside him. "Something's off. I've been all over this place, and I can't find a single threat. That either means we were wrong, or it's so well hidden, even I can't see it."

"We weren't wrong. And Thomas doesn't strike me as the kind of man to make idle threats."

"Exactly. Which means there's something brewing we're missing." Rigs motioned toward Henry. "Is Red's dad on board?"

"You know she hates being called that, right?"

"Yup."

Russel snorted. "He said he was. Quinn seems to think he's a man of his word."

"You gonna call it in?"

"Was just waiting for you. Didn't want to leave her alone."

"I'm good. This floor has shitty service. You might want to go over to that glass walkway. It's pretty close. You'll be able to hear Bridgette there."

"Hold the fort. I'll be right back."

Rigs gave him a roll of the eyes then took up Russel's position beside Quinn. She looked up and smiled at Russel, and damn… There was that hard thump. That burning ache right in the middle of his chest.

He quickly exited, reminding the officer not to let

anyone who wasn't authorized inside, then headed for the walkway. It only took a couple of minutes to go down one flight then over to the corridor. Waning sunlight streamed in through the large expanse of windows from a rare patch of cloudless skies before already starting to dim. The sky had turned orange near the horizon, a hint of indigo overhead. He kept making a point of scanning the area, looking for anything that might be out of place, when Agent Springer rounded the corner at the far end, quickly disappearing around the corner.

Great. Now, he'd have to play nice with the feds while waiting for the US Marshals to show up. Not that he had an inherent dislike for feds, but Springer rubbed him the wrong way. He didn't like the way he'd talked to Quinn, as if she were part of the organization.

He contemplated how he might get a chance to pop the guy in the jaw as called Bridgette. She answered on the third ring.

"Hayward."

"Do you seriously not have a special ringtone for me? That hurts, Bridg."

"Hello, Russel. And, yes, I do, but you've all been using burner phones, so I don't ever know who's calling. Though, I hope you're about to tell me some good news."

"I am. Quinn talked to her father. He's weak, and I doubt you'll get much out of him for at least another week, maybe two, but he said he was in. Well, nodded it. But Quinn assures me he's a man of his word. And, honestly, I think he'd do anything to keep Quinn from going to jail. The man really loves her."

"That's just what I needed to hear. I'll get Jeremy on it,

pronto. He'll just need a few signatures, and we can get the Marshal service over there. Forty minutes, tops."

"That's fine. Rigs is with her, and I'm heading back up. Damn nurses don't like you call from the rooms on a cell. And I just saw Springer head up, so... I'm sure there won't be any lack of irritating conversation."

"Springer? Special Agent Mark Springer? But..."

"But what? Isn't he heading the James' case?"

"Yes, yes, of course, and he has every right to be there. It's just... It's generally standard protocol for the agent in charge to stick with a suspect until after they're done questioning him. And Thomas Carlson isn't your ordinary perp. I can't believe that the Bureau is finished with him in under twenty-four hours. They've been trying to get the man for years. By all accounts, they should have the creep locked up in an interrogation room for the next two days, with Mark Springer masquerading as the man's worse nightmare."

Fuck.

Russel took off running, heading for the room. He took the corridor at a full sprint, juggling his phone to his other hand as he reached for his weapon. "I'll call you back. Tell Sam to get his ass over here. Now."

Russel cut off the call, taking the stairs two at a time then racing down the hallway. A couple of nurses yelled at him to slow down, but he barely heard their voices. Every neuron was focused on getting to Quinn. Making it there before it was too late.

His heart rate jumped as he rounded the corner, the door to Henry's room unguarded. He barely paused before he was breaching the door. Going in low then diving over toward the bed. He rose gun in hand, muzzle sweeping the room. The incessant beeping of Henry's heart pinged away in the distance, the rest of the area deadly quiet.

The cop who'd been standing by the window was down. Body splayed out across the floor, a pool of blood slowly thickening beneath his head. Russel checked for a pulse, sighing at the stillness beneath her fingers. Fuck.

He took a deep breath. Quinn and Rigs were gone, but there was no missing the large splatter of blood staining the floor off to his right, a trail of it leading out the door. He bit back the hard stab of fear. The shiver of dread that wove down his spine. Losing it would only guarantee Quinn died.

He stood, switching into PJ mode. While he'd had a hard time making the transition before, it happened seamlessly, now. One minute, fear had him by the balls, making him choke on his own saliva, the next—cold, hard focus.

He was getting her back. Simple as that.

Russel followed the drops, turning left out of the room before pausing at the corner. He counted to three then popped out, sweeping the corridor before racing down it. He did it, again, at the next corner, still following the blood until he reached the stairs. A massive bloody handprint smeared the smooth silver surface, a drop of blood half visible under the door.

Russel growled then kicked the fucker open, clearing up then heading down. He didn't need the droplets to know he was going in the right direction. He could feel it. Smell a hint of her perfume, or maybe it was just her skin. Her hair. Whatever, it was like a damn beacon calling out to him.

He took the corners hard and fast, building up speed only to stop cold. Rigs was propped up against the wall, blood drenching his shirt. He had a gun in one hand, his phone in the other.

"Fuck, Rigs." He knelt beside him, opening his shirt, cursing at the puckered wounds on his chest. Two across his rib cage. One to his shoulder. He watched Rigs take his next labored breath—no bubbling at the puncture sights. Not gurgling breaths. Lungs should be intact. Heart probably wasn't compromised. And no arterial bleeding or he would have died two floors ago. But the guy was losing blood at an alarming rate.

Rigs shook his head, trying to push off Russel's hands. "I'm fine. Quinn… If they get too far ahead, the tracker won't work."

Tracker? He didn't know when Rigs had slipped a tracker on her, but he loved the man for it,

"You're not fine. You're bleeding out. Fuck, you need surgery. Now."

He wrapped his arm around Rigs' waist then lifted, bracing most of his weight as he all but carried the man down the last few twists of stairs, all the while having Rigs trying to shove his phone at him, telling him to go after Quinn. "I can't help her until I know what happened. I need to have an idea what I'm up against. If she's alive and you're tracking her, then she has a couple of minutes to spare. You don't."

Rigs groaned, trying to carry some of his own weight but failing. "I was standing there, right where you left me, when that fuckhead Springer walks in. He starts talking to Quinn about Wit Sec and how she'll have to say goodbye to her dad. That they won't be able to contact each other. There was something in his voice—irritated me, but...fuck. The guy's a fed. Then, Henry's heartbeat started soaring. He's gasping into the mask, eyes white. Fingers desperately trying to fist around the blanket. I watch him for a few moments when I realize he's trying to motion to Springer..."

He coughed, spraying bits of blood across his hand. "Fucker already had his Glock out. Shot me point blank then turns and pops the cop. Double tap straight to the head. Quinn grabbed the bedpan, threw it at the bastard's head, but he was on her before she could do anything else. He starts muttering something about taking her to Thomas. He was aiming at Henry, but I got off a shot. Clipped the asshole in the arm. He stumbled back. That's when the cop from outside came in. Told him he better clear out. That someone was bound to have heard the shots.

"They high tail it out of there. I think he drugged Quinn or hit her because he had to carry her. I managed to get up, follow but..."

"But you were a bit busy bleeding out. He say where they were going?"

"Nope, but it doesn't matter. I've got their location on my phone."

"When the fuck did you have a chance to put a tracker on Quinn?"

"At my place. Before I woke you up. Sex obviously makes her sleep like she's in a coma. She didn't so much as twitch. It's skin-colored. Waterproof. Just below her hairline. I would have told you after the threat was over, but..."

"I'd punch you in the face if I didn't want to kiss you, right now. How much distance do I have?"

Rigs shoved his phone into Russel's other hand. "That blip is her. Signal's good for about fifteen or twenty miles. But that's all."

Russel took it, glancing at it as he opened the last door then stumbled through. He started yelling for a doctor, all the while watching the pulsing dot. They were moving northwest. Had to be in a car.

Several people came running, dragging a gurney. Russel placed Rigs on top, looking down at him when he grabbed Russel's wrist.

His pale face searched Russel's. "I had a buddy of mine go to that bar and get her bike. Had him drop it off out front. Ninth street. Left of the doors. I was going to ride it back. Shadow you two. Keys are under the seat. Go after her."

He kept hanging on when Russel turned to go.

Rigs coughed, again, then collapsed back. "This isn't over as long as they're both breathing. You know that, right?"

"Never liked that idea of letting Thomas spend fifty years in jail. Like it even less, now."

Two doctors swarmed the scene, yanking Rigs' hand free then barking out orders for IVs and chest X-rays. Russel pushed down the flutter in his stomach. Fuck, Rigs had better make it, then he ran toward the exit, calling Sam as he went.

"I'm five minutes out. Talk to me, Ice."

Russel slipped in an earpiece as he continued toward the big doors at the end of the hall. "It's Springer. He killed one of the cops and caught Rigs twice in the chest. Once in the shoulder. Stubborn bastard nearly got all the way down to the first floor before I found him in the stairwell. Thankfully, one of us was thinking with the right head. He put a tracker on Quinn. They're heading northwest. Along the water. I've got her bike. I'll patch you into the map."

He tapped on the screen, busting through the doors then heading left. Her motorcycle was next to a planter, helmet bungeed to the seat. He pulled it over his head, then felt for the keys, shoving them in the ignition as he swung his leg over. He hit the button, smiling at the growl of the engine.

"Okay, Ice. I've got it. On my way."

"Sam."

Nothing but silence. Sam knew what was coming.

"Rigs said Thomas was with them. This ends. Permanently."

CHAPTER 18

God, her head hurt. Every little movement sent a pulse of pain shooting across her temples. It felt worse than when she'd woken up with a hangover after having Russel drive her...

Russel!

Quinn inhaled, collapsing back on the hard, cold surface when she tried to open her eyes. The scenery washed across her vision—dull shapes entrenched in deep shadows. There was a steady hum beneath her, interrupted by the occasion squeak and groan. She wasn't sure where she was, but she remembered seeing Special Agent Springer walk in. Listening to him talk about the Wit Sec program. Then, her father's heart rate had gotten all jumpy, and the small bit of color he'd had in his cheeks had blanched out.

That's when everything had happened at once. Springer had calmly pulled his gun and shot Rigs while the man was trying to move in front of her as he'd reached for his own weapon. She wasn't sure how Rigs had clued in, but he'd been tossed across the room before collapsing onto the floor. The cop by the window had yelled at Springer to freeze, while drawing his pistol, but it was too late. Springer simply turned and capped him in the head while the man was still aiming.

She remembered the sound. The dull pops then the crack of the young man's head snapping back, hitting the window before he fell forward. He crashed to the floor, the loud thumb reverberating through her shoes.

She'd reacted. Grabbed the bedpan and launched it at Springer's head, but he'd fired some kind of dart at her. Hit in her the shoulder. She vaguely remembered Rigs getting off a shot—hitting Springer in the arm—before he'd passed out on the floor.

Tears burned her eyes. He was dead. He had to be. Blood had splattered everywhere. And he'd been so…still. Pale and unmoving and looking exactly like she'd imagined that man from the café looking. Limbs loose against the floor. Eyes closed. Skin already an eerie shade of white.

That was her last clear image, until now.

She blinked. She was lying in the dark, hard angles all around her. There was a hint of muted red light off to her right, reflecting an odd glow. She watched the shadows moving beyond the blurry surface for a few minutes before everything shifted into place.

Shit. She was in the trunk of a car, hands and feet bound in front of her. They hadn't put anything in her mouth, not that she could talk. Scream for help. It took every ounce of strength just to open her eyes—look around. She managed to wiggle her fingers just enough to know they still worked before passing out, again.

When she woke the second time, the scenery stabilized. She took a few breaths, allowing her eyes to adjust to the darkness. There were what looked like tools shoved in one corner, a set of jumper cables wrapped around her legs. A bit of light filtered in through the crack where the hood closed, the steady drone of the tires roaring in the background.

But beneath that were mumbled voices, echoing through the vents next to the backseat. It took her a few moments to place them. Springer and Thomas.

She should have guessed. That's what her father had been trying to tell her. That Springer was on the take. That must have been Thomas' plan all along. Why he didn't put up a fight. Hadn't looked remotely scared when Springer had taken him away in handcuffs the previous night. They'd planned it together.

Quinn took stock. She doubted she'd be able to fight both men, but that didn't mean she was helpless. If she could crack one of the lights, there was a chance they'd pass a cop—get pulled over. It was a long shot, but at the moment, it was all she had.

She concentrated on moving—reaching out to grab whatever was rattling against the trunk's wall. It made a metallic clang every time the car went over a bump, knocking Quinn's head against the hard edges. She fought against the nausea, finally managing to wrap her fingers around the handle.

A screwdriver. Maybe things weren't quite as bleak as she'd thought.

Served the fuckers right. If they'd had half a brain between them, they would have tied her hands behind her back. Given her more of that drug Springer had used. Instead, they'd simply dumped her in the trunk and made a half-assed attempt to incapacitate her. If nothing else, she'd be able to shove the slotted end into one of their guts. Watch the asshole's eyes widen in surprise.

Yeah, she could get behind that. They'd still kill her, but she might take one of them with her. She'd read somewhere that stomach wounds were an excruciating way to die. They were agonizingly slow. Just what the bastards deserved.

First, she used the tool to break the zip straps around her ankles. She tried to do her wrists, but all it did was gouge her skin, cut into her flesh. So, she concentrated on the light.

It took her a while to steady her hands—gain enough motor control to slip the tip between the thin gaps in the metal and thrust it against the plastic covers. But with a little patience, and a shit load of luck, she was able to punch a hole in the right side.

A swirl of fresh air breezed over her, and she took a minute to breathe it in. It carried traces of exhaust and the salty scent of brine, but she didn't care. It smelled like freedom.

She'd come so close. So close to actually being free. Starting a life with Russel. Even if Thomas had gotten off, she'd known Russel could handle the constant threat. Could deal with anything the creep sent their way. She only wished she'd told him she loved him. Face to face, without his buddies looking on. Allowed him to search her eyes—see her honesty.

More tears burned her eyes, but she wasn't sad. She was angry. After all she'd endured, she deserved a chance, and there was no way she was going to give up. Russel wouldn't. He'd find a way to bust out. Come back to her. She knew he would. Which meant working harder. Maybe if she could break enough of the light to see better, she could wedge the screwdriver under the latch and jimmy it open.

She worked at the plastic, chipping off bits until over half the covering was gone. Black asphalt stretched out behind her with the occasional glimpse of the ocean. The water was on the right side, which meant they were heading north. Probably to an industrial district. Or further up to one of the parks—somewhere they could dispose of a body without witnesses.

Except for the part where she was going to pop open this damn trunk and jump out. She could run with her hands bound, and she'd been tossed enough times in jujitsu to know how to roll. This toss would be harder and faster, but it was essentially the same basics. Tuck, lift her head enough to avoid contact, and keep moving to absorb the impact. Then run like hell.

Quinn used her feet to push up on the trunk until she could wedge the tip under the latch. A few hard twists and it gave. Lifting the lid slightly, she held her breath, gripping the edge with her bound hands. She'd wait until they were close to a park or a subdivision, then launch herself out.

The car wove along the street, nothing but warehouses and the steady rise of fall of the waves against the breaker walls. If they stopped before she jumped out, she'd never stand a chance. They'd be on her before she could do more than stumble to her feet and take a few steps. It had to happen, now. To hell with waiting for a better opportunity. Was the car slowing down?

She took a deep breath, readied herself then froze. Because what she saw defined logic. And it made her heart swell with hope.

Russel revved the engine, twisted the throttle and took off. It had been a couple of years since he'd ridden a bike. But he'd taken advanced driving courses during his training—all Special Forces soldiers did—and there wasn't a vehicle he couldn't handle. Couldn't wrestle into submission.

He started off easy, going through the gears as he reacquainted himself with the feel of the machine beneath him. The rumble of power between his legs. He took a few sweeping turns, let his muscles regain the sensory memory of leaning into the corners. Of being one with the bike.

Two minutes in, and he was flying. Shifting up and down, working the gears to get the most thrust, as he wove through traffic, passing on the inside, outside. Hell, he jumped a curb and shot across a crosswalk when the road ahead got congested.

He didn't blink, didn't flinch, using the tools he'd learned to stay ahead of any possible pitfalls. He'd check one direction, mentally note if there were any obstacles, then glance in the other, making the turn without wasting time checking, again.

He didn't have any time. They must have jumped on the freeway. The dot was pulling ahead, sitting at the edge of the zone Rigs had mentioned. If Russel let them disappear, he might never find Quinn, again. Might have to spend the rest of his life knowing he'd failed her. Stare down at her dead body when it finally surfaced—if it ever did. Or maybe he'd have to live never knowing. Always holding out hope for the woman he loved but would never see, again. Never touch or kiss.

No. Not happening. He'd told himself repeatedly that she was his mission, and he didn't fail those. He'd broken ranks, had gotten kicked out, but he'd never let his brothers down. Never left them behind when he'd had even a remote chance of bringing them back.

And Quinn wasn't just any teammate. She was *the* teammate. His. The other half of his soul. The part of him he'd thought he'd lost when he'd stared down at the words scribbled across his discharge papers. One look, one smile, and he felt whole. Completely content.

He leaned down closer. Reduced his friction just enough to edge the bike faster. He was already screaming along the road, passing everything in a blur of color. Cars. Trucks. They all disappeared behind him. Forgotten. He hit the freeway and really opened her up. The revs whined, the needle pegged over to the right. He didn't care. He'd buy Quinn a new bike. A hundred new ones if it meant he got to her before they'd hurt her. Taken her past the point he'd be able to help. What he'd told her was true. All his training. His years stitching soldiers up under fire. Carrying them across hostile territory. Keeping them from bleeding out. But he couldn't raise the dead.

Images filled his mind. Quinn bleeding. Quinn lying in a pool of her own blood. Quinn limp and lifeless in his arms, those beautiful green eyes dull and unseeing. There'd be no heartbeat beneath his palm. No warm skin against his flesh. Just icy death.

Fuck that.

He glanced at the phone. He'd wedged it inside the instruments, half blocking the speed and tach. But he didn't care. He wasn't looking at the instruments. He was driving by feel. By the hum of the engine, the whine of the transmission. It didn't matter how fast he was going, only that he needed to go faster. Close the gap more.

His earpiece buzzed. Sam.

"Looks like they're heading for the warehouse district. I'll cut over—try to get ahead of them."

"Roger."

He couldn't manage more than a single word. He was too focused. Too obsessed at watching the dot slowly move closer. On milking every possible ounce of speed out of the motorcycle. On catching up.

The dot veered left, and so did he. Down the exit ramp, across the street and into an alley. A park loomed up on his right. He hit the curb, hopped a small planter then took the paved trail through the center. A few joggers jumped out of his way, shaking fists at him as he flew past, kicking up stones and dirt.

He kept going, kept pushing. An older woman appeared in front of him, and he shoved the bike into a slide. Sparks crackled around him before he was up, again, and popping out the other side. He'd cut the distance in half, Quinn's beacon drawing him forward.

He hedged his bet that Sam was right and took

another shortcut, dodging through a few open warehouses then rejoining the route. That got him closer by half, again. Just a few more minutes, a few more jumps and slides and skids and—yes. Red tail lights up ahead.

That was the car. Had to be. And, if they were still driving, it meant he hadn't lost her, yet. Hadn't failed.

He followed behind, slowly gaining on them. He didn't want to let them pull away, but he couldn't get too close without them making him. And, without knowing where she was in the car, he couldn't anticipate which tactic to use. He could probably force them off the road, but the impact could hurt Quinn, or worse.

He could follow until they either pulled over or arrived where they were heading. But, if she was medically compromised, she might bleed to death before he reached her. He could shoot out a tire, but if the driver couldn't handle the sudden shift in balance, he'd be back to crashing the car. And that was assuming they wouldn't just turn around and shoot her.

Then, everything changed because bits of the rear right light were breaking off and bouncing along the ground. They scattered across the pavement, like tiny spotlights that winked at him when they caught the light. More chunks, each one bigger than the last until a hole appeared. He couldn't see in but there was something sticking out. Something metallic that was glinting off the last of the sunlight as it started to dip below the surface of the water—flashing at him every time it poked through.

Shit. They'd put her in the trunk. It was the only explanation. The only way the plastic was slowly disappearing. She was conscious and trying to break the light—maybe hoping she'd get lucky. Have a cop see it and pull the bastards over. Russel edged closer, trying to stay in the driver's blind spot when the entire trunk cracked open. The lid bounced on the hinges, lifting farther up with every bump. The car went around a bit of a corner, and Russel sped up, not wanting to lose a second of it in his sights. He banked left, and his heart stopped. Just stopped.

She was peeking out through the opening, looking as if she was going to jump. Actually, jump out of a moving vehicle. Then, her gaze landed on him, and damn if she didn't smile. Whether she recognized his silhouette or her bike he didn't know. But she knew it was him. He was sure. The way her eyes rounded, then her mouth lifted—it wasn't just relief. It was joy. Joy and hope and, damn it, love—for him.

Was the car slowing down?

They were in an industrial area. Warehouses and shops. Was this their end game? Where they'd planned on leaving her body?

He cranked the throttle. This was ending. Now.

The bike roared, and he shot forward, quickly closing the distance. He thought he saw two heads in the front, but the light was fading and the seat rests were hiding most of his view. Then, the passenger window opened, and an arm appeared—a barrel pointed his way. He ducked left as shots flew past. But he was streamlined, staying too far over for the asshole to clip him. Quinn was still watching him, bouncing roughly as the car hit every bump. Every damn pothole. She cracked her head against the trunk, but she didn't lose focus. Didn't try to protect herself. She stayed vigilant, watching him, probably still looking for an opportunity to leap out.

She'd kill herself at these speeds, not that she seemed

to care. They rounded another curve, and she opened the trunk more, placed one leg on the edge before the driver punched it. The car leaped ahead, knocking her into the trunk then backwards. He lost sight of her as the trunk snapped shut.

Another few hits, and they might end up killing her.

Anger burned beneath his skin. He wasn't going to lose her. He'd ram the damn car. Throw himself on top or snatch her out. Anything but watch her die.

He hit the throttle, picking up speed, not worrying about if the fuckers could see him or not, when tires squealed ahead of him and Bridgette's Jeep shot out from a small side street. Or alleyway. Fuck, it looked like a damn bike path, not even big enough for the vehicle. But there it was, fish tailing on the pavement, skidding until it was barreling straight at the other vehicle. Sam wasn't holding back. He had the Jeep pegged at some insane speed, heading directly at Thomas and Springer.

This wasn't a game of chicken. It was a damn head on collision in the making. Russel knew Sam wouldn't back down, wouldn't flinch. He'd take those men out or die trying. Russel backed off enough he'd be clear of the wreckage. He couldn't help Quinn, drag Sam's ass out of a burning vehicle if he got caught up in the carnage.

Whoever was driving—Russel was pretty damn sure it was that mother fucker Thomas—swerved at the last second, hit the curb, rode up and through the barrier, then disappeared over the edge. Water exploded into the air, raining down on the pavement as the car torpedoed into the ocean twenty feet out from the break wall.

Russel watched it all happen in slow motion. Playing out like every damn mission he'd been on over the past fifteen years. Saw the trunk jerk open, Quinn's head pop up as she tried to climb out, only to get bounced back inside as the car tipped forward. He heard the horn blast through the relative silence, dying off when it hit the water, sinking beneath the inky surface. Even the droplets hovered in the air, like tiny specks of glass glinting in the setting sun, as the scene paused...

Then, it came rushing back. The car cutting through the water, the sound of metal twisting, glass breaking. He aimed at the spot where they'd gone over, with every intention of driving the bike in after them. Save the few precious seconds it would take to stop it, jump off, then dive in. He'd survive the impact, no question.

But, just as he went to gun it, give himself an extra boost of speed, Sam scrambled over the edge, paused to take a couple of long, deep breaths, then dove in.

Russel screeched to a halt at the lip of the curb. He dropped the bike, ignoring the metallic scrape as it hit the cement, and ran to the edge. White-tipped waves curled in toward the land, an expanding ring of ripples the only proof the car had impacted the surface. A faint glow penetrated the darkness—the headlights mapping out the path of the vehicle toward the bottom.

He mentally counted the seconds since the car had struck the surface. Sam, Russel, Hank and the others—they could hold their breath for a couple of minutes while carrying out an op. Maybe three if they were still. But civilians... They didn't practice prolonged dives. How to regulate their movement to use the least amount of oxygen—give themselves a few more moments of air. And, if Quinn had hit her head... Been knocked unconscious... She'd have breathed in the water the moment it filled the trunk.

Forty-five seconds.

It was taking too long. The water was cold. Even in the summer, people died of exposure in the Pacific. Couple that with the growing darkness and having to navigate the sinking car—Sam might not be able to get her out.

Fifty-five seconds.

He'd wait ten more, then he was going in.

The waves crashed against the wall, spraying a soaking mist into the air, as Russel ticked off the last five seconds. Surely, Sam would be topside, by now, if he'd been able to get Quinn out.

Russel started a series of deep breaths. He needed to oxygenate his lungs—fill them as much as he could. Maximize the amount of time he could stay submersed. The cold would slow his heart rate, but it might not be enough.

He focused on the last hint of light, calculating his impact point—the one that would get him the closest to the sinking vehicle—when Sam crested the water, gulping in air. Quinn was limp at his side, eyes closed, arms dragging behind them. Sam swam for the edge, boosting Quinn from below as Russel grabbed her arms and lifted her clear of the wall. Five steps and he had her on the ground, head tilted back, ear pressed to her mouth, fingers along her carotid.

No whisper of breath against his cheek. No strum of blood beneath his hand.

He gave her a couple deep breaths, watching her chest to see it rise, then started chest compressions. "Sam."

His buddy dropped down beside him, water dripping

off him and onto the pavement. "The damn trunk got jammed. I had to pry the fucker open with my knife. I don't know if she hit her head or couldn't hold her breath that long. She was limp when I finally got in."

Russel nodded, counting out each push. "When I tell you, position her head and give her two deep breaths. Just two."

Sam moved into position, bending over and breathing into her cold, pale mouth when Russel called it out.

Nothing.

He resumed the compressions, still keeping a running clock in his head. "Water's cold. That's good. Less chance of her sustaining any brain damage. You were only down there a minute. Pretty fucking fast for having to jimmy that damn trunk. Again, Sam."

Sam followed Russel's lead, breathing every time the man motioned to him. Two minutes turned into four. Then five.

Russel kept working. "Come on, sweetheart. Just one breath. That's all I need. You're stronger than this."

Sam bent low, again, giving another two breaths, when she coughed.

"Rolling her."

Russel tipped her over, keeping her head aligned with her spine as she coughed and heaved, emptying everything in her stomach onto the asphalt. It took her a minute to get it all up before she was gasping in air, her arms and legs moving in an effort to sit up.

He checked her mouth, ensured it was clear, then rolled her back, waiting to see if she'd stay conscious, ready to do whatever it took to keep her alive.

She blinked a few times then kept her eyes open, staring up at them. She squinted then smiled. "You came."

Russel did a quick body sweep, checking her reflexes, then pulled her into his chest, holding the back of her head with one hand and her waist with the other. "Of course, I came. Can't get rid of me that easily."

"How?"

"I'll explain everything, later. Just...let me hold you."

She wrapped her arms weakly around him. "Is it over?"

Russel looked up at Sam. The guy nodded.

"It's over. Thomas can't hurt you ever, again."

She nodded, her fingers fisting around his shirt. "Good. Bastard deserved far worse, but I'll take what I can get."

"You scared another ten years off my life, tonight. Firefights. HALOs. Getting pinned down by fifty cal rounds. Nothing came close to how I felt when that car went over the edge. When Sam dragged you up. Promise me you won't ever do that to me, again."

Quinn pulled back enough to stare up at him. She placed a small icy hand on his chin, her thumb stroking his cheek. "Sounds like you might need to stick around to make sure I stay out of trouble."

"I'm not sure merely being by your side is enough. I'll have to take more drastic measures."

Her smile flourished. "Is that so? Like what?"

"Like legally binding you to me. Maybe then, I can tame that stubborn streak of yours."

"Unlikely. But it's worth a shot."

"Is that a yes?"

"Was there a question?"

He laughed. "Damn, I love you. So, what do you say, Harlequin? Marry me?"

Quinn's face lit up. "I love you, too. And, yes, after you tell me one more thing."

"Anything. What do you want to know?"

"What's my new last name?"

CHAPTER 19

"I SWEAR, Ice, if you don't help me get out of this bed and out of this hospital, I will blow up your damn truck."

Russel chuckled as he eyed Rigs from the end of the bed, casually flipping through the man's chart. The jackass had come dangerously close to dying, a fact he seemed more than willing to ignore.

Russel placed the clipboard back on the foot rail. "Do you know how much blood you lost? Three liters. Most people are dead by that time."

Rigs shrugged. "We both know I'm not most people."

Russel continued. "And then, there's the tissue damage from those bullets ricocheting around inside you. Not to mention a couple of broken ribs. Bitch all you want, but you won't be blowing up anything for a while longer."

Rigs glared at him. "You willing to put that Tacoma of yours at risk? I know how much you love that truck."

"But he loves you more." Quinn ambled up beside Russel, planting a kiss on his cheek, a brown bag in her hand. "You guys think you're all so tough. But it's a regular bromance in here."

Rigs grunted. "If that's chick-speak for wanting to kill one of your best buddies, then, hell yeah."

She merely shook her head then held up the bag. "I brought you a burger. And fries."

Rigs arched a brow. "Pickles?"

"Extra. Told them to load up on the ketchup, too. It's practically drowning the meat."

He motioned with his fingers, rustling the paper as he opened the sandwich. "Fine. I won't blow up the new bike jackass got you. But his truck is still on the line if I don't see some pants by the time I finish this burger."

"Is he still bitching about his damn pants? You'd think he'd be kicking back, enjoying all those free sponge baths."

Russel grinned as Hank walked through the door, stopping next to him.

Rigs gave the man a death stare. "You might not want to get too cocky. You've got even more fun things I could wire up."

Hank laughed. "You wouldn't want to cripple your own company, would ya, Rigs?"

Russel looked from Montana over to Rigs then back. "You got Rigs to sign up? Was the devil involved? Someone have to hand over a golden fiddle?"

"That's right, Ice. Keep joking, and I might forget to tell you where I put *your* tracker."

Quinn giggled beside him, pursing her lips when he looked at her. She smiled then turned back to Rigs, giggling, again. She hadn't been overly amused when she'd discovered *her* tracker, even if it had saved her life. She'd had Russel check every square inch of her skin for more—

he'd enjoyed that part. Had been tempted to pretend to find one just so he could do it all over, again.

Hank crossed his arms over his chest. "So, Harlequin. How's your dad?"

Quinn had decided to go back to her full name. Had said that, with the threat over, she could honor her mother without worrying about being pegged as a crime heiress. Not that she cared, anymore. She also said it went well with Foster.

Russel's chest squeezed tight. He still couldn't believe she'd said yes. It had been insanely quick. He knew it. He just didn't care because the proof of her love was in every smile. Every touch. Plan for the worst. Hope for the best, and this was definitely the best.

Her smile faded for a moment before she sighed. "He left with a contingency of US Marshals last night. From what I heard, he's being extremely cooperative. Bridgette says they'll have him in a variety of safe houses until the trial, which won't be for several months at the earliest. I guess there's a lot of files to go through. Connections to make. And, with Thomas gone, my family's empire pretty much imploded."

"You okay with all of that?"

"Still a little shell-shocked but…" She looked up at Russel, and the world dimmed as her face glowed. "I've got all I need right here."

"So, I heard. Congratulations on the engagement. Still baffled how a thug like Ice landed such a beautiful lady, but we'll chalk it up to intervention by a higher power."

"As long as that higher power sees that she gets to the chapel without being kidnaped or shot at or run off the road, I'm good." Russel arched a brow at Rigs. "You think you'll be able to stand up long enough with Midnight to be a witness? Or will we have to get married in this room?"

"Watch it, or I might just steal the bride." Rigs winked at Harlequin. "The girl's got a soft spot for me."

"Probably has something to do with you taking a bullet for her. Which reminds me… Did Henry's files uncover any other moles inside the Bureau?"

"Two." Hank shook his head. "Half a dozen police officers, too, including the one who was instrumental in Harlequin's abduction. I think it's safe to say none of them will be seeing this side of a jail cell for a very long time. I did get a personal thank you from the feds. Said if we ever needed a favor…"

"A favor from the Bureau? Not sure I want to know what that looks like."

Hank nodded at Harlequin. "I only wish we could use it so you and your father would be able to communicate after the trial. Must be hard having to let him go."

She snorted. "Please. My father evaded federal prosecution for thirty years. Ran a high-level money laundering scheme. I'm pretty sure he can find a way to give me a call if he wants."

Hank chuckled. "I suppose he could. Then, it's a good thing you've got Ice around. I have a feeling this isn't the last time trouble might come knocking on your door."

"Trouble can knock, but… My kickass PJ won't let them in."

Rigs huffed. "Of course not, because I'll make sure I show him how to rig the damn door. You two really need to start embracing the art of blowing shit up. Now, about those pants…"

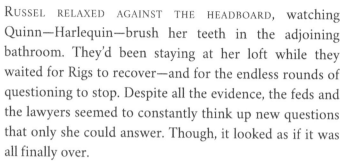

Russel relaxed against the headboard, watching Quinn—Harlequin—brush her teeth in the adjoining bathroom. They'd been staying at her loft while they waited for Rigs to recover—and for the endless rounds of questioning to stop. Despite all the evidence, the feds and the lawyers seemed to constantly think up new questions that only she could answer. Though, it looked as if it was all finally over.

He'd caved and allowed Rigs to talk him into leaving the hospital. But only on the condition that he hung out with them—was on a twenty-four-hour watch. If Russel thought for a second that the man's condition was worsening, he told Rigs he'd have his ass back at Harborview quicker than Rigs could blink.

"Penny for your thoughts."

Russel blinked. Quinn had made her way over to the bed and was sitting on the side, those stunning green eyes fixed on him. God, he could stare at her for a hundred years and never get tired of the way she smiled back at him. Eyes bright and full of love.

He rubbed the spot on his chest where it hurt then offered her his hand. She took it, climbing over him until she was straddling his legs. He inhaled as she settled her butt right over his erection—the one that never seemed to go away whenever she was in the room. Or the house. Or on the same planet.

Her eyes widened as her breath released in a raspy hum. She wiggled against his dick, grinning when it swelled beneath her.

"Looks like someone's happy to see me."

"Extremely happy. Possibly happier than I've ever been. But…"

"Again, with the but."

"It's late. Rigs is in your spare room—"

"Rigs has heard us before. We're not going to shock the man."

"And," he continued, "you're still recovering from your concussion followed by nearly drowning on me." He shivered at the thought. Christ, as long as he lived, he'd always remember the fear. Her limp body held in Sam's arms as he dragged her over to the wall. "You're just lucky I didn't crack any ribs. I was so focused on getting you to breathe…"

Her eyes softened, and she leaned forward, cupping his face as she nuzzled his nose. "Thank you."

"You don't have to thank me, sweetheart. It was purely selfish. Couldn't imagine living without you."

"Not just for that. For driving a drunk girl home. Then giving her back her life."

She pressed her lips to his, slowly teasing his skin before licking her way inside. She tasted like sweetness and heat—a combination that short-circuited his brain and made him run on pure instinct. He slid his hands down her sides, holding her still as he lifted against her. If it weren't for his boxers, he'd already be inside her.

She eased back, breath curling around his jaw. "Why don't I help you out with that?"

"What about your ribs? Your head?"

She arched a brow. "They won't be involved."

"Harlequin."

She shivered at her name, a rash of goosebumps prickling her skin. "God, the way you say that. I have to focus not to come."

"Then, I'll say it, again. Harlequin."

"Call me crazy. But I thought being engaged meant you'd finally stop trying to talk me out of making love to you. Is this an indication of what the next fifty years are going to be like?"

"God, I hope so. And what I was going to say is… looks like you made it to the bed without falling down or puking, so…"

"You'll pound me into it?"

"All night."

"That's one of the things I love most about you. The way you throw yourself into a mission. I suggest you take a deep breath, because I'm not letting you come up for air until the sun does, too."

MIDNIGHT RANGER

BROTHERHOOD PROTECTORS WORLD

KRIS NORRIS

Midnight RANGER

BROTHERHOOD PROTECTORS

KRIS NORRIS

CHAPTER 1

SEATTLE. Ten months later...

"DON'T you ever keep regular hours?"

Bridgette Hayward looked up from her desk, smiling at the man standing in her doorway. Tall, dark, handsome, dressed in Armani with his hair perfectly styled—Jeremy Brenner was the classic image of an assistant US attorney. In the two years she'd been working for the United States Attorney's Office, she'd never once seen the guy sweat or lose the calm demeanor he wore like a shield, regardless of the circumstances. And the man had gone up against some intimidating clients.

Bridgette leaned back, twirling her pen around her fingers. "Says the man standing in my doorway at...oh, nine o'clock on a Friday night."

"I just came back because I forgot a brief I needed. You, on the other hand, haven't left, yet."

"Big case means extra time, and I can't afford to screw this one up."

Jeremy's eyes narrowed, and he glanced around as if looking for others, despite the fact the office had been closed for hours, before stepping through the doorway. "You know I think you're one of the best lawyers we've had come through here, right?"

She frowned. "Why do I sense a 'but' at the end of that statement?"

"Not a 'but'. I'm just…worried about you."

"That's sweet."

"Seriously, Bridgette. Alexander Stevens has been heading his family's drug business for longer than you've been alive. It's taken that many years to make a case against him, and it was essentially a fluke. Which means he's got more connections than anyone knows. The kind that's kept him out of jail and gotten other people killed." He nodded at her. "You still getting threats? Calls? Letters?"

A chill beaded her skin, the ghostly echo of a gravelly voice on her cell sounding inside her head before she shoved it aside. "Nothing I haven't gotten before. And, as usual, I'm being cautious."

"If you were being cautious, you'd either have a bodyguard or you'd be working remotely until the trial starts, and we can petition for police protection."

"I'm fine, Jeremy. Promise."

He shook his head. "I realize this is a huge leap forward in your career, and you deserve every bit of it. Your record here is more than impressive. I'd just hate to see you get hurt over it."

"I promise I'll be more vigilant. And if things

escalate—"

"If things escalate, it'll be too damn late." He huffed, running his fingers through his hair. "You *are* stubborn. Anyway, I'm heading out. You ready to go? I'll walk you to your car like a perfect gentleman." He winked. "Or not, if you'd prefer."

She smiled—the guy had been trying to get into her pants for months. "Thanks, but I have a few things left. I'll be out of here soon, though."

"All right. Be careful."

"Always."

He shook his head then left, his footsteps fading down the hallway. Bridgette focused on the written testimonies, again, noting any concerns or questions she wanted to discuss, until the words started blurring together. She sat back and glanced at the clock—nine forty-five. She closed her eyes for a moment, rubbing the bridge of her nose in the hopes of lessening the ache building between her eyes. Jeremy was right about one thing. She needed a break. She could look at the files, again, in the morning, but reading the same paragraph over and over wasn't helping.

She stood and stretched, hoping to ease the tight press between her shoulder blades. A few more weeks like this, and her colleagues would start calling her Quasimodo. Maybe she'd take a hot bath. Spend the night curled up on the couch, watching a movie. Anything not related to Alexander Stevens or this case.

The thought made her smile as she packed some folders into her briefcase then placed it on her desk. She filed any remaining papers then grabbed her case and her purse. A quick trip to the ladies' room, and she could head out.

The building was eerily quiet as she walked down the hallway then into the bathroom. Usually, she enjoyed the silence after everyone else had left, but tonight felt different. Whether it was the storm raging outside or Jeremy's words, she wasn't sure. But she'd be happy to get home—lock herself inside.

Her boots clicked across the floor as she made her way back to grab her jacket. If she'd been thinking clearly, she would have taken it with her and locked up, already, saving her the return trip. But the long days were definitely taking a toll, and it seemed as if she forgot simple things more often, lately.

She sighed, stepping inside, before coming to a halt. A large yellow envelope sat kitty-corner on her desk, her name scribbled across the front. She glanced around, staring at the shadows lining the hallway. She'd been gone less than ten minutes.

Her heart rate kicked up as she walked over to her desk, staring down at the offering. No return address. No mail stamp. She thumbed the corner, debating on whether to open it or call the cops. Though, if it turned out to be nothing, she'd never live it down. And she hadn't been there long enough to bring that kind of attention to herself.

Bridgette took a breath then gently lifted the tab. It hadn't even been sealed, which hopefully meant it didn't contain any kind of deadly virus. Her pulse thundered in her head as she slipped her hand inside and removed a collection of photographs. A small note was stuck to the front, familiar handwriting scrawled across it.

I'm coming for you.

The words glared up at her, the simple statement

making her stomach roil. She bit her bottom lip then flipped through the images. Whoever had taken them had followed her from her apartment to her office. There were even a few of her at the boxing club—her hands in gloves as she moved around the ring. They'd obviously been taken over a few days, which meant someone was stalking her. *Had* been stalking her for some time, and she hadn't even noticed.

Memories surfaced in the background. Distant, like a clock ticking in another room. But there, just the same. She pursed her lips then stuffed the photos back into the envelope. If Alex Stevens thought some creepy phone calls and a few pictures would be enough to intimidate her, the man had a hard lesson ahead of him.

First, she'd go home. Lock up. Double check her alarm system. Then, she'd make copies of everything. She knew firsthand that evidence had a way of "disappearing" with the right amount of motivation. And Stevens had more than enough motivation at his disposal.

In the morning, she'd head to the police station. She'd give them the envelope and half of the photos. Have them add the images to her growing file of harassment since she'd first been handed the case months ago. But she'd send the note and the other pictures to her friend, Special Agent Jack Taylor. See if the Bureau could match the handwriting or get some kind of DNA off the paper. It wasn't that she didn't trust the local precinct, she just trusted Jack more.

Her briefcase felt heavy as she slipped the envelope inside then headed for the bank of elevators at the opposite end of the hallway. Different scenarios bounced around in her head, trying to take shape, when a distant noise stopped her. She paused, trying to pinpoint it when the dull echo sounded, again.

Footsteps. Behind her.

Bridgette swallowed against the punch of fear cooling her skin and began walking. Faster, this time. The footsteps followed her—two for every one of hers. She reached the elevator and hit the button. The arrow lit up, accompanied by the hum of machinery as the unit began moving.

She glanced down the hallway. Had she only imagined the footsteps? Wouldn't the person have rounded the corner by now? Was it another coworker returning to their office?

No. There hadn't been any other lights on. All the doors had been closed. She looked at the number pad clicking off the floors then made for the stairwell. At least she'd have some control by taking the stairs. No surprises when the silver doors opened, and she could easily detour to another floor if she heard someone approaching from below.

The heavy metal fire door clicked shut behind her as she bustled through, descending as fast as she could without making too much noise. She'd gotten two floors down when another click resonated through the air above her, followed by hurried steps.

Bridgette raced down the stairs, sticking to the outer wall, in case anyone tried to see her over the railing. She didn't stop, winding her way down to the bottom level. Why had she decided to park in the damn garage today? It was like asking to become a victim. But the rain had been falling in steady sheets, and she'd been too rushed to try and find a spot on the road or in a neighboring lot. So, she'd opted for the staff parking. A key-activated sensor and garage door were supposed to make the area secure. But no such thing existed. There were always ways in, and if someone wanted her bad enough, they would have found one.

The exit door squeaked as she shoved on it, darting to her right once she'd cleared the small glass enclosure. Only a scattering of cars dotted the large space, a patchwork of shadows masking the glare of the overhead lights. She headed for the wall, keeping herself between it and the front of a few vehicles in case she needed to disappear. She'd made it halfway to her Jeep when the inner door bounced open.

Bridgette hit the concrete, crouching behind the grill of a large Suburban. The plate caught on her pants, ripping a line across her hip. She cursed under her breath, yanking the fabric free then slowing peering around the left side of the SUV. A dark figure moved down the outer edge of the parking stalls, head swiveling from side to side.

A man. No question. Wide, thick shoulders with a broad chest and narrow waist, the guy looked athletic beneath the snug black clothing and matching ski mask. As if he could chase her for hours and never get tired. Judging by the size of his biceps, she had no doubts that he packed one hell of a punch. The kind that would knock her out with only a single blow. Something glinted off one of the lights, the silver gleam winking at her.

He had a gun, though the barrel looked strangely thick —shit. A suppressor. This guy meant business. He wasn't there to threaten her. To beat a warning into her. He was there to kill her. Period.

ALSO BY KRIS NORRIS

SINGLES

Centerfold

Keeping Faith

My Soul to Keep

Ricochet

Rope's End

SERIES

'TIL DEATH

1 - Deadly Vision

2 - Deadly Obsession

3 - Deadly Deception

BROTHERHOOD PROTECTORS ~ Elle James

1 - Midnight Ranger

COLLATERAL DAMAGE

1 - Force of Nature

DARK PROPHECY

1 - Sacred Talisman

2 - Twice Bitten

3 - Blood of the Wolf

ENCHANTED LOVERS
1 - Healing Hands

FROM GRACE
1 - Gabriel
2 – Michael

GRIZZLY ENCOUNTERS
1 – Iron Will

THRESHOLD
1 - Grave Measures

COLLECTIONS

Blue Collar Collection

Into the Spirit, Boxed Set

RE-RELEASING SOON

WHAT REMAINS
1 - Untainted

2 - Wasteland

3 - Mutation

4 - Reckoning

ABOUT THE AUTHOR

Author, single mother, slave to chaos—she's a jack-of-all-trades who's constantly looking for her ever elusive clone.

And don't forget to subscribe to her newsletter to get the latest scoop on new and upcoming releases as well as exclusive free reads.

https://www.subscribepage.com/krisnorris

Kris loves connecting with fellow book enthusiasts. You can find her on these social media platforms…

krisnorris.ca
contactme@krisnorris.ca

facebook.com/kris.norris.731
twitter.com/kris_norris
instagram.com/girlnovelist
amazon.com/author/krisnorris

ORIGINAL BROTHERHOOD PROTECTORS SERIES

BY ELLE JAMES

Brotherhood Protectors Series

Montana SEAL (#1)

Bride Protector SEAL (#2)

Montana D-Force (#3)

Cowboy D-Force (#4)

Montana Ranger (#5)

Montana Dog Soldier (#6)

Montana SEAL Daddy (#7)

Montana Ranger's Wedding Vow (#8)

Montana SEAL Undercover Daddy (#9)

Cape Cod SEAL Rescue (#10)

Montana SEAL Friendly Fire (#11)

Montana SEAL's Bride (#12)

Montana Rescue

Hot SEAL, Salty Dog

ABOUT ELLE JAMES

ELLE JAMES also writing as MYLA JACKSON is a *New York Times* and *USA Today* Bestselling author of books including cowboys, intrigues and paranormal adventures that keep her readers on the edges of their seats. With over eighty works in a variety of sub-genres and lengths she has published with Harlequin, Samhain, Ellora's Cave, Kensington, Cleis Press, and Avon. When she's not at her computer, she's traveling, snow skiing, boating, or riding her ATV, dreaming up new stories. Learn more about Elle James at www.ellejames.com

Website | Facebook | Twitter | GoodReads | Newsletter | BookBub | Amazon

Follow Elle!
www.ellejames.com
ellejames@ellejames.com

facebook.com/ellejamesauthor
twitter.com/ElleJamesAuthor

Made in United States
Cleveland, OH
01 April 2025